# Invitation to a Bonfire

_Adrienne Celt_

R A V E N BOOKS

LONDON · OXFORD · NEW YORK · NEW DELHI · SYDNEY

RAVEN BOOKS
Bloomsbury Publishing Plc
50 Bedford Square, London, WC1B 3DP, UK

BLOOMSBURY, RAVEN BOOKS and the Raven Books logo are trademarks
of Bloomsbury Publishing Plc

First published in Great Britain 2018

A catalogue record for this book is available from the British Library

ISBN: HB: 978-1-4088-9514-6; TPB: 978-1-4088-9515-3; eBook: 978-1-4088-9516-0

2 4 6 8 10 9 7 5 3 1

Typeset by Westchester Publishing Services
Printed and bound in Great Britain by CPI Group (UK) Ltd, Croydon CR0 4YY

To find out more about our authors and books visit www.bloomsbury.com
and sign up for our newsletters

# A Note on the Text

This collection of papers was assembled as a project of the Donne School Alumnae Society of Goslings, from statewide archives, 1984.

The project was funded by a posthumous grant from one of the Donne School's most generous benefactors, Mrs. Vera Orlov (née Volkov), who wished, she said, for the research to make a definitive historical mark. After the tragic death of her husband, the writer Leo Orlov—who taught briefly at the Donne School in the days preceding his murder in 1931—Mrs. Orlov returned to her family home in France, but remained a dedicated supporter of the school.

The section of Mrs. Orlov's will that earmarked this money for the Society of Goslings also bequeathed a number of documents, many still in probate. One important document, however, arrived alongside the funding: a diary seemingly written by the young Donne School employee Zoe Andropov, who died under hotly debated circumstances the same year as Mr. Orlov. Its presence in Mrs. Orlov's possessions remains a point of inquiry, especially as documentation about Mrs. Orlov herself remains in such short supply.

This diary, along with a previously unseen package of correspondence written by Mr. Orlov, forms the backbone of the enclosed research. The findings are separated into three main categories: Ms. Andropov's diary (under the section heading "Zoya"), Mr. Orlov's letters (under the section heading "Lev"), and all other primary or secondary source documents (newspaper clippings, police reports, interviews, et cetera), with editorial notes as appropriate. The documents in the second and third categories have been included wherever they were found in Ms. Andropov's diary, or else wherever the Gosling alumnae felt they would offer the most useful perspective.

The personal records in this collection make frequent use of Russian name variations, patronymics, and diminutives, and these, for disambiguation, are listed here:

**Leo Orlov**: also referred to as Lev, Lev Orlov, and Leo (or Lev) Pavlovich Orlov

**Vera Orlov**: also referred to as Renka, Verenka, Vera Orlova, Verena Petrovna Volkova, and Vera Volkova

**Zoe Andropov**: also referred to as Zoya and Zoya Ivanovna Andropova

We hope that readers find this project to be in keeping with the institution's mission of honesty, clarity, and revelation.

# VOLUME ONE

# *Zoya*

*Editor's note: All entries from this diary appear to have been written between June and July of 1931.*

## *1.*

LET ME BEGIN BY SAYING I DID NOT THINK it would end this way. No—let me begin by saying I will burn this diary shortly. There's a fireplace here in the cabin where I'm staying, complete with an iron grate and a long pair of tongs, and I've been practicing every night with bits of drift-wood, though it makes me over-warm. Summer air, hot blaze. The New Jersey coastal breeze not enough of a balm to keep sweat from rolling down my forehead. I'm reminded of my childhood in Lipetsk, how even on sweltering nights we had to set bonfires in order to do away with the weeds in the sugar beet fields, and there were always two or three spots charred black amidst the green leaves. I was good at it then, striking the match in just the right place. My father would rumple my hair with his enormous, practical hands, and my mother would gather me up in her skirts as I ran away from the burning brush. But it's been years since I had reason to do more than light the stove to put on a kettle.

I wanted to make sure I could still arrange the heat, maximize the incendiary consequences. So I've been crumpling paper balls to varying degrees of tightness, stacking logs in a crisscross pattern, then log cabin–style, then teepee. Once, a gust of wind blew down the chimney at just the right moment, and the whole pile went up with a *woof,* throwing me backwards and singeing my eyelashes. I've been trying to re-create it ever since.

Maybe I'm too worried about the diary. After all, this cabin—small and shingled, cheap but sufficient—wasn't rented in my name. I'm a ghost here, same as every occupant who's come and gone, invited for the weekend to enjoy the brisk delicacies of the eastern seaboard and leaving promptly on the Monday train. Everyone who's dipped their toes in the waves and then come back in to wrap a sweater round their shoulders. I'm—say, a photo in a lost locket, dropped between some godforsaken floorboards. No one will think to look for me here, and so they won't look for the diary either.

But. Why not burn it, just to be safe? Already I've burned my ties to home, to the school and all the people I knew there. All the people I loved. Why not these pages too? My aim, anyway, is not posterity, but instead to take a sharp, bright pin and use it to bore a hole—one might say a pinprick—in the swollen history that rests on my shoulders. If I don't let out some of that air, I think I will go mad, or at the very least confess to someone unwise. And she would not like that. I think she would not let me. Little Vera with her tall shoes, her black hair, her long and perfect nose.

I took her husband. Or at the very least I tried. Many afternoons he took me, whether out in the garden or in the hazy light of my bedroom, always filtered through the screen I placed in front of my window to offer privacy while changing. He sniffed me out in whatever room I happened to occupy, or whatever restaurant in our small shared city where I might have been tucking into a pork cutlet and sipping a glass of sweet white wine. Once he approached me from behind in a very nice place, and bent down in full view of the room to smell my neck. I felt the soft skin of his appendage brush against the nub of my spine, felt the small hairs there pulled upright in thrall to his breathing. The knife dropped from my hand—just a short ways, but it hit the plate with a crash, chipping off a small bit of china and turning the subcurrent of attention in the restaurant into a mass of unabashed stares. By the time I gathered myself to turn around, though, he'd disappeared, leaving behind him only the soft ping of the bell at the top of the door.

You'll think (you! I suppose I have to imagine someone to talk to as I write, a sympathetic ear. Though even you I picture with a hint of disapproval, listening more for the tickle than the truth) that I only want to confess this passion. The affair. Stolen hours, eyes meeting across some distance and fizzing with sin. People love broken rules, after all. The rise of a pesky, risk-taking underdog. We have, on the whole, so little of our own that when we rip things from the hands of the ruling class they take on new value, offering us a reflected glow. I knew this every time I met him, my Lev, my life. I knew that the oblong of his head and the irony of his eyebrows would have meant nothing to me if he were young and poor and free. If I hadn't read his work for years, first in periodicals and then in volumes, and hadn't already loved his mind, slept with his books pressed between my knees for safekeeping. I knew he belonged to Vera when he came to me, came for me, came into my hands as if dropped there by parachute. And it's true, his unavailability only made me hold him tighter.

But I have no need to exorcise his possession of me from my mind. It's what Vera did that threatens to sink me. And to get it right, to tell it whole, I have to start at the beginning.

2.

FIRST: AN APARTMENT IN MOSCOW, where my mother gave birth to me on the kitchen floor because she could not get to the hospital in time. Neighbor women, hearing her screams, ran in to help and turned the room into a grimly efficient medical theatre, with water boiling on the stove and sterilized cooking forceps at the ready. They coached her, offering bits of crushed ice, shoulder massages, compliments. "*Otlichno, krasavitsa!*" the women cried, and then they peeked between her legs and decided it was time to push, counting up to the moment of crisis. "*Raz! Dva! Tri!*" Most of them had been through the same thing themselves, and when my head emerged the oldest woman gripped it firmly with the forceps and tugged. She showed no hesitation, and sometimes when I'm over-tired I still rub the small indentations she made behind my ears.

My father, offering around vodka we couldn't afford and rolling cigarette after cigarette, was ecstatic at this vision of communal spirit. When one of the women, herself eight months pregnant, went into sympathetic labor and had to be hustled away, he applauded her out the door and strolled back in shaking his head with pride and flicking his dark hair away from his eyes. He and my mother had come to Moscow from the fields of the Lipetsk Oblast, following my father's revolutionary tendencies and his faith in the common man. They still went back to Lipetsk in the summers, for the harvest—he wasn't formally tied to the land, but he believed in it: the soul of the earth, and the brotherhood of the field workers. He believed less so, of course, in the noble estate that crushed the workers and profited from their labor—this, my father had privately sworn to dismantle. But we needed the money, you see.

In Moscow, he drove a taxi part-time, leaving him ample opportunity to attend secret meetings and contribute his ideas to unpublished manifestos, or else to walk around the house half-drunk, gloating about the coming ascendancy of the peasant class. In boisterous moods he threatened to wrestle things: a pony chained up in the park with ribbons tied all through its mane, a friend's large dog, a hedge shaped like an elephant. But beneath the surface of his voluminous personality, my father was a clever man. Instead of picking fights in the street or talking out of turn to aristocrats, as many of his radical friends were only too happy to do, he chose to work quietly, tirelessly, behind the scenes, for a revolution he was sure would change everything. The poor would rise up and make ours a better world; the rich would cede, or die, he said. And I wanted so much for him to be right, for some snap of our collective fingers to polish my shoes and fill the kitchen with rich aromas, transform my little bed with eiderdown. Maybe not quite the change he intended, but still. Small problems never fazed my father, because history was on his side. When the taxi he shared was broken into and ransacked, the seats stolen for who knows what purpose, his co-owners Dmitri and Misha collapsed into a deep despair. But my father simply found a set of folding chairs to install in the car and went about his business.

I know all this because it was a famous story in our household, his zeal and my violent birth, always illustrated with a gesture to the bloodstained kitchen parquet. The family news, *novosti Andropova*. Besides one another it was all we had, really, and, looking back, I would have traded it for a pair of new shoes and a comfortable winter hat—traded it without a second thought—but I didn't have that choice. I was a child. My mother snorted at my father's talk of a glorious future, rolled her eyes, but she also wove her fingers between his and squeezed. Even the day I was born, as she lay on the floor in a pool of her own blood, she let him stroke her hair while she pushed and be the first one to hold me after the neighbor women wiped me clean. "A true child of the revolution," he called me. "A child of ideals." Whatever that meant. I wish—I remember a time when I felt his words as magic, vibration. I remember thinking that he would change the world, give me everything, just by wanting to. Where has that girl gone? Where did she run off to?

## 3.

THESE DAYS I TRY TO KEEP MY MIND AWAY from Moscow—thinking about it is too painful, a scar that burns to the touch. But sometimes I can't help drifting back there. To the crib where I slept in our tiny apartment, before the harvest began and after it ended. Our city home. We didn't have a dacha we could escape to for summers in the country, no short brick wall surrounding a garden of grass and trees. No small yard buxom with flowers or little house with a wood-burning stove. No banya out back, thick with steam, and for that matter no grandmother to soak birch branches in a plastic bucket and hit my naked skin while we bathed to improve my circulation. Not like the better families. Instead, we had a field of sugar beets in Lipetsk, and it wasn't even really our field. The region dated back to the Tatars, and my mother said we were bred to it by blood. Obligated in our servitude, if not to the landlord then still to the soil and the trees, to generations of seeds sprouted there, and all the rooty flesh boiled into sweets and sold for someone else's benefit. Sometimes when we were there, she pointed to the landlord's family riding by in the distance on their pretty horses and told me there was no reason I shouldn't follow their example of nobility and pride. But she said it while we knelt in the dirt with sweat pouring off our faces. No wonder I preferred the high-rise in Moscow, however heavy the air was there, however many dogs roamed the streets outside and crawled onto the trolleybuses in search of scraps. At least in Moscow there were times when I felt free—free, if nothing else, to make my own mistakes.

My crib stood under our living room window, and sometimes the heavy curtains got caught up in the bars along with threads of heavy city light. I always made it worse, pulling the dusty blackout brocade and twisting it around my fingers until the curtain rod buckled underneath my weight and the rings clacked together. My mother would sweep in then to scold me, clucking. Swat my fingers and give me a kiss on the head before disappearing again through the kitchen door. Most of the time my parents left me alone, though, working at one thing or another. I had a soft rabbit that I rubbed against my cheek for comfort. A terribly sweet feeling. Little nubs of fabric fur, its nose made hard by thick embroidery. I caressed myself, ran the long ears up and down my arms. Tossed the toy to the end of my bed and picked it back up with my toes. I can still feel the rabbit tucked under my shirt, pressed hard against my beating heart. As a child, I had muddled ideas about pregnancy and believed that this was where women carried their babies. Curled behind the ribs for safety.

One day as I idly passed the rabbit's face across my own, one of the eyes popped off from wear. It was a black sphere with a hole through it for thread. Smooth to the touch. I remember being glad that it was round on every side: I'd sometimes wondered if the eyes had flat backs, and the idea had disturbed me. Children love their verisimilitude. The surface of the bead was scratched—probably my fault, from the way I tossed that doll around. But it was black all the way through, and the scratches looked raw, almost as if they could be smoothed back together. I put the rabbit's eye into my mouth, thinking it might melt there.

That, of course, did not happen. Though what did seemed just as remarkable to me, then. I clutched the bead between my teeth, and my mouth watered, the water seeming to flow directly from the little eye. It made me feel strong, but also afraid, like I was rising and sinking all at once. The darkness of the bead made me think it had no beginning or end; perhaps I was half-sleeping, and the feeling was half dream.

My mother made a sound in the kitchen. A metal spoon clattering into a pan. I looked up and saw her turn towards my crib, checking to see if the commotion had woken me. Her eyes met mine, and seeing the tenderness of her concern, I wanted to ask her, beg her, to help me. But I had no words for what was wrong. She came in and put a hand on my head, her palm wet from cookery. "*Vsyo horosho,*" she told me, petting my hair. Everything is alright. "*Zasiypay.*" Sleep, now. I swallowed the bead. Then, under my mother's soft gesture, I lay back down and clutched my rabbit, stomach roiling. In my childish way I knew that I would never get the eye out of me now. It would spin behind my heart, and it would give birth to something. God knows when, and God knows what.

That was the beginning of me.

## 4.

But I want to talk about Vera. The little face hovering over my shoulder, even when she isn't there. I want to examine the places where the line of her life passed over mine, where we crissed and crossed or ran at a distant parallel, so I can figure out how I got to where I am. Moscow to the New Jersey shoreline: hardly a straight trajectory.

I knew Vera when we were young. Before I came to America, before any of that. Not that she'd have admitted the association—even after the revolution she was out of my league by ten thousand paces. A girl with a riding crop in her hand, a girl who snuck cigarettes from soldiers and wore a new gown for the season's every occasion. Her family was pure White Russian—the rich old guard—but even so I'm sure that all the soldiers courted her when they could. The Bolshevik Reds were still red-blooded, after all, and no one could resist a girl like that. Invited to everything, wanted everywhere. She played piano at her parents' parties, looking up from underneath her dark eyebrows with a smile that each man in the room hoped was their secret. Lev told me that in her teen years, when it was fashionable, she wrote poetry for exile magazines and did translations by candlelight. Set typescript until her fingertips were black with ink.

I knew her, but we didn't run in the same circles (except once, but I'll get to that in its proper time). While she was being tutored at her family's estate on the outskirts of Moscow, and later—having finally fled the Reds who won the war—at their dingy Paris apartment, I was educated in a string of cramped facilities paid for by the Soviet State Commissariat, perfecting my handwriting and avoiding any historical facts that might have been deemed counter-revolutionary.

My parents were on the right side of the war between the Reds and the Whites, of course—which is to say, the winning side. They embraced the changes in our country, from the ideological to the typographical, purging the aristocracy and the last remnants of Old Slavonic spelling from our lives in one fell blow. I remember when the signs and posters in the city quietly rid themselves of the *tvyordi znak*, a silly little mark that looked like a ъ and did—well, it didn't do much, but the new regime understood that words and symbols meant something. That changing the language was the same as changing the fabric of reality and the shape of the human mind. It was an exciting time. Occasionally people burned their old typewriters in enormous civil bonfires. Occasionally, too, the Party called for more serious sacrifices.

There's a reason, you see, that I didn't stay on in the country of my birth and apprentice as something useful and hardy: a machinist, say, or a land surveyor. A reason that I am, instead, a young woman huddled in a small cabin by the seashore, scratching out stories in the terrible quiet. My parents died a few years into the new and glorious union of our country. First my father, then my mother, and all official memory of our family as a unit. At fifteen I was taken to an orphanage—a bleakness that I've worked hard to scrub from my mind, without success—and then at sixteen was smuggled into the U.S. on a hush-hush transport ship along with a hundred other children, all of us plucked from our uncomfortable beds and promised a better life, which we needed very much.

What do I remember of the orphanage? The shock of being there. The cross-stitched portraits of Party members framed and hung along the walls, with eyes that watched you move around. It was considered beneficial for us to work on those cross-stitches together in the common room no matter how badly we sewed, and even once I landed on the transport ship I felt pricks in my inept fingers and thumbs from where my needle had pierced the skin. In the orphanage we were told how lucky we were to be raised not by parents but by the motherland herself, and our caretakers frequently used this excuse to smack us into place when we strayed. Rulers sharp on the back of the hand, backs of hands across the cheek, all in an effort to vouchsafe not only our own futures but also those of the Party and the *bratstvo,* the brotherhood of all mankind. I remember being hungry. I remember a great many dark walkways, blank and featureless faces. And then I remember being carried out in someone's arms, and told I was going to sail for America.

A beautiful voice offered me amber fields and purple mountains. Majesty. I had studied English in school, but still I assumed there was some misunderstanding, because who would bother giving anything like that to me? A new home. A new life. I didn't know then that the mountains and fields were just lines in a song, which the man hurrying me towards the boat was probably singing to keep himself warm: it was a bitter evening. But I decided to put my faith in this new place, just in case. I figured it had to be better than fighting to remain where I'd been.

## 5.

WE DIDN'T HAVE AN EASY TIME GETTING there, though. During our voyage to America, waves of flu swept through the ship and bad weather dogged us. The girl who shared my bunk turned green within a day of setting sail, and took to moaning and shivering beneath our quilt, asking for death. Little Marlenochka. I spent hours trying to find a spot of healthy pink on her skin to report to her in the hopes of earning a smile, sometimes searching from her hairline to the soles of her feet with no success. The attention didn't soothe her much, even as I scratched her gently with my fingernails and traced her ear with my thumb. She heaved up what seemed like gallons of saltwater, though of course that can't be right, since I never saw her eat more than a few bites of dry cracker, or drink more than a sip of bouillon tea. I can't imagine what became of her after we landed. She was so briny, so continually moist. And not alone in that. The bunkrooms belowdecks stank of vomit, and those of us who could still walk would stroll the deck for hours in search of a clean breath of air. But it was slippery up there, and we were weak; many children disappeared without a whisper. I didn't get sick until halfway through the trip, but I remember trembling against the rail of the ship, staring into the ocean and seeing, to my utter shock, the dinner-plate eye of a whale rise up just a few feet away, clear though untouchable. Was it, I wondered, a hallucination? Certainly it seemed unreal. The eye was wet with tears and seawater, full of sympathy I'd never earned or even dreamed of. The giant grey body moved beside us silently, ruffling the water like it was rearranging a blanket. I began to cry, and then to pray to this giant creature—badly, I'm sure, having never prayed before. The waves were colorless, and I reached towards them. Then the whale sank out of view.

Despite the hardships we faced in transit, my faith in the American promise remained unshaken. Altered, perhaps, when there was found to be a shortage of aspirin on board, and our fevers were treated with rest and stale tea. Further transformed when we arrived at port and were told that, for reasons of national security, we might not be allowed to disembark. But this only made me more eager to kiss the American soil when I finally stepped down onto it. Everyone smiled at you in America, whether or not they meant it. I found that interesting.

# *Lev*

15 June 1931
Airmail via London

VERA. EVEN YOUR NAME INTOXICATES, incinerates. Veer-a. A swift turn on the road, a gasp at the end of the act. My Vera. You were Renka, standing on your tiptoes at the edge of the bridge, peering at the line where the water and the air connected. Verena Petrovna behind your black mask at the ball, lit by lamplight. But for me, you were always Vera, first.

I know we've been cold to one another lately, my darling, more so with every step I took towards the realization of this plan. My return to the homeland, a rescue mission for my lost manuscript, which you told me I should never find. I've been repeating the steps to myself every day and hour leading up to my departure: Locate a map with likely updates to the Soviet roadways: check. Befriend the American military and their biplanes: check. And now, traverse the ocean and land on a distant shore: check. But I don't want to leave things that way, and the closer I get to the streets where we first met, the more it seems the perfect time for honesty. You used to press me for stories about my early romances, and I always said no, not wanting to diminish in your mind the vision of our ideal connection. But now I think I see your point: how can you trust that my feelings for you are unique if you don't know my feelings for anyone else? Alright then, Vera. As always, you win. If it brings us closer, it will be worth it.

Of course there were girls before you. In particular there was one, a sweet thing of sixteen who I knew through my father; we went hunting at her country home near Tsarskoye Selo, just outside of Leningrad. It was a quaint place, just seven bedrooms and a sitting room full of brocade and exposed stone, which they always brightened up at night with candles. They left the curtains open for evening cocktails, and I remember coming towards the house after a walk in the dark; above me a sea of stars fell in every direction as if a divine huntress was shaking droplets of water from her hair. And through the window, another set of bright white points, one of which was in the hand of the girl. She moved from one end of the room to the other towards an object I would never know. Her chestnut hair shone upon her head; her skin was white, almost frozen. That passage, no more than a few footsteps past the window glass, seemed to contain within it my whole life's purpose, my whole mysterious volition: delicious, untouchable, motivated by something just beyond my grasp.

When I went inside I felt certain the spell would break, and for a moment it seemed to. The room was stuffy with the musk of men—her father, my father, both of her brothers—and the fireplace flue was not quite open, so a hint of smoke lingered round the ceiling and the corners. As I walked through the door one of her brothers said something quiet and the other laughed—a sound that made my shoulders itch with the anticipation of a fight. They were tall, hulking. I was long and lean. I went to the sideboard and poured myself a glass of wine from the ready decanter, trying not to let the smoke bother my lungs and thinking how I might make a polite escape. Perhaps fake a chest cold? Pretend exhaustion? Even a girl was not worth this, surely. Then I turned. A single pivoting step that severed one part of my life from the next.

In the far corner of the room, she perched on an armchair much too large for her, so she looked like a child in her father's study. But such a serious child, and with such poise that I could have balanced my wine on her head without fear of spilling a single drop. The candle she'd carried sat on a small table beside her, lighting her up from below. Her eyes were dark with little points of light, galaxy marbles, runic hints. It was impossible to tell if she was breathing, so still did she hold herself. Not like a doe in the woods, alert to danger. Like the hunter that doe has scented. Patient. Glacial.

Without knowing what I would say, I started to move towards her, but at that moment the maid came in and rang for dinner, and we were all ushered through into the cramped dining room for undercooked veal and a few stabbing attempts at conversation. Once or twice I tried to strike up a topic with the young lady, whose name was Diana, or Dina, but she was half the table away and stuck telling my father about her study of painting—a theme on which he was routinely tiresome, his own mother having dabbled in watercolor. Once or twice she flashed those eyes at me, and my body seized with wanting. Then we all went up to bed.

The week transformed into a series of excuses designed to push me into Dina's company. I switched from the steady gelding I'd been riding to a mare Dina thought a better companion for her own; the mare and I were bitter enemies from the start, she always pushing my leg into trees and intentionally stumbling over shallow creek beds, and me driving her so hard with my heels that she ended each day sweated half to death. We tore after rabbits instead of foxes. Plunged down embankments too steep to escape and trotted back and forth in twin pique. Dina just laughed at our rivalry, and rode her horse with the grace of a centaur. One afternoon I let her walk me to the river that bordered her family's property on the pretext that I give my opinion on opportunities to fish it, a practical task I could not have been more ill-suited to as a boy of seventeen, primarily enamored of books and cigarettes and the sound of my own voice. I knew nothing about fishing, and in fact forgot the explanation for our excursion as soon as we were out of sight of the house, though plenty of the creatures wallowed fat in the shade with speckled sides and deckled tails, confident and lazy. Dina let the back of her hand brush my fingers, and as we approached the water's edge I pulled her into an embrace. "We can't," Dina whispered. She pressed her bosom against my breastbone, laid her head on my chest and clutched at me with her little fingers as I bent and ran my hands underneath her skirt. An hour later when we returned, her father asked about the fish and I was at a loss to give him any answer, until Dina smiled guilelessly and said, "He found the river quite singular."

Her father was no fool, and as you can imagine, our opportunities to be alone together were swiftly curtailed: the greatest satisfaction I would derive from that point onward was in watching her astride that wicked mare from my wicked own. We were seated far apart at meals, and during the cocktail hour Dina's brothers took up all her attention, asking her to sing them songs they remembered from childhood or playing keep-away with ornamental jewels they plucked out of her hair. They endeavored to make a little girl out of her, but every childish game they concocted just emphasized her bloom into womanhood, a background of dishonesty illuminating a pure truth. Once, while passing me in an ancient narrow hallway, Dina touched my leg high enough up the thigh to ink the pressure of her fingers permanently into my skin. But she did not slow her pace, and soon disappeared around a corner, the tail of her skirt flicking back in a smirk. After we left I thought of her constantly, counting the seconds until we might be reunited. But when my father and I tried to make plans for a return trip later in the fall, we were met with the news that Dina had been shot through the waist by an incompetent hunter who mistook her brown riding jacket for a hide, and died of blood loss some five hours later, fevered white skin almost invisible against the bleached linens of her bed.

I used to dream of her laid out on a funeral bier, her burial gown flowing over the edges like snow. I dreamed that she stood up and stretched, sweet and sleepy, and truly believed that I might bring her back from the grave using only the force of my will. Girl on horseback, jumping death. She was my every fascination, my nightly rhythm, my dream upon waking. She was the only girl I ever loved. Until you.

# *Zoya*

*6.*

I ARRIVED IN MAPLE HILL IN JANUARY, halfway through the school year, and spent my first New Jersey winter wandering around and marveling at my good fortune. We suffered ice storms nearly every week, bad enough to take out the city's power, but cold was nothing new to me. When I woke up and saw my breath, I dressed practically, in layers, and topped myself off with the grass-green wool coat I'd bought at the local department store with the ten dollars offered to all combat orphans by the American committee that took on our care. They mistook the moth-eaten look of my old coat for war-torn: a bit of luck. Each day I tucked my hands into my clean new pockets to protect them from the wind and also to hide the holes in the fingertips of my gloves—I'd never owned anything brand new before, and I was grateful to the winter weather for giving me an opportunity to show off, however minimally. My lips in that freeze looked bitten, and my skin achieved a nearly fashionable pallor, though I would never quite lose the hardy peasant complexion that was my birthright. My roommate, Margaret, slept under an electric blanket; she kept it plugged in even during blackouts, and when I got up on those winter mornings all I could see was the tuft of her hair beneath her pile of supplementary quilts, and the electric wire snaking hopefully down to the floor.

Despite my coat stipend I was given nothing for shoes, and since the tread on my old boots was worn almost completely away I was forced to walk slowly along the slick roads to keep from falling. I didn't mind. Everything was covered with a film of ice that looked, to me, like sugar glaze. On the bone-bare trees, on the holly bushes with their prickling leaves and poisonous red berries. On white picket-fence posts and holiday lights; on lost purple mittens and the occasional squirrel, fallen from its treetop nest as heavy as a paperweight. The cars lining the streets sported wipers shellacked to their windshields, and every mailbox was sealed tight, whether bearing secret gifts or only more cold air. (Sometimes, I admit, I imagined prying one open and seeing a living bird fly out; I'm not sure why this image appealed to me so much, but it was strong enough to push me once or twice into standing in front of a box and tugging at the metal lip, hoping for some give. Always, though, the approach of a car or some movement in a nearby window forced me to abridge my efforts.) There were no houses in Moscow, at least not like this, small and sweet and personal. There was beauty, of course: art nouveau and cracked gilding, windows that were stories tall. But nothing so pretty or pedestrian. Nothing, since I lost my parents, that felt so immediately like home.

Each day I made my way through the neighborhoods that surrounded the Donne School, sometimes taking deliberate steps, sometimes gliding along like a skater until I reached the strip of stores that constituted our downtown, where the sidewalks were salted dry. There was a bookshop I entered rarely but with great reverence, a market that didn't open until ten A.M., a dress shop next door to a tailor, and, most important, a little café that seemed to have prophetic hours, as no matter when I slid out of bed, I was always their first customer of the day. I never bought more than a single coffee, but it was refilled as long as I wanted to stay, and occasionally the proprietor—an old maid named Marie who wore gypsy skirts but sensible earrings—would slip a biscotti onto my plate alongside the white ceramic coffee cup. There, I would labor through the reading that allowed me to scrape passing grades in my classes. It had been expected that I would enter school a bit behind, with the limited English skills and (sadly temporary) refugee sheen I imported from abroad, which earned me some pity in those early days. But more than the language, I found it difficult to mimic the bravado of my classmates as they went about their work, offering answers—in front of the teacher!—which were not only wrong but impertinent, while I crossed and recrossed my legs at the back of the room, trying to memorize my textbooks.

It wasn't that I didn't try, but it was all strange to me. The Donne School lecture halls were full of unfamiliar cheer, with paper murals and stacks of books you were welcome to pick up, flip through, argue with. The matching desks and chairs arranged throughout the rooms stayed somehow neat and refinished all year, despite the girls who put their feet up, leaking winter salt and ice onto the wood, and the girls who scraped at the varnish with their fingernails, peeling away long, almost weightless threads. Sometimes they picked out hairpins and used them to carve their initials, but even these small marks seemed to disappear within a few days or even hours, a handyman bustling in with a pocket full of sandpaper. Back home I would've considered these girls feral, scribbling their indecipherable notes and wearing stockings with the seams all twisted, full of runs. But here, the messier they were, the more abominably casual, the richer their families tended to be. And though I didn't understand it, I liked it. I liked them, from afar. They had pink book bags and they threw away half-eaten chocolate bars, which I had to stop myself from picking out of the trash. One or two of them chewed on their hair, calling up the memory of deep, inerasable hungers that I knew none of them had ever felt. I liked knowing that they hadn't. They flowed together through the halls, giggling and holding hands, studied in the library carrels with heads pressed together in dim lamplight, and I watched them, wanting to swim in that same easy water. We were often asked to give presentations or make speeches in class, and under this attention the other girls preened every bit as much as I recoiled. Because something unimaginable happened: when they finished, people applauded. Every day, every time. And I applauded too, as vigorously as anyone else.

Expressing a firm or independent opinion felt unnatural to me, and this made composition papers a struggle. I also didn't care to write about my family history, to the consternation of teachers and counselors alike. "Wouldn't it make you feel better to talk about what you've been through?" they asked me, and I always answered with a firm "No." It's interesting how time changes a person. I never would have relented to keeping a diary back then.

Between the bodies that eventually filed in and the radiator steam, Marie's café was endemically overheated, and I have many fond memories of sitting at a round table by the fogged-up window, sipping from my bottomless coffee cup. I remember that the room always smelled of the rosemary Marie baked into her scones, though I never had the money to buy one, and that the bathroom had the familiar, bouillon scent of a home whose inhabitants eat a great deal of cabbage. I often wondered if Marie, too, was in exile from some former life, but her nasal American speech made it hard to imagine what that life might be. (A limitation of inventiveness that I have since overcome.) We sat in companionable silence: me turning pages and slurping with unmannered indifference, she ringing up change and wiping crumbs off of tabletops, occasionally humming a jaunty tune that, despite being stuck in my memory, I have never been able to identify.

I was at Marie's when I made the discovery that turned school—or, at least, schoolwork—tolerable. The winter sun was halfway down, streetlights buzzing on outside, and I was exhausted by the effort of doing poorly, day after day. You have to remember, my studies were all I had at this point; everyone I knew or loved was back in Moscow, most now dead. As it was, I sometimes initiated chats with the Donne School gardeners just to feel connected to the earth again, and to get back a sliver of the confidence I used to feel among the sugar beet fields of Lipetsk. In the café, I leaned my head against the window so I could watch the hazy figures clip by on the sidewalk in their dark coats, heading home. Out of the corner of my eye, I noticed the faint outline of a heart drawn into the steam—some other child must've done it, on some other day. But when I pressed my finger to the glass and traced the line, a man walking by outside smiled. At me. My perceived whimsy. My perceived joy. And I realized: maybe I knew what to do, after all. There were plenty of opinions in the world, and any of them could be mine, if I only said so.

I took the theory to class with me the next day, thinking I'd start small and test the waters, nodding along during someone else's argument or raising my hand in a group of "pro" or "con" opinions during Civics 102. Back in Moscow I'd had plenty of practice trying on beliefs like sweaters and socks, to see which ones had holes in the lining and which might help me to survive. But that had been a matter of life and death. This was just participation points, adding up to a small percentage of our term grade. Still, I didn't want to fail.

Civ 102 was doing a unit on the Greek *polis* system and the students had been divided into four groups, each assigned a different city-state. We got points for presenting compelling insights about our home *polis*, and the winners had been promised ice cream. My corner of the room was Corinth—not objectively the most exciting, the height of neither scholarship nor war. But the project had inspired a cliquishness that had little to do with the realities of ancient Greek life. "Athens was the center of everything important," sniffed a girl named Abigail. "Of course we'll win." "Sparta will *kill you*," hissed her best friend, Denise, pencil gripped in her fist like a dagger. I'd been conducting diligent research and offering up a trove of facts about Corinthian exports each class period—which was, I thought, the point of the exercise. But other girls wrote snazzy jingles. They made lightning bolts out of yellow paper as offerings to Zeus, and used the popularity of their projects as proof of their superiority in Greek society. Several of my teammates had complained privately that Corinth's financial status—as a center of trade and a source of fine pottery—was being unjustly ignored because Athens had better temples.

"We're the rich ones," they whispered. "Who wouldn't want to be the rich ones?"

*Yes*, I thought. *Who?* It was a fashionable enough sentiment that everyone would agree with it, general enough that anyone could have come up with it. And so, mid-period, when the teacher asked for arguments designed to win the daily rhetorical challenge, I raised my hand while the rest of my teammates were distracted arranging a row of flowerpots painted with black tempera.

"I think it's been overlooked—"

"What's that, hon?" asked the teacher, leaning closer as if to hear better, but also interrupting me. They were all eager to be the one to "get through" to me, or else (I suspected) to prove I was at heart a Soviet spy. I frowned, and muddled on.

"I said, I think we've forgotten how wealthy Corinth was. A, um, a—" I struggled to remember the exact term I'd underlined in last night's reading—"seat of commerce and industry."

Silence in the room for a beat. Then one of the Athenians said, "So?"

My cheeks flushed. "So I mean, they were rich."

"So *what*? Did they have *scholars*?"

"They had, um, the Bacchidae, an aristocratic—"

"Boring. We had Socrates."

Behind me, I heard a pair of girls whispering, "Sure, *until you murdered him.*" This was my chance. In truth, I didn't care about the ice cream social or even being right. But people were watching me, almost interested. The teacher was taking notes. No one was asking me about my parents, reminding me how I'd left them, how they'd vanished one by one—

"Maybe Athens had Socrates," I said, "until they killed him. But money is power. Money is always power." *New sweaters,* I thought. *Angora wool. Penny loafers. Midnight cookies. Nail polish.* The right to walk into a store and see the counter girl turn her smile up extra bright, and the ability to buy and buy, to change your life in small but measurable ways.

"That's . . . Well—" The teacher peered around the room, waiting for a rebuttal. None came. "That's a very vigorous position. I think we'll give the rhet point to Corinth today."

I let out a small puff of air. *Really, it worked?* And so easily, too. My teammates surrounded me, patting my back and offering congratulations. One called me "buddy" and another told me to keep it coming with the good stuff. Even the teacher gave me an encouraging nod, placing a gold star next to my name in her activity log. I squirmed under the unfamiliar touch of so many gentle hands, but still—I smiled.

## 7.

I HESITATE TO DESCRIBE THE WORK THAT earned me Bs and Cs that year as plagiarism: every word I wrote was my own. It's just the ideas that were borrowed, and the passion for them. My instructors were all relieved to find my papers suddenly passable—no one likes to fail the war orphan. And for my part, I came to enjoy whipping up a textual froth from the enthusiasms of Tolstoy, Thoreau, or de Tocqueville. If my ideas contradicted themselves from one assignment to the next—well. That was seen as the purview of youth. No one minded theft or inconsistency, even vitriol, so long as it meant you were making a statement. This was my first great lesson in being American, and I took it to heart.

## 8.

OF COURSE, VERA HAD NO PLACE AT the Donne School then, except as a faint part of my memory, which I was always trying to excise. A character from the motherland, the life I left behind. Back where we met, there were no cozy split-levels or so-called French fries, no one calling you "little miss." Moscow was a different beast. We had dancing bears, and the Arbat. We had underground businessmen with overlarge hats, and a winter so long and dark that it brought sense to fairy tales: why wouldn't you make a deal with a witch if she promised to bring out the sun? Our Moscow was a city of men slurring and ruddy with vodka, of old women competent, by necessity, to swing an axe—or at least, my Moscow was. Vera breathed a more rarefied air. But we shared the Young Pioneers scout troop, whether she remembers or not.

Our scoutmaster would call: *Vsyegda!* and we would shout back: *Gotov!* Always prepared. The cry of scouts across the globe. I joined the group at twelve, a little later than most, as I'd spent all my previous summers working in the countryside, and Vera showed up halfway through that same year, though I was never clear on her age. Older, surely. That was the brief, golden period in which my father was thriving in the new world order, and our house's star seemed on the rise. It would not last long, nor would it end well, but I didn't know that yet.

I remember walking into the meeting hall that day, following close behind two girls named Lidya and Marta whom I'd been hoping to befriend. I was watching their shoulders move up and down as they skipped along, the slender points of them rising up almost like the tips of wings. There was something about the turn of their ears, the tapering of their ankles that I couldn't keep my eyes off of, a magnetic drag in their every shift and shrug—I was terribly intent. My lips parted slightly, ready to speak if only I could find the right words. So while they saw the new girl right away, for a moment I missed her.

When Lidya and Marta stopped abruptly, I ran into Marta's back, sending both girls bubbling across the room in a fit of giggles. I looked up, face burning. But Vera took little notice of us. Who knows how long she'd been there, alone. Sitting on the edge of a wooden folding chair, one foot perched on the other. Red scarf cheerful and knotted, just like the rest of us. Her white shirt, though, was darted in here and there to fit her figure, and her skirt was hemmed an inch too high. Our chairs were organized in an imperfect circle and I sat opposite her, each of us at an apex. I admit I didn't like her then. Something in her gaze, which wouldn't rest on any face and just kept flitting around, to the top of the corrugated wall, to Lidya's inexpert fingernail polish, to the ceiling, to the floor.

The hall was enormous, an emptied-out warehouse lent to the scout troop on a weekly basis. We came in through a metal door on one end and sat under blinding fluorescent lights, occasionally using the space to run bomb drills or practice marching in formation for parades. The concrete floor was smudged with black in places where we'd lit preparedness fires; one day our scoutmaster had asked us to bring in kindling and then handed matchbooks to us in groups of three. By the end of that hour, half the troop had inhaled dangerous levels of smoke, but we were so proud of ourselves that most stayed overtime, toasting bacon on camping forks. Now, anyone could see that Vera would have none of this. Game play. Camaraderie. There were charcoal smears on the bottom of her smart little shoes, and with a shuddering foresight knew I'd find those same shoes in a charity bin a few weeks later, and be forced by my mother to take them.

"*Rebyata! Posmotritye!*" The scoutmaster stuck her cigarette in the corner of her mouth and clapped as she called us to attention. "We have a new comrade today, Verena Petrovna Volkova, so please make her feel welcome." Fifteen pairs of eyes turned to Vera, bored into her. The scoutmaster clapped again. "Remember that we are stronger together." In response—whether to our scrutiny or simply the idea that she might not be perfectly self-sufficient—Vera crossed her legs the other way.

We spent the afternoon learning how to track, and, more importantly, learning how to evade detection if we should ever find ourselves in the woods and facing heavy enemy fire. It wasn't one of our more practical lessons, given that we lived in the city center, and it ended in a kittenish game where each girl was given a ball of yarn to mark her trail. The object was to walk around as much of the room as we could without crossing paths. My yarn was blue. Vera's, red. She passed it from hand to hand, stretching her fingers away from the staticky threads and then squeezing them tight. The scoutmaster, her hair in a perpetual wave, leaned down by Vera and told her it was ok if she wasn't very good at the activity yet. Everyone had to start somewhere. "*Poprobuytye, pozhaluysta.*" Try.

As we unspooled the first of our yarn I was mostly interested in Lidya and Marta, who had taken to holding hands when they saw me, and running away. It didn't take long, however, for me to realize how poorly they were playing the game. Every few feet their threads intersected, orange over green and then green over orange. They shrieked when they ran into other girls, and made mock guns with their forefingers and thumbs. Even their attempts to be serious led mostly to slapped wrists and volleys of useless admonition: "*You* go left." "No, *you.*" "No, *you.*" All the while, Vera walked the room's long perimeter, occasionally hopping over a box or dodging under pieces of sharp-edged machinery. Staying unnoticed, if not unseen. I began to follow her.

In the years since, I've learned that there are veins in the human body so long that, if uncoiled, they'd span city blocks. City limits, even. I've also learned that the blood inside our bodies starts to look blue if it's buried deep, and needs to be pumped with oxygen. It's appropriate that the image of me trailing behind a young Vera would be one that mimics a trajectory towards the heart. The door to the hall was cracked open, and from time to time a bit of wind would lift the yarn, and then settle it back down. A red string and a blue string, side-by-side. Two little rivers, rushing.

I followed Vera for a good five minutes, careful to keep my own trail far enough away from hers that they wouldn't be shoved together somehow and lose us the game by stupid default. She never turned around or glanced over her shoulder, so I assumed she didn't mind. And why, after all, should one person reach the finish alone when two could go just as easily? The meeting was almost over, and my heart began to pick up speed as I imagined the scoutmaster praising us for following her directions so well. The other girls would look at me with new interest—me and Vera both—as we held our hands aloft in victory.

Vera slowed down as she approached one of the room's far corners, and I paused too, holding my yarn in place with the toe of my shoe. Based on what she'd done so far, I expected Vera to duck around a stack of crates and continue down the length of the wall. But there must have been something else in the way, because instead she turned sharp on her heel and stared at me, her face as blank as paper. I realized the reason she'd let me follow her wasn't charity or goodwill: she just hadn't known I was there. Within seconds of starting the game, she forgot the rest of us existed.

"You need to go that way," Vera said, indicating me back with the flick of her wrist. The first words she ever spoke to me. And the last for many years. When I saw she was instructing me to cross another girl's line in order to clear her own path, I felt an unexpected resistance.

"No," I said. "I'm winning."

She shook her hand at me again, nodding her head in the direction she intended, but I stood firm, weaving the loose end of my yarn around and around my fingers. And then I saw a shutter go down behind Vera's eyes. She looked at the yarn on the ground, all the various threads intersecting around the room, plus our two paths in perfect perpendicularity. A pile of wool, all across the floor. Not just her path. A dozen of them.

Vera could still have won, then. Made a few careful pivots, dodged around me, headed back to the center of the hall. But I knew that she wouldn't. She had only been interested in playing when she thought she was making up the rules as she went. As soon as she realized she was part of something larger, and something entirely outside her design, the game lost all its value for her.

Dropping her remaining yarn into a red puddle on the concrete, Vera walked across the floor, past the circle of wooden chairs, and out the door. As she went she pushed a few of our threads around, smudging them together with everyone else's in a hopeless tangle. Not, I thought, out of malice. She just didn't care enough to pay attention.

The scoutmaster called us all back to our chairs and took a ceremonial puff from her cigarette. "Ok!" she said. "*Spacibo, rebyata!* I'll see you next week."

Of course, Vera never returned to those meetings. No one mentioned her absence the following week or the week after that—probably the scoutmaster had been informed that her presence would be provisional, and was then told, more curtly, that the experiment had failed—until I began to think I had imagined her. Such a delicate girl, with her perfect, tailored uniform. Erect in her bearing, total in her indifference. I did become friends with Lidya and Marta, after a fashion, sitting in dingy teahouses together and taking up the hems of our skirts. Though we lost touch a few years later, when I was smuggled out on the orphan ship, and I have no idea what became of them or any of the others.

As for Vera and me, it would be a long time before we came face to face again.

9.

MY ATTEMPTS AT MIMICRY, SO SUCCESSFUL with the Donne School teachers, didn't go as well outside the classroom—friendship being, after all, more delicate than intellect. You can fake your way into fear or respect or passing grades, but not affection. Or at least, that's how it seemed to me when I tried to imitate my roommate, Margaret, who was the most beloved person I knew.

I watched her carefully whenever we happened to be in the room at the same time, or whenever we met in the halls: the way she poked her friends in the ribs with delight when they said something particularly nasty, and the way she laughed, scrunching her nose up to just the degree that her few light freckles were hidden by her mirth. Her beauty, compounded by her happiness. Though I liked the freckles, actually: she was the one who powdered them to death each morning, trying to pretend they didn't exist.

When she was away in class or out with a friend, drinking soda and smirking at the outfits of the passersby, I opened her drawers and lifted her sweaters up by the handful, pressing them to my nose and smelling the rosewater her housecleaner had sprayed them with after washing. Periodically, she sent a box of clothes back home to be cleaned and received a fresh shipment, which wasn't something I could aspire to, personally. (To whom would I have sent them? To what address? The past, c/o my deepest wishes.) But I saved up and bought a bottle of light cologne to scent my own wardrobe, which Margaret did in fact compliment, one time.

I watched, and I calculated the ways I could pick up her American habits: walk like she walked, smile like she smiled. Still, something was lost in the translation from her body to my own, the dialect of my limbs never quite tracking the lilting way she tossed her hair. To be American was to take what you wanted; to be American was to sit and laugh just so. Early on in my first semester the cafeteria served fries alongside their "famous" chicken-fried chunks of steak, and I noticed that Margaret alone ate them with both ketchup and mayonnaise, dipping one end in each sauce before taking alternating bites. I thought it was elegant, or maybe just efficient. Clever, in any case, and I found I liked the taste. Ketchup on its own was too sweet for me, but Margaret's method simulated the mayo-thick salads I was used to from home, served as treats with our most celebratory meals—I never did quite get used to the idea of "salad" denoting iceberg lettuce and cold tomatoes arranged on a plate.

Following Margaret, I dipped once, twice, with perfect confidence, savoring the bite of oil and the kiss of vinegar on my tongue. That is, until a girl named Sandy turned around to ask me for the salt and pepper shakers and visibly blanched at my behavior.

"What in God's name," she asked, "do you think you're doing?"

I went still, one half-doused fry hovering above my paper ketchup cup. "Eating?" I said. But since she caught me off guard, I didn't have time to affect the cool voice I was piecing together from Margaret's intonation, and so it sounded like I suggested I was *Yeeting?* Which likely didn't help my case. Sandy squinted, taking in the ketchup, the mayonnaise, the little piece of potato pinched between my fingers.

"How very *European*," she said, at last, making it clear that she did not consider Europeanness a compliment. After that, I endured several days of girls piping up in the halls with whatever little foreign phrase they could pin down, their aim so broad that I got as much *Parlez-vous français?* and *Voulez-vous coucher avec moi?* as I did hearty shouts of *Comrade!* accompanied by punishingly affable smacks on the back. Only Margaret kept out of it, responding with a mild shrug to any comments made about me in earshot of her.

We all talked about ourselves in terms of colors and seasons that year, a game thought up by a rising senior that quickly spread throughout the school: I was a spring, what with my light hair and the green undertone of my skin. Margaret considered herself a winter, but she was more accurately late fall. Soft browns, mustard yellows, certain shades of roseate pink all set off her skin and hair, turning her from a spirited girl into a kind of forest nymph. She tied her loose curls back in a ponytail, or let them tumble down over her shoulders with delicate twists pinned up behind her ears. She often wore tartan skirts and polished oxfords, pressed white shirts with pearl buttons that somehow managed not to look too sweet. In vain I tried to read her like my personal Rosetta Stone, but no matter what I did to emulate Margaret, it wasn't enough. My true self always leaked through to the surface, sometimes frightening even me.

10.

"You."

I was in the library one late-winter afternoon, grinding my teeth and trying to read Schopenhauer in an English translation. Marie's café had seemed, for once, too far to walk, in part because the wind that day was so frigid and sharp I felt sure it could peel the bark off trees and the skin off my back. But also, I had woken up with an unfamiliar nesting instinct. *Stay close*, I thought. *Stay here. Stay home.* So I'd hunkered down in a study carrel, twisting myself into a tight ball of irregular verbs and borrowed pessimism. When the tap came on my shoulder I jerked around, knocking my book off the table and startling the girl I found standing behind me into taking a step back.

Cindy Pink was a peripheral friend of Margaret's who also happened to be in my math class. In general she spent a lot of time managing her cuticles, nibbling them until they bled or pushing them back with a small black emery board. You could judge her mood that way: if her nails were ragged, then class work was going poorly, or else she'd gotten into a fight with her mother, angry missives arriving by mail and the phone ringing off the hook in the dorms. There was a lot of gossip about it because sometimes those fights ended with Cindy receiving apologetic fruit baskets that she parceled out to her suitemates. That day, however, her hands were neat, with a thin layer of clear polish giving her naturally pink nail beds an extraterrestrial gleam. She crossed her arms over her chest and nodded to me.

"Hey, you," she said again. "Are you busy? What are you doing right now?"

"Studying?" I looked at my book, splayed out on the floor. "Why?" No one really talked to me, as a rule, except in class or else to tell me that the loose buttons on the side of my skirt had come undone. And even then, sometimes girls just poked their fingers through the hole to my stockinged leg, looking up at me as if to ask, *Well?*

Cindy pursed her lips and glanced down at one hand, inspecting the glossy manicure there. She seemed conflicted. "You're kind of weird, right?"

"I'm not sure I know what you mean."

"Sure you do." Her hair was black and straight: she was a true winter, with pale blue eyes she narrowed at me, now. "You're a spooky one. You know," she gestured around her head, as if chasing off a cloud of gnats. "Woo-woo. So anyway, we need you to help us with a project."

At this point a touch of affront might've done me good, or at least a bit of skepticism. But I was dazzled by the idea that Cindy, or anyone, had thought about me as any kind of person at all. I didn't know what *woo-woo* meant, but between her nervous stance and her hand-waving, I could guess. And in fact I wasn't opposed to having a reputation for witchiness. It meant there were girls who had looked at me, girls who had whispered and seen something in me that I had no idea was there. Plus, it was a lot less pathetic than I expected.

I leaned down and picked up my Schopenhauer, placing it facedown on the carrel desk so that the dour portrait on the front of the book, which always gave me the creeps, was out of view. Then I crossed my legs and lightly folded my hands on top of my knees.

"What is this . . . project?"

"Ok, I knew you'd be into it." Paying no attention at all to what I'd hoped was a very sophisticated posture, Cindy grabbed my elbow and pulled me away into the library, weaving through the stacks and then looking back and forth behind us before slipping into a small stairway in the building's rear. "Shh," she said unnecessarily as we tiptoed down the stairs.

We emerged into one of the library's sub-basements, a supposed research area so poorly outfitted that half of the shelves were empty, and in some places graffiti had snuck onto the walls, eluding the watchful eyes of the facilities crew. Pencil scribbles mostly, though sometimes a haunting slash of lipstick: CHERYL WAS HERE and I'VE GOT YOU NOW followed by WHO? followed by WOULDN'T YOU LIKE TO KNOW? Sometimes girls snuck down here to hide books they were using for class projects and wanted to keep from being recalled; at the end of every semester a librarian was dispatched to collect and re-catalogue them. Cindy and I made our way to the back of the room, where a few shelves had been pushed around to create a circle, like a clearing in the woods. Several girls were already there, sitting cross-legged on the worn grey carpet.

"Oh good," said a girl named Adeline, who lived on the floor below me. "You got her."

"Why am I here?" I asked. My elbow hurt where Cindy had been holding it, and I tried to rub away the pain while still looking cool, collected.

"Right, right, we'll get to that." Adeline raised her eyebrows at Cindy and surveyed the room. She asked me: "You know everyone?" Besides us and Cindy, there were three other girls from our year—Bernice, Leslie, and Louise—plus a first-year named Marion who would later transfer out. A senior named Olivia.

"I guess so," I said.

"Perfect. Well, listen, we've all heard about you"—again, I was flattered and confused to hear it—"and we think you can help us with something we need to do. How is, uh, how are your grades going?"

"What?"

"You know," Adeline said. "Are you doing ok in your classes?" She seemed uneasy, clocking my reactions, as if she was as scared as I was that I would say the wrong thing.

"Sort of. It's fine." I didn't want to get into it. Cindy smirked, and I threw her a look from the corner of my eye—math was one of my better subjects, actually. Dispassionate, and a universal language. "Why, is this a study group? I like working . . ." I paused, considered my phrasing, not wanting to lie. "I *prefer* working on my own," I said, which I did, because it cut down on the stress of conversation.

"Well, that's really great for *you* and all, but not everyone feels that way." Olivia, the senior girl, had her back pushed up against a bookcase, and she kept rocking into it, making it shudder. "Some of us aren't doing so great, and some of us need to graduate on time."

"Oh." It wasn't clear to me how I could help them. Olivia and Marion, in particular, weren't even in my classes.

"Anyway." Adeline stared at Olivia until she sat still; until everyone was perfectly still. "Anyway. Studying is fine, but sometimes it's not enough. We want to do everything we possibly can to make sure finals go well this year. It's important. For all of us."

"Do something, like what?"

"Hmm," said Adeline. "Have you ever heard of the Gray Governess?"

"No."

"Well, she's the ghost of the library, and she's going to help us pass. And you're going to help us talk to her."

## *Excerpt from* The Donne School:
## History and Legacy, *by R. B. Stinson*

THOUGH MANY CONSIDER THE METAPHYSICAL poet and cleric John Donne (b. 1572, d. 1631) the institution's primary spiritual forebear, the Donne School has long maintained a second connection to the mysterious and much-debated Lady Donne, also called the Gray Governess. A recluse and a scholar from the eighteenth century, the Governess lived in Devonshire, England, as heir to and proprietor of her ancestral castle The Goss, where she acted as ward to a group of orphaned young women from all over the county who called themselves the Gray Goslings. This group was viewed with some apprehension by the community; reported Gosling activity ranged from advanced hermetic scholarship to unsubstantiated, likely slanderous accounts of witchcraft and necromancy, though it is widely believed by serious historians that the girls spent most of their time cultivating the grounds around the castle in order to provide food to the local poor. After The Goss burned down in 1826, all firsthand records of the period were lost.

Although her mark on history is fainter than that of her literary namesake, it can be seen in her limited remaining writing that Lady Donne shared many of the poet's philosophical concerns, including the mercurial essence of nature, flux and momentariness in all existence, and the transmigration of the human spirit into the physical world. Lady Donne, however, also believed in the transmigration of God's spirit into man, and was notable for her insistence that the exercise of human will is a vital method of communication with the divine. In simpler terms, she believed that what we do is what God is, and that this fact endows humanity with a number of grave obligations, particularly when guiding young people toward productive lives.

At the Donne School, our primary responsibility is to the welfare and education of our students, and we believe Lady Donne provides them with a unique example of modern (if not quite contemporary) femininity. Robust in her challenge to the idea that young ladies must be seen and not heard, Lady Donne was heard, but not seen; she offered shelter and education to the unfortunate without seeking any personal visibility or reward, and was bold enough to insist on a causal link between base corporeal actions and the transcendence of the soul. Her work was, in a word, visionary, despite the limitations placed on her sex during her lifetime. Stonework rescued from the ruins of The Goss can be found throughout the Donne School campus, serving as a reminder of the Gray Governess's commitment to education and as an extratemporal link between today's Goslings and those of yesteryear. A chalice of earth from Devonshire, likewise, evokes the Governess's spirit in the library.

*Editor's note: This page, torn out of a Donne School reference book, was found tucked into the Andropov diary. A thorough comb-through of the Donne School library, including the sub-basements, located the exact tome from which the page originated, including the shredded remnants where the page was removed, and a smudged fingerprint in the nearby margins.*

# *Zoya*

*11.*

"HERE'S THE BASIC IDEA," CINDY TOLD me, stepping in for Adeline. She seemed nervous again, allowing herself one small nibble at her pretty thumbnail. "There's supposed to be this library ghost? And if you ask her things, she can help you with your schoolwork? Because she believed in education?"

"Ok," I said. "And?"

"And we want her to help us? According to the legend, you're supposed to find this dirt, see. That's the first thing. And then you get a sensitive person to be the ghost's, um, mouth. Voice. And, um, we thought, you seemed pretty sensitive."

I looked around the room, waiting for one of the girls to burst into laughter. But they were nodding, attentive. Leslie and Bernice held hands, and despite my fear of being made a fool of, I was intrigued. Back in Moscow I'd been raised by the state to believe in sensible ideas, focusing on practical knowledge and hard work instead of fairytales about life after death. God was forbidden in my childhood, and spook stories, too, those hair-raising articles of the capitalist imagination, designed to lull the overrun masses into a submissive stupor, while the revolution was designed, instead, to wake us up. But the pragmatism required by my Soviet education never quite took, with me. Maybe because my mother had been full of superstitions—sit on a cold stone and lose your child-bearing abilities; go to sleep with wet hair and you'll wake up with the walking flu; whistle below the full moon and you're inviting something malign to tea—or maybe just because I didn't feel that my physical senses were perfect enough to grasp everything the universe had to offer. And then, too, my parents died, which felt like something that might happen to somebody else, suggesting that I wasn't living my own proper life. Anyway, beyond any ghostly concerns, I hadn't been completely honest with Adeline when I said my grades were fine. They could've been better. They could always have been better.

"So how do we get the dirt?" I asked.

Cindy nudged Marion with her toe, and the younger girl reached into a knapsack, pulling out a paper bag. She shook it, and I heard the soft sprinkling of earth.

"Open your hands," Marion instructed, and I did so, making a little bowl. She shook a bit of the dirt onto my palms.

"And you all just thought I could do this? Because I seem . . . open?"

"Well, that," Cindy agreed. "And, honestly, none of us wanted to. We figured if you said no, we'd tell Margaret you follow her around copying her every move."

"What?" I retracted my hands a bit, losing a light dusting of soil.

"Careful!" Cindy said. "Look, it's no big deal. We just thought, if *we* were Margaret, then *we* wouldn't want our creepy roommate tailing us like a creepy shadow. Not that you're necessarily creepy," she assured me with a shrug. "And I mean, you said yes, so we don't have to tell Margaret anything anyway."

My face burned. In a way, it had worked: my plan to get noticed and find my place among the other girls. But this was not the place I had wanted, or the notice I was hoping for. The ghostly dirt felt cool in my hands, and gave off the vaguest scent of grass and stone.

"What do we do now?" I asked, not looking up.

"Now we're going to say a poem," Marion told me. She was the calmest of them, and her voice was pleasant. Lulling. "You just listen to the poem, and each of us will light a candle. Then the Gray Governess is supposed to speak."

"Ok," I said. It didn't sound so bad. Around me, everyone nodded, and Adeline gently pushed me into the center of the circle. I sat down, and they arranged themselves at an even distance, pulling out short tapers and passing a box of matches hand to hand. Louise stood up and turned off the lights. There was just the soft glow of the candles.

Later I would realize the poem was in the Donne School charter, and I would wonder how they came to select it for this particular task. But at the time I barely caught the words—all I took in was the sense they were talking of honesty, clarity, a peculiar girl. I supposed she must be me. I closed my eyes, and the poem rumbled across me like waves. I thought of the whale, which I'd seen from the ship that brought me to America. I thought of my mother, singing gentle lullabies. And my father, frowning at me, beginning to change from the lighthearted man I knew in my early childhood into someone suspicious, hollow-cheeked, and stern.

He had been a true believer in the revolution that killed the centuries-old Tsarist regime with the aim of redistributing all the aristocracy's land and wealth. He was, too, a passionate advocate of the idea that the workers of the world would unite, that we shared a spirit which would help us ascend to a place of equanimity and humble goodness. I loved his faith, as it was all that I knew, and loved it more when he began to rise in the Party, bringing home meat from the most recalcitrant butcher and offering us little presents: a comb or a ribbon, a locket with his picture inside. The modest lift in our household status seemed to confirm that his faith was justified, that the Party was right in all it said.

But as the years went by in Moscow, something changed for him, and then, slowly, it changed for me. Though I was still obedient, my political observance stopped pleasing him, somehow—even simple expressions of enthusiasm for the Party or our brave new world made him look at me with suspicion. When he told me we wouldn't be going back to Lipetsk because the Party thought his skills were needed elsewhere, I was over-joyed at the idea of staying in the city and danced around the room, singing a little song I made up on the spot. (*Kto yez-dit? Ni-k-to. Kto sidit zdes'? Ya, horosho!* Who's going? No one. Who's staying? Me!) But he was ashen.

"Don't you see?" he asked me. "It isn't right. If I'm not there to help with the harvest, who will do my work for me? Someone will have to do it for me." I didn't understand why this upset him. But he wouldn't stop talking about it, or about the other items on his growing list of qualms. Opulent meetings. Peculiar methods. Privileges withheld from the many for the benefit of the few.

In very little time our social ascension slowed, then stopped. I pestered my father with questions—innocent ones mostly, about when we'd be getting more food rations and why it was that the Party wasn't happy with us. Hadn't we all been happy before? Apparently I pressed this particular issue hard enough that something in my father snapped. One day as we were setting the table for dinner I asked again, and he grabbed my shoulders, stopping me on the way from the stove to the table and upsetting a platter of food in my hands. "It's better to be good," he told me, "than to be happy. Remember that, Zoya." His eyes scared me. I threw the platter down and ran away from him, hiding my tears behind my hand. It wasn't long before he was gone.

All these scenes drifted in front of me as I sat in the Donne School library with my eyes pinched shut, carpet scratching against my thighs. At some point the other girls stopped reciting the poem, but I didn't notice. There were images in front of me. People in the shadows. Someone with something urgent to say.

"God, snap out of it." It took me a moment to realize that Adeline was shaking my shoulder. "It's no good if you don't speak English. What was she saying?"

"What?" I blinked, as bleary-eyed as if I'd just awoken from a deep sleep. "Was I talking?"

"Oh my god, yes, it worked, but you were just saying, like, gobbledygook." She rubbed her forehead. "How are we supposed to know what she told us?"

"Who?"

"The Gray Governess! The whole *point* of all this?" Cindy piped in now, looking just as cross as Adeline. "Is there something we're supposed to do? So our grades are good? Did she tell us to eat dandelion leaves or something?" A few other girls turned to Cindy, curious, and she blushed. "I heard that somewhere, that she told people that."

*Ti' budet bolshe,* I suddenly remembered. *Ti' budet luchshe.* There had been a voice of some kind, after all.

"I think she told me we'd get better?" I said. I didn't know how to explain what that meant, or that the grammar of the words spoke only to me. *You'll be more, you'll be greater—you* in the singular, meaning not the rest of them. As the girls around me perked up, I sensed now was not the time to try to make them understand.

"That seems kind of promising," Olivia said. Then she peered at me. "Are you sure that's actually what she told you though? You seemed kind of—I don't know. Sick. Off."

"Off of what?"

"It's—Who cares. It's an expression. But you didn't look normal. Your eyes were all weird."

"Weren't they closed?"

"Oh my god, you didn't know you opened your eyes?" Cindy looked horrified. "Ok, this is getting creepy. Somebody turn on the lights."

Marion started to cry, softly. "Jesus wouldn't love this," she said.

"Oh hush," said Adeline.

The lights came on and the girls blew out their candles. No one seemed to be paying much attention, so I let the dirt fall through my fingers onto the ground, brushing my palms together to get them clean.

"Uh, we'll see you later," Cindy said as she stood up to leave. "And, um, thanks, I guess."

"Sure," I told her. I let the other girls disperse without me, not quite trusting myself to stand while they were watching. My legs were jelly: I had to use the stair rail to keep myself on my feet as I made my way back into the library proper. Back at my desk I was startled to find the Schopenhauer book upright, the philosopher's dyspeptic face staring straight into my own. I knew that someone had probably just come by and turned it out of curiosity, but the sight made my throat tighten up. I returned the book to the woman at the front desk without finishing it, and simply skipped that assignment—a book report, which, curiously enough, our teacher never collected.

Later, alone in my room while Margaret had dinner in town with friends, I took out the last few possessions I had from home, and held them up to my face, one by one. Looking, I suppose, for secret messages in the tattered threads I had left. My locket. My rotten gloves. A little box with a few seeds in it, which I'd collected from the Moscow lilacs which in springtime grew out of every window box and every crack in the city streets. I wondered if they'd still grow for me, here. I thought I might try to find out.

## 12.

In the weeks and months following our botched séance, my school assignments began to take on a more personal quality—the teachers all seeming to draw on some obscure archive of my disquiet that I assumed had been awakened in that basement room. For instance, in art class it was announced that we were going to make busts of our fathers from papier-mâché threaded over balloons on the theory that the round balloons would provide healthy apple cheeks and funny foreheads. And on the theory, too, that this would be fun for us, which everyone but me seemed to agree with. Quality time with dear old dad. Some of my classmates brought in photos to work from, passing them around so we could all laugh at the way that fathers are: so embarrassing, so sweet. A couple of girls asked me if I had any photos of home left, and I thought of the locket, safe in my room, which I almost never wore. "No," I said, firmly. It seemed easier to tell them that everything was lost, when almost every-thing was. I claimed to not quite remember what he looked like.

We wore smocks to protect our clothing, and spent an hour diligently pasting newspaper strips into smooth lines, trying to smear together the edges and adding layers for eyebrows, bent strips for the nose. I didn't mind so much when the faces were anonymous, and could've been anyone—I just didn't like the idea of calling yet another person up from beyond the grave. I figured I would make a brown-haired, frowning no-man, and everyone, acting on misguided pity, would tell me it looked a lot like me. I would get a decent grade. "You're not my father," I whispered to the blank, beige face in front of me as the other girls laughed and kissed their plaster papas on the cheek. In spite of myself, I thought of the real man, my *papochka*, the day he went missing. His hair messy and uncombed, and his clothing rumpled as he slouched out the door. We never saw him again. Counter-revolutionary ideas, my mother and I guessed. Pulled around a corner by rough hands. Leaving us to survive alone, because he wanted so badly to be good. Despite my efforts the balloon man began to look more and more like him, and I quietly wished it ill.

The next class period we were supposed to pop the balloons beneath the dry papier-mâché and get on with painting them. But instead we found that half the balloons had deflated overnight, caving our fathers in from the top. It was—I was surprisingly shaken to see my secret curse enacted in such a gruesome manner, even if they were just art projects, toys. Worse still was the fact that my balloon was intact, while others around me suffered the stupid indignity I'd wished on myself. I saw one girl run her fingertips over the dent in her father-balloon, as if she could heal it by longing, or make some sort of emotional splint. She couldn't, though, and I felt a wave of guilt.

Can you cause a small tragedy just by wanting to? It seemed that way to me. That cause and effect were intertwined, impossible. And hadn't Cindy and Adeline implied I was a witch? While we were cleaning up, the girls decided to stomp the balloons and get their revenge for being made to feel they'd failed; the semi-deflated ones wouldn't burst, having already lost their tension, but the pristine ones exploded and split the papier-mâché back into scraps.

The whole classroom was uproarious; people were shrieking. We ran around screaming, "Kaboom! Kaboom!" For a second I thought I might belong among these girls, as I had sometimes felt I did with the Young Pioneer scouts back in Moscow, just one in a great blur of bodies, one cell in a great hive mind. But the affection of the room cooled as they ran out of heads to smash. Of course I could've given them mine and prolonged the mood: one eager classmate even held out her hands. But now that I had the chance, I couldn't seem to let it go.

## *13.*

LET ME GET BACK TO VERA, THOUGH, dear reader. Just for a little while, to cool my mind, move away from Cindy and Adeline and Marion, who all got decent grades that year after all, though Marion ended up leaving anyway, for a Catholic school even farther upstate. Silly girls, with their simple lives and simpler troubles. I wish I could go with them and escape what came next for me, the dark deeds that stumbled across my path, from a kiss on the lips to a slap on the cheek. Not to mention the darker things, which are still coming, even now. But I can't go with those girls, and so I'll go to Vera instead: the one who'll have me, however reluctantly.

I doubt Vera had a dacha either, at least not the sort I dreamed about as a child. Too small, too peasant-inflected. And why would she need one, anyway, when her family lived on a country estate? As big as our whole apartment building, surrounded by forests, veined with creeks and rivers. The house bright yellow and white, like the palace at Peterhof. Probably the land was farmed, but Vera's hands would never have touched soil. She would've had smart calfskin riding gloves and a white Lipizzaner, its mane in braids. She would've learned to make the horse dance from side to side within a ring, but preferred to trot through the countryside and listen to birdsong, watch the secret life beneath the trees. Perhaps once or twice she came upon two peasants fornicating in the bushes, and this would have been the first time she saw the white of a thigh, the curve of a buttock, the hasty motion of stolen passion.

I doubt, too, that she told anyone about them. Not from pity or under-standing, you see—she just wouldn't have known any peasants well enough to name names.

It soothes me to remember Vera as she must've been then, during the time that stretched out between our meeting as children and the moment when we were reunited as women and rivals; adults of sound body and mind. Thinking about her youth is restful for me in the same way as looking at a beautiful painting, where a few flicks of the brush come together to create a tableau so warm you want to crawl inside. She had so much that I did not. Silk stockings, piano lessons, an enormous harp in the family's sitting room, set up by a window that stretched ceiling-high. A peaceful image. I imagine her running her fingertips over the strings, not quite playing, but not without a certain sensitivity to their rhythms. At one point, I know, the family brought in a young scholar to guide her reading—a pleasant fellow, if somewhat foppish. Flopping hair. (Lev told me about him once: never met the man himself, but always thought Vera had a crush, from the way she said his name.) Not quite aristocratic, but attuned to the elegance of mathematics, and selected by her father with help from his connections at the university. Her father: an ordinary man, not over-bearing, attached to his things. So attached that later, in Paris, he'd die clutching a golden cuckoo clock that had belonged to his grandfather.

Perhaps you'll wonder how I can be sure about any of this. And I can't be, of course: all I have are pieces, stitched together with wobbly thread. I know what little is in the public record, and what she told her husband, up to a point. Lyrical Lev, Lying Lev, Lev the Lothario, or so he liked to think. He used to give me bundles of their letters to riffle through, as a gesture of closeness, knowing that I liked his handwriting, and some of those contained traces of her past. Just jokes, recollections. The rest I have to make up. Not an act of intrusion, in my opinion, but just embellish-ment and embroidery: we talk about our own lives this way all the time, stretching the truth to fit our feelings. And Vera and I have become so tangled together that in order to tell you my whole story, I have to tell you hers, too. (A nerve-wracking thought: that I am not complete until she is. Well, then, let's continue.)

Vera and the scholar would've been given a schoolroom, I think, but Vera never did like being contained. They would've gone to the library for their lessons instead, to her father's study, to the sitting room, on a divan beside the harp. Wherever her parents were not. The servants would bring in a samovar of hot tea, and dishes of honey and lemon and jam. Blue and white china cups. Vera's lip on the rim of one, puckered out as she sipped. Her eyes peering sideways between dark lashes, and the scholar watching so intently that he spilled all over a rare collection of eighteenth-century anatomical prints which the two had been innocently perusing. Biology hour. His hand running along the inner, upper quadrant of her thigh. Explaining it to her as a surgeon might see it, while her cheeks flushed but her gaze remained steady. Her neck flushed and she let her mouth open. The thighs themselves flushing as they parted just a little wider, as her hand reached out and found something to hold.

But wait.

Let's leave them alone for a moment, our young lovers. It's the decent thing to do, and more than that, I'd like to walk around the room while their attention is otherwise occupied, removing Vera as the focal point in favor of the space at large. You see, if her life is like a painting, then the details are important: sometimes it's only by studying the background that you understand a picture's true meaning, its actual subject. (Not the pink cheeks of the child sitting for the portrait, but the skull on the shelf behind, the fly on the rotting fruit in the bowl, that tell you what the painter thought about youth and mortality.)

I want to see, if only in my mind's eye, her oak poster bed and the cherry-wood tables that line the walls of her chamber. Her hairbrush, bristles chock with black strands because the maid hasn't yet been in. Even the bedclothes, tossed. I want to smell her buttery sleep as I back out the door, so it becomes mine, just a little bit. Run my fingers along the Japanese vases lining the hallways, and see the automaton set behind glass that could, when wound, spin its cane and whistle a frightening tune. I want to sit deep in their sofas, all down-stuffed. Even if it makes me sneeze. To walk through the lemon and chicken-fat air of their kitchen, see the calf strung up for roasting. Take a bite out of a candle, leave tooth prints in the taper and flick wax onto the rug, knowing it'll be vigorously beaten away. I want to see the servants scurry behind secret doors, order the gardeners to stand by height and by age and by favorite rose. Hellebore here, there gallica.

Oh, but they're finished now. She and he. So young, their love is instantaneous. It's over in a second, and it lasts forever. He'll go back to Leningrad, and she'll be given a lady instructor. An older lady, compared to the girl. Perhaps thirty, thirty-two. Hair of dun. Glasses perched. Only the memory of Vera's young scholar remaining, and the hope of meeting again.

## 14.

BUT THEY WON'T. Sorry, Vera.

# *Lev*

MY VERA. MY VERENKA. YOU AREN'T cross with me, are you? I don't think I could bear it. After all, before I left you pestered me to tell you about the women from my past, because of those beastly rumors, I suppose. And I gave in only because I wanted to soothe you after that series of fits you threw—your version of a fit. A pout. This has been a long time to go without seeing your face or getting a letter, even if I am *en route*. A long stretch without at least the tender animals of your handwriting creeping out across the page in front of me. Do you know I used to hold every one of your letters up to my face, so the words could caress my skin? I'm imagining it now. How I'd breathe them in, the perfect soliloquies of your *q*s and *s*s, the hot hint of the *h*, the burning uproar of the ж. And did you know your handwriting is identical in every language? That's not true for everyone. It takes real strength of character.

The scent changes, though, as you hop between tongues. I'm not sure how you achieve the effect, but you can trust me. I am fluent in you. Your Russian is full of pepper and thyme, all the old world and the new—there's a bit of whisky in it, too, an undernote which I appreciate. It's the way you smell on a hot day. After a walk, picking a piece of hair off your forehead, leaning down to pull a bit of grass from your shoe.

Grasshoppers flicking by, pinging off the nearby stones and kicking up dust so it sticks to your skin. Intoxicating, of course. Breathy. Sun-bitter. You might think it would all be gun smoke and snow, but no. It's not the country. It's you, in the country.

Your French begins with mineral water and ends with a thin slice of apple. It's simpler: starvation diet. The middle is miles of unsmoked tobacco and piles of thin paper to roll it in, with sticky ends. But you'll be curious about the English. You've never liked the way you sounded in America, complained that people thought they knew you just by the way your voice hollowed out over certain vowels. You moaned that your vocabulary took on a martial edge, and now you'll want to know: on the page, is there any softening? And I say: of a sort. But I doubt it'll endear you to hear that your American letters are thick with the scent of asphalt melting in the sun. Just pliable, giving under the heel. Bitumen, hydro-chloride, diesel drippings. The road one great roasting pan. I wish I knew how you did it. Perhaps you have different pens, but I've examined the ink, and would swear it's all identical.

Come, Vera, have you smiled at all to learn how carefully I categorize you? Even a little? That's my nightingale, my night-blooming flower.

I hope you aren't moping over poor doomed Dina. Such a minor crea-ture to make such a great red stain over our lives. Don't let her. Dina's hair was dark, but not so dark as yours. Her skin was white, but yours is milk. Yours is clean teeth, and the tongue that licks them. You know this. The tongue my tongue, counting your incisors and bicuspids, counting your fingers and your toes. Poor Dina had a single candle in her hand, whereas you have ignited a thousand fatal fires with just the tip of your thumb. Judicious and useful. *Les petites morts de Vera*. I could recite them in front of bishops and have them declared holy, like the deaths of saints. This one in a moving car. This one leaning against the door frame. This one on a fainting couch, your father in the very next room, waiting to pour us glasses of gin. Whereas Dina had just one death, slow and dumb. Lying in her bed, as still as a virgin.

You know, I have at times considered shooting you in the gut just to see how differently you'd take the pain. The distinction, I think, would be enormous. Not wan, but angry. Your face alive with terse revenge until the moment it was not. Every second a mortal danger to me, as your precious blood drained out into a puddle round my feet. I would not want to cross you, Vera; it would be safer to kill you. You're more formidable than I am. We both know that.

Please write and let me know about your plans for the rest of the summer. I sit in tense anticipation.

# *Zoya*

## 15.

I WAS A STUDENT AT THE DONNE SCHOOL for a year and a half, spending my one interim summer mimeographing research notes for an anthropology professor before graduating without particular honors. Margaret, for reasons unknown, withstood me the whole time—perhaps it was the frequency with which she awoke to find me gone, staying out the entire day at Marie's café, or in class, or at the library. Perhaps it was my clothes, never any competition for her own. On the rare occasions when we left the dorm together I looked like some downtrodden child she'd picked up on the street so she could warm me up with a cup of soup, which only made me avoid her more earnestly—as did the fear that Cindy or Adeline might tell her about my shadowing campaign, despite their promises to the contrary. Anyway it was embarrassing to be seen together. I was used to a discount-bin wardrobe, but not to being surrounded by so many people who could afford to do better. In the spring my green coat became too warm, and so I lost even that small piece of armor.

It was a relief not to need a new roommate for my second year, though. Other girls pressed their foreheads together and giggled, plotting to get peak real estate in the towers, with garden views and proximity to the caf. Sometimes they exploded into spectacular arguments: one ingénue slapped another in our history seminar upon finding out she'd been dropped in favor of a rival classmate. For the whole hour, the slapped girl sat stiff and tall, her face shining red but still triumphant. I didn't have any friends I could ask—it was exhausting enough to speak to strangers in a language I struggled to understand, never mind confidantes—and I didn't want to learn any new behaviors around sharing toiletries and room temperature and ambient sound. In Moscow the heat was controlled by the state, turned on each fall to identical levels city-wide, give or take the functionality of your building's furnace, so the idea that you could adjust a room to suit your exact—even momentary—pleasure was new to me, and I saw how quickly this power went to people's heads. Temperature was at the heart of many domestic battles royale, with girls daily arriving to class covered in sweat, or shivering and wearing fingerless typing gloves. Girls came down with unnecessary head colds. Each room had a gas coil heater that clicked and hissed, burping out alarming sounds in the middle of the night if their settings had been recently changed, and I let Margaret keep ours a bit too high—"I have lizard blood," she told me, "I need to sit on a hot rock"—because otherwise I couldn't sleep for all the clinking. The idea of adjusting to a new and unpredictable set of preferences alarmed me.

Still, Margaret had plenty of followers, and I figured she'd drop me as soon as she could. Social dynamics among the girls required constant maintenance, and choosing a roommate had the potential to elevate or destroy you, depending. Someone as popular as Margaret might choose a classmate with access to good contraband, or a pretty girl to decorate her room like a flower. Or a less pretty girl, to help herself shine in comparison. She was smart enough not to need a study buddy, or a patsy to do her homework, but everyone needs something. I figured she'd choose to room with her friend Sharon, whose father owned a plant that manufactured skin cream, or Lucy, who had a pert nose and a lisp. Or any of the other moon-faced things that scurried to vacate my bed when I came through the door every night. But no.

"Oh, you," she said one afternoon near the end of our first year together, returning from class. Always the tone of surprise when we ran across one another in the middle of the day. I was tearing apart my side of the room, throwing thin-elbowed sweaters onto the floor and shaking out textbooks by the spine.

"Have you seen my form?" I asked, not bothering to stop in my search. "Room requests are due."

Margaret clicked her tongue and sat down in her desk chair, twisting her neck so she could still face me. "I turned it in for you," she said. "I thought you knew."

"What?" I inspected the sock in my hand. Unmatched, and unmatchable. I balled it up and tossed it in the wastebasket. "Why would you do that?"

"Well, technically I threw it out." She flipped her hair down over her face and then back up, catching it into a voluminous ponytail. "You only have to submit one if you're requesting together."

"What?" I said again.

"Yeah, so because of your whole orphan thing, we got early pick. St. Paul's Tower, third floor." She raised an eyebrow at me. "Not bad, right?"

I gaped, speechless, and Margaret took this for agreement. Fair enough, I suppose, given our relationship pattern of silence and distance. She turned her back to me and propped open her French textbook, proceeding to read aloud in an atrocious accent about going to the cinema, meeting at the cinema, having been at the cinema, having met.

When I arrived at the Donne School I thought I'd be embraced. Looking up at the tall stone halls after stepping out of the taxi that had been provided for me, I imagined hundreds of girls leaning out the windows waving handkerchiefs, streaming through the doors in white dresses, their hair in very American ponytails, all of their limbs long and healthy and tanned. They would throw their arms out, so many girls crowding around me at once that we'd move and shift like a flock on the wing, wavering back and forth in ferocious tandem. We'd lift up, our toes just barely scraping the ground. Instead, a single matron came out with a clipboard and showed me to my room, where I found Margaret, whose previous roommate had disappeared when her appendix burst without warning. Even after Cindy's threats I occasionally held Margaret's clothes up to my body, imagining what they'd look like on. She came back from the bathroom once rather quicker than I'd anticipated and found me trying on her lipstick—just a dab, as I wasn't brave enough to wear much color. "No," she told me. That was all she had to say. I gave in like a puppy, rolling over to expose the soft pink of my belly, hoping she might pick me up in her mouth and carry me with her wherever she went. Which is what I really wanted. Not the whole school in tennis whites, but Margaret at least.

What I got was Margaret. And I was glad not to lose her, not to have lost her, to keep her at least for a while, to have kept.

## Donne Girls Spring Into a New Role

From the *Gosling Herald*, April 15, 1927

MAPLE HILL, NJ. EVERY YEAR THE Donne School student body is faced with a problem: how do you throw a good spring formal with no gentleman dance partners? This year, thrifty girls got into the spirit of making-do and decided to use the number-one resource they had on hand: other girls.

A week before the Mix-n-Match Fling, every student entering the caf was asked to throw her name into a hat, and once a quorum was achieved, half the names were drawn to play the role of women, and half were drawn to play the role of men. The lists, posted outside the dorms after dinner that night, caused a great deal more excitement than your usual spring dance theme.

Some girls (we aren't allowed to call them *sad sacks* in print, but readers may draw their own conclusions) were disappointed to find themselves assigned to the male gender, though most (including this reporter) accepted the responsibility with the enthusiasm it required. The girls assigned as "girls" were also looking forward to the event. "I feel like I'm about to meet my new beau!" a sophomore from Rhode Island was heard to say, followed by a cascade of appreciative laughter.

The night of the dance, Donne girls (and boys) were surprised to find the gentlemen better outfitted than the ladies—and slightly outnumbering them. It turned out that finding a decent "boy's" outfit was such good sport that even some of the assigned "girls" got in on the fun. Never let it be said that our ladies don't relish a challenge! When asked about the meticulous detailing on his cravat, one Donne "boy" (also known as Sharon Lisby) looked affronted and replied quite witheringly, "Of course I wore my very best. What else would be good enough for these young beauties?" Well put.

In the days since this successful party, it's safe to say that all the Donne girls are looking at their classmates with renewed admiration. Margaret Rathburn of New Canaan, Connecticut, described the suit she'd acquired as "one of [her] new favorite ensembles" and the dress she chose for her roommate, Zoe Andropov, as "entirely demure," adding, "She sat there like a little angel and let me do her face. Turns out she has lovely eyes, once she lets someone line them!" Miss Andropov, tucked in the corner of the room as this reporter conducted her interview, was seen to blush. She did, indeed, look becoming with pink cheeks.

The *Herald* is firm in our opinion that the Mix-n-Match Fling indicates triumphant future endeavors for the entire Donne School community. After all, if we can make gentlemen out of ladies, what can't we transform to our advantage?

*Editor's note: Found in the Andropov diary, with several passages underlined in felt pen.*

# *Zoya*

## 16.

A FEW TIMES IN THE FOLLOWING MONTHS, Cindy and Adeline badgered me back into the library to try and contact more spirits, though we didn't have much luck. They pared down the people and the accessories, so it was just the three of us, and instead of candles they brought cigarettes. Mostly we sat around while they smoked. There was just one other occasion worth mentioning. It was early in the spring of my second and final year, when the grass was still covered with frozen dew in the mornings, and they made me show up before first bell, slipping a note under my door to indicate the time and place. I walked over with a scarf pulled tight around my neck, coat hanging off my shoulders, grumbling inwardly about missing breakfast. I'd become very fond of morning coffee, and without it I felt sluggish and low. Scratchy throat, itchy nose. Icy wind and early pollen. As I approached the library Cindy poked her head out of the door and indicated I should hurry, so I picked up into a jog and followed her to the basement, rolling my eyes just a bit.

There was another girl there, no one I knew, who introduced herself as Caroline Geiss. A fellow fourth-year and an aficionado of field hockey, hailing from Minnesota. Her legs were covered in bruises, which she wore with pride.

"What are we doing here so early?" I asked, throwing my bag down and shaking the cold morning out of my hair. "Grades? Peeking into the future?" I looked at Cindy and waved my fingers. "Woo-ooh?"

"Why don't you tell her?" Cindy said to Caroline. The girl colored, which was unexpected. All those muscles and wounds, she seemed like the type who could hold her own.

"My friend," she said. "I miss her." Apparently, before her parents shipped her off to New Jersey, Caroline had been close with a girl named Laura Shipman, who she'd known since childhood. During the first week of classes at the Donne School, Caroline found out that Laura had had a bad reaction to a bee sting, and had died following a severe attack of anaphylactic shock. Her parents wouldn't agree to bring her back for the funeral, for financial reasons or something else that Caroline wouldn't go into. Now here she was, and as she looked at me her spine straightened out with hope and sincerity. "They said you could talk to her."

"I don't know." I frowned. It seemed unkind to promise anything when my past attempts had ended so badly.

"But you can at least *try*, right?" Adeline tugged my hair until it hurt, and I slapped her hand away. Then I nodded. Because really, why not?

"We better hurry, though, if we want to get out of here before classes start."

The four of us sat in a circle, Caroline fidgeting beside me. Cindy and Adeline started reciting that same strange poem that always sent me into a stupor, and I closed my eyes, waiting. I didn't expect anything to happen, not again. I thought we'd sit there for five or six minutes growing increasingly bored, until someone stood up and said they were going to get an apple before the caf closed, and that would be that. But then there was a breeze on my face, the scent of clover and cut grass. I reached out and took Caroline's hand, and she squeezed it, tightly.

"Laura?" she asked. "Is it you?"

"Yes," I said.

I knew it was really me, but then again, I didn't. I was playing the game the way they wanted me to, and for a second it was sweet. A rush of familiarity and bubblegum, swimming pools full of chlorine and toys that could float. It fuzzed around my awareness, bleaching out parts of me I knew to be basic: language, history, loss. And the girls surrounded me with sudden interest, whispering, "Laura, Laura," as if they all knew and adored me. When I peeked out at their faces to see again if they were joking, they opened their eyes one by one and beamed at me with total love. A moment in which we were infatuated with each other. And then, the room grew uneasy. Maybe I smiled too wide. Maybe they just came to their senses. When I started squeezing back on Caroline's hand, I felt the bones beneath her skin crunching together like a fistful of crab's legs, and she tried to tug it away. But I tightened my fingers and pulled her towards me, crashing her head into my shoulder a bit harder than I intended to, and holding her there.

"Ouch," she said. First a whisper in my ear, and then a yelp, a shout, as the others came to her rescue. "Ouch! Get off me!" I gave her one last tug, then let go.

Those girls, they liked me so easily and so much the second they saw me as one of their own. *Laura, Laura.* A girl from their same world, where houses got drafty from size instead of poor craftsmanship, and your uncle came by just to take you and your girlfriends out for chocolate milkshakes, which you sucked up through colored straws. Where you slept in on Saturdays, and could accomplish anything you set your mind to, and where you were given a bright red bicycle with streamers on the handlebars, which whistled as you rode. They'd never known how to make do, to sew the covers back onto old schoolbooks. To sneak into the cloakroom at restaurants and gather tobacco from men's coat pockets in order to make a cigarette with which to bribe the greengrocer. To watch their parents turn into strangers before their eyes, and then be told by those strangers that they didn't deserve any more than what others had, because why would they? The girls didn't want to know those things. And they were equally afraid of the fact that I did, and that I could shed the appearance of that knowledge so quickly. Like slipping out of a skin.

Or maybe they were just scared about the tightness of my grip, the red lines I left on Caroline's hand, and the bruise that formed there the next morning. Not my chameleon face but my strong fingers. None of them ever talked to me again after that. But it didn't occur to me for some time how ordinary and impersonal their fear might have been.

## 17.

As it turned out, I had bigger problems at school that year than rooming or even ghosts. I had to think about graduation. A concept that had somehow never occurred to me until it was almost on top of me: a hasty exeunt to an invisible offstage. Where could I go? What expertise could I offer? Other girls, I knew, were planning on college or secretarial school, or being set up in New York by their parents. A few were going home to Boston to help their mothers throw DAR parties, and at least one from our class married a dentist and moved to Detroit, having first spent three months showing off her ring and moaning about the impossibility of wedding dinner place cards. One joined the circus, I think. The actual circus. She said she was starting out as a makeup girl but planned to work her way up to an acrobat. I couldn't tell if she was serious, but like the rest she disappeared in a car after graduation and never came back.

Whatever wartime good graces landed me in Maple Hill to begin with had long since worn off. As the date of my dorm eviction loomed I haunted the mailroom, hoping for a letter from the Office of Orphans that had paid my tuition. Perhaps, I thought, they knew a wealthy benefactor. Perhaps they could set me up as someone's assistant. I could make a passable campfire with twigs and leaves and a single match; I could negotiate black-market transactions using only nylon stockings for currency. There had to be something I could contribute to, but despite my fine secondary school education I had no idea what this might be. A university was out of the question, because it cost money, and I thought with some bitterness about the wealthy Moscow girls who'd fled ahead of me to Europe and the new world, their furs and jewel earrings one day scattering to the wind as if they expected to be next in line for a bludgeoning now that the Romanovs were gone. At first I had been glad to be rid of them, elated to skate through a Moscow magically lightened of its bratty debutantes. But as winter lifted and my father disappeared, I did come to find some pity for them, deep within me—pity that they had been forced to leave home and all that they found dear. Now, thousands of miles away and years later, I realized they were fine. Probably getting ready to matriculate at Radcliffe or Sarah Lawrence, or else perhaps the Sorbonne. The revolution having changed—nothing. Vera once took issue with me on this point, arguing about lost estates and bank accounts absorbed into the national fund, but I'm fairly certain she arrived in Paris with diamonds sewn into her skirt hems.

Well, I shouldn't say the revolution changed nothing. It took my parents, after all.

That last semester as a Donne student I shook out the Moscow lilac seeds I'd saved and used my father's method to sprout them, first soaking them and letting them rest in a wet towel before transplanting them into a window box. I had, at that point, a deep sense that no more good would ever come to me from the country I'd abandoned, and those lilacs were the first hint that maybe I was wrong. The first hint that maybe what I deserved would not be the same as what I got—that I might do better. By making some educated guesses and reading a few pamphlets suggested by the Donne School gardening staff, I managed to adjust the mineral content in the soil just enough for the seeds to germinate and bloom. There was a fair bit of superstition involved, too: thinking they might miss the smoggy Moscow air, I borrowed a cigarette from a girl named Charlotte down the hall, and sat in front of the open window blowing clouds of smoke onto the soil. When the first buds opened that April—in the morning, with muted light gracing the petals as if through heavy-handed stage direction—it softened something in me. There were, after all, a few things in life untouched by people and the things we did. A few things that happened if the conditions were right, no matter who you were. Seeds had their own systems. After that I took to researching horticulture in the library, alternately calling forth and smudging out my family with every turn of the page.

At any rate, with a few weeks still to go before graduation, I had just unlocked my little brass mailbox and pulled out a handful of advertorial trash when one of the Donne School groundskeepers ran up to me. We'd always had a good rapport—I asked them questions about planting seasons and bulb hibernation, and they took pleasure in talking to a young woman who'd actually spent time in the dirt. They taught me things, a second education in seed varietals and local mulch tucked behind the lapel of my official degree. Most of the Donne girls acted as though the facilities crew didn't exist; at least, not until those same girls had a clanking radiator or a mouse chewing through the walls near their bed. They walked the swept paths and commented on the comeliness of the flowers, all while ignoring the men in brown duck cloth who were weeding under the begonias. Sometimes they got their hands on a bottle of sherry and threw up on the carpeting, taking it for granted that the stain would be scrubbed clean by morning and never bothering to apologize.

I wasn't in the mood for a conversation. Not even with this particular groundskeeper, John O'Brien, who was especially kind and always took an interest. *What are you planning to do next?* I knew he'd ask, and the harrowing silence which would follow that question was more than I could bear. I honestly thought about pretending not to know him, or else hitting him in the face and running out of the room. Throwing the few clothes I had into a bag and making my way to the bus station, scraping together my last few dollars for a ticket to anywhere. For weeks I'd been agonizing over which of my paltry possessions I could carry with me on my back when I left and which I'd have to part with. Now I sparkled with clarity: a couple of sweaters, a week's worth of socks. The skirt I was wearing and perhaps a pair of pants. What else could a girl need?

"Zo! Zoe!" John, as always, was happy to see me—and as always, mispronounced my name. He never quite wrapped his head around *Zoya*, though it is, to me, more obviously mellifluous than the nasal *Zo-ee* most Americans insist on. I gave up on *Zoya Ivanovna Andropova* early; here, I was just Zoe Andropov. Sometimes Zo. "I was looking for you," John puffed. Apparently he'd been running around campus; his face was pink. "I just found out, and I knew I had to tell you right away."

"Tell me—what?" I crumpled newsprint between my fingers. He seemed enthusiastic, but what was there to get excited for? Had the fellows put together a collection and bought me a balloon? Americans loved useless presents, I'd noticed. Rewards from bubblegum machines, wooden trinkets.

"There's an opening," John beamed. "Right up your alley."

"My alley?"

"Your—I don't know—area of expertise?"

I had trouble with idioms, but even more so with the idea I might be an expert in anything. "You must be mistaken."

"No, honey, that I am not." He puffed again, put his hands on his knees, delighted or perhaps on death's door. A redhead, his skin was almost translucent, and veritably boiled under any provocation. "They're building a greenhouse." He gestured to the rear of the building. "Behind the science hall. Your little green thumb. Gonna be perfect."

"I could—" I hesitated. "Work there?" He nodded. "Where would I live?"

"Probably let you keep campus housing until you save up for a place of your own." John stood up straight at last, expelling a great gush of air. "We're all rooting for you, sweetie pie."

"You are?" My eyes filled up with tears, and I leaned back against the wall of locked boxes. A weight off my shoulders, but still my knees were jelly. They knew, after all. They knew, already. And here I'd been desperate to escape John's high expectations.

After I recovered myself we hurried over to the facilities office; there had been some argument about who was in charge of the greenhouse project, and whether the hiring should fall under the domain of groundskeeping or the biological sciences. But as it turned out, both sides of that coin were keen on my potential, and I was hired with the title of Manager and Caretaker of Hothouse Plants. Following a provisional year, I could be offered a long-term contract, and though I would not be allowed to remain in the room I'd shared with Margaret, a small single would be made available for me until I could secure my own accommodations. In addition to maintaining a selection of fruits and vegetables for the cafeteria and observing student projects (my presence being a failsafe against those girls who slept through their watering or weeding sessions, and those too prim for fertilizer), my purview would include curating a display of exotic flora—a perfect showpiece for the school when anxious parents came to visit. What could be more soothing than warm, green stems bending overhead? And what more appealing than the waxy pink leaves of Stonecrop firecrackers and shock-yellow stamens of Dutch twink daffodils bursting with life while snow gathered in drifts beyond the windows?

And of course, a girl in an apron and dirty dungarees, walking throughout with her hair pinned back, clutching a spray bottle. Her face pink with intelligence and care. Tending something vulnerable and helping it grow to its best advantage.

## 18.

BUT WHERE WAS VERA IN ALL THIS? Parallel. Elsewhere.

Soon after her maiden tutoress arrived she was whisked off to Paris to live in her father's wretched pied-à-terre. On the way there was a masquerade ball in Leningrad (*Leningrad!* she must've thought), because even her escapes were plush, whether or not she admitted it. She wore a black gown à la *Madame X*, and a black silk mask tied on with a ribbon. Her mouth turned down as she walked from room to room and realized her young tutor was not there. Could not possibly have been there, amidst the champagne and the desperation of the old guard, a few wearing tuxedos that were feathering and fraying at the seams. Vera stood by a little table, one weighted down by a tall potted plant. An aloe all the way from Arizona, with sharp points and rigid leaves on which the staff had secured candles, using epoxy. (My opinion as an expert: not an advisable approach if you have an eye to the plant's longevity.)

She was thinking of poetry. Dark and spleen-filled stuff, apropos her new situation, fueled by the glass of wine in her hand. A few men offered dances—older men, friends of her father's—and she refused, in no mood to please her *cher papa*. Behind her, a balcony. Below that, the Moika. Dark water shimmering with applied light, and in her fit of teen pique she let herself think *All is vanity*, before mentally slapping her own wrist for adopting such a quotidian sentiment with such real feeling.

Her wrist, which—suddenly there were fingers there. Not the sturdy hands of her once-beloved, but long, elegant digits smudged artfully with ink. She looked up, glad for the mask, because she hadn't yet decided on an expression.

Though she would, soon enough.

# *Lev*

22 June 1931
Airmail via [Redacted]

DEAREST VERA. GRANDEST AND MOST terrible Vera. I know you're upset—
shall we be very American and even say *peeved?*—to be left alone in that
drafty Craftsman bungalow while I skulk around the border trying to
persuade some young patrolman to sneak me across into the country we
left behind. I know you disapprove of my entire project, from its concep-
tion to its most probable bitter end: a waste of money, a waste of talent, a
waste of time. Not to mention the danger to my person, though I think
this is the only part of the affair that might thrill you a little, your studious
*pyatnik* turned buccaneer. Black-bearded and ready for anything, buckle
or swash. I've even bought a gun, Vera. It's tucked in my waistband, a
gleaming black pistol. I made the seller give me lessons.

I know you think it's beneath me, darling, but I need that manuscript
if I'm to go on as a writer. As a man. It was my first: proof I can finish something once begun. You'll say that's silly, because it's *first*, not *only*, unless
indeed you mean *only still unpublished, only repudiated and rejected, only
unloved.* You'll say that in any case I won't possibly find it: a stack of yellow
pages tied together with a bit of twine, which I buried in an old tin box
outside the last trolley station on the outskirts of Leningrad. Maybe so, my
dear one. Maybe so. But the spirit of the whole endeavor—my entire *raison,*

my vision and scope—lies in those pages, and it would be a violation of the artistic compact not to try and retrieve them from their early grave. Anyway, I told my publisher, and you know he's quite enthusiastic.

In the meantime it pains me to picture you bumping around alone in that house. (Or, let's be honest, sitting behind your typewriter catching up on correspondence. Making a perfect cup of tea, stirring three times counterclockwise. I'm not so foolish as to imagine my absence has entirely undone you or your routines.) And of course my own incompetence prolongs our separation; I don't have your talent for knowing which hands to shake, which guards to bribe with cash and which to slip bottles of vodka, cognac, or rum. If you were here, the pages would already be a *fait accompli*, but instead I've now wasted a week with my bumbling attempts at travel *incognito*. Not that I'm bitter, no. The unseasonal wind claws at my face beneath this thin balaclava, and you sit solo, tucked in that ugly wingback chair by the window. No doubt disapproving of me doubly: abandoner, and inept. And here I've been writing to you about my old love affairs. What rot, in this besotted brain.

Let me do better, Vera. Let me tell you the story of us, how the past echoes the future, how our separations always end with reconciliation, reconnection, reconnoiter, coitus. For example: you in Paris, me still degrading in Leningrad. Do you know how I obsessed over you then? Your nose, straight and slender. Your hair, which melted on my tongue like tar.

I couldn't stand imagining you crouched in that stinking room in the fourteenth, with your father smoking on the balcony, head lost behind the ambient cloud. Your hips zipped into last season's skirt, fingertips weary with the cold Paris spring as you set type. None of the essays worth the effort. Don't argue, it's true. You read them too. You cranked the printing press that duplicated them duplicated them duplicated them as that dreadful nursemaid sat knitting in the kitchen. What did she teach you, Vera? Bravery? Unconquerable hope? At least I hope she showed you how to mix a proper martini or choose the quality bottle of red from an otherwise weak cellar, but I suppose she was a teetotaler too. Did she know history? Botany? Interdimensional geometry? Where to find the best *café au lait?*

(And yes, now I'm being sour to remove the sting of my own betrayal, made clear by the tart kiss you placed on my cheek instead of my lips as I walked out the door. At least your *préceptrice* stayed by your side, Vera. She had that much on me.)

Your letters from that time told me so little about your days that I was forced into furious strolls along the canals, inventing villains for you to subvert or be perverted by; enemy soldiers behind your lines. I hope you forgave my petty jealousies, darling, then as now. The sad sketch artists I invaded you with, the bathos of the bad poetry I serenaded you with. I was so thwarted. My heart one grand thrombosis. Lev, minus levity. *Lev, mal.*

It wasn't just your body I missed. (Though I don't want to mislead you, my youthful mind was far from pure. You've always been my poison tincture, turning the most solemn occasion to lust and stardust.) It was the whole of you, how you echolocate the walls of every room and press them ever outward, expanding the space. How you turn yourself into a pinpoint against the enormity, the only thing worth looking at in the whole wide world. Everything grows in your presence, Vera. Everything grows. (And yes, a black little pun still buried there, but I'll pretend you didn't see it. Some false solemnity, the better to corrupt you from upon our inevitable reunion.)

The day we met ruined me, you see. Made me. You won't begrudge me the reliving of it now, all the better to pepper my mind with flashes of your face: false idols relayed to the real.

It was a grim soiree. I'll set the scene: some seven years ago, one Lev Pavlovich, his face sallowed by hunger, which is endemic in the room but admitted by none. Seen as a class weakness. The party nonetheless thick with smuggled alcohol and pickled quail's eggs, a hundred days' rations traded up for a single ostentatious display. A sea of suits, unbespoken by time and tragedy. A sheen of masks, to pretend gaiety. Whispers of experiments performed by enemy combatants: kerosene secreted into the veins of all the comely Russian dolls, hoping to make them into ticking-tocking walking time bombs. Or maybe these rumors are mixed up with past indecencies; no one can tell heartless exaggeration from reality anymore. A man breaks down in the corner and says that the homeland is lost to them, they will never return once they pass the borders, their memories will be ghosts. They are already ghosts. All the room's inhabitants. Partygoers shift nervously, and change the topic to something brighter.

A curfew is in effect; electricity *verboten* after eight P.M., so the room is reduced to candlelight, which has an admittedly charming effect. Warmth implied by the glimmer and flicker. You know how I feel about candles, Vera. Even then, you felt it too: I know, because we have the same heart.

But still. I was bored and glum. There wasn't a single gentleman present who was fit to converse with, and every Leningrad lady was avoiding me after an unfortunate botched engagement. (Unfortunate for Lev, then. Not for this Lev. Our Lev. Now we can look back on the *flagrante delicto* in which he was caught with a certain affection that borders on sympathetic arousal. The girl was no match for you, but she was useful in her way.) The waiters circulated mostly wine, but I'd come upon a bottle of scotch stashed, or perhaps simply forgotten, behind a mirror in the marble hall.

Enter here: the darling imp. Her fingers light on the stem of her glass, tongue reaching out to lips to catch an errant drop. You stood by that grotesque cactus, soft body hitched and stitched into a defiant geometry. Behind you, the balcony. Below that, the Moika. How many times have I repeated this image to myself, wondered what you were thinking? Were you drawing a map of escape in your mind? Tracing lines in the carpets that hung for insulation on the walls? Had you spotted a cockroach and watched it climb into the pocket of an ex-counselor to the tsar? You wouldn't tell me. Still haven't. Your imagination is yet a locked box. Of course I didn't tell you, then, how you dragged the shadow of Dina behind you, catching my eye with her lost silhouette but keeping it with your impudent own. It seemed, after all, unimportant. As I approached you I understood anew the role that Dina had played in my life: not a tragedy, but a guide. Not perfection, but a mark of my own poor imagination, which saw in her the *ur*.

I picked up your wrist and turned it over, watching the sweet blood run beneath your skin. You looked at me, quizzical. Mouth turned down. Hair squeezed by the black velvet ribbon that secured your requisite disguise. And then you smiled.

# God Save the Motherless Child?

## A look back at the so-called "orphan boat"

From the *New York Register*, Opinion Page, May 1928

NEW YORK, NY. MOST READERS WILL remember the daring rescue undertaken by the Committee on Futurity (commonly referred to as "The Furies") some three years ago, when a group of orphaned Soviet children were secreted onto a passenger steamer in the hopes of bringing them to our country and offering them the best of American values. Details of the children's liberation were popular news at the time, particularly the unlikely series of tactics supposedly employed by the Furies, which included subterfuge, scout troops, coded newspaper articles, special whistles and hand signs, and the implausibly named "Cat Burglar Escape." But now, with the arrival of the "orphan boat" at Ellis Island safely in the past, what do we really know about the children themselves and their plans for our nation? Attempts by this newspaper to track down and interview any of the orphans were firmly stonewalled by Fury spokesman Roberts and his team.

The notion that these children may not be innocent—that they may, in fact, have been part of a plot to infiltrate our home life with spies—first emerged along with the news that the orphans were not from German and Polish ghettos as assumed, but instead from Soviet orphanages all around the USSR. Suspicions only increased during the ship's two-week quarantine in harbor, which many hypothesized was due not to flu (as the

Furies reported) but instead to the heightened political tension around the ship's passengers. During this period, lights were frequently seen on the boat at night, and sometimes figures were spotted moving around the dock. Sources close to the *Register* insisted that occasionally the lights would "change color" or "move funny" in the dark, but these reports were never substantiated.

Thanks to an anonymous tip, *Register* reporters were on the scene when the children were finally released and sent on to their new American homes on a quiet night in December. Two hundred small figures were removed from the boat, huddled beneath coats and blankets, before being placed into waiting vans and taken to the nearest train depot. Although the crowd was told the orphans were young and sick, bystanders eager for a closer look continued to press toward the children, and flashbulbs popped regularly in the darkness. One onlooker even waved a knife in the air while declaring himself "ready to act" if necessary, and though this man was quickly subdued by authorities, there were some present who questioned whether his actions were those of a crank or a hero.

Three years later, we are still left with the same uncertainties. Was it charity to place these children with American families, or a boondoggle of the greatest order? Did they grow up to contribute productively to their households, or did they wait and watch for the moment they might undermine them? With the Furies still closely guarding their whereabouts, we're still no closer to finding out.

# *Zoya*

19.

WHEN I WAS ONE OF THEM, THE GIRLS of the Donne School all seemed unique to me, each equipped with her own set of interests (which I knew of) and hidden talents (which I sometimes suspected), and peculiar embarrassments (which I rarely understood), not to mention a pair or two of infrequently laundered pajamas. They all had names: Jenny Hollinger, Leonora Torrance, Margaret Rathburn, Cindy Pink. Josephine Toff and Ashley Pearson, Regina Anderson and Leah Wills. It was only once I joined the staff that they became as one to me, a sea of girls washing forward out of classroom doors, dredged back into seats with the chime of a bell. Totally tidal and predictable. Utterly furious in their force.

It's true I endured my fair share of snubbing as a student—as I've said, I didn't really have friends. But it was accepted that I was supposed to be there. A little exotic, a little pathetic. Their mascot European exile with her heavy accent (embarrassing: I rid myself of this as soon as I could) and quietly ridiculous turns of phrase. Many fellow students recognized me as Margaret's roommate, and put me under their wing for that reason, helping me pick the one good dessert from a table full of sticky canned puddings, or stopping me outside the bathroom to point out the toilet paper attached to my shoe. (It took me years to get the hang of throwing soiled tissue into the toilet instead of a wastebasket, as I'd been taught to do back home. Especially considering the dented tins placed in every stall

for items of feminine hygiene; how was I supposed to know the difference? Lucky for me, none of the girls ever knew. I think I'd have been
lynched, or would, at the very least, have acquired a sickening nickname.)
At graduation we all wore black gowns and hugged on the lawn, creating
a tableau not unlike my original dreams of the Donne School, but in
reverse. Good-byes, not hellos. Dark clothing, not white. Still quite tender.

I expected things to carry on more or less the same way when the new
semester started and I began my work in the greenhouse, after spending
the summer reading horticulture periodicals and receiving daily tutorials
from John O'Brien. Yes, it was unusual for a graduated senior to remain
on campus, but I was hardly older than the rest of the girls. In fact, most
of the returning students already knew me: as a former upperclassman,
albeit an unpopular one. In perhaps the last gasp of my socialist-optimist
naïveté, I really thought this familiarity would work to my advantage.

The first day was flush with move-ins, slammed car doors. I heard
shrieks of greeting as I trudged to and from the greenhouse, carrying sacks
of fertilizer and seedling pots from the back of John's pickup. We were
behind our original schedule, still fixing things into place, but were confident about finishing on time, and anyway it added visibility to the project,
having us work so vigorously in such plain view. Already that morning
we'd scrubbed the glass clean and checked all the window seals, and
we'd spent the past two weeks testing how well the space held its temperature when set to various levels: mild, tepid, hot, steaming. I had a
hanging basket of spray bottles, some full of water, some nutrient-rich
soil enhancers, some a mild dish soap solution to discourage pests. One
had nettle tea. Now we were bringing in the plant life, and I felt an unexpected wave of maternal awe. Holding a flat of young tomatoes, I wanted
to cry at the great vulnerability there at my fingertips. The spice smell, the
fragile stems, the sticky hairs—it all combined, for me, into something
quite infant-like, a cold and shivering tray of children being shuttled away
from the only home they'd ever known. I wondered what it was like for
them to ride in the bed of a truck, *en plein air*. If it was stunning. If they felt
fear. Rocking gently back and forth like children on the deck of a boat in
a storm. But never mind.

After we'd settled the fruit and vegetable selection, the more glamorous flora would be brought in. Some I was planning to start from seeds: a tree called Voon's banana that I had found in a catalogue, which purported to grow complexly flavored fruit and electric-pink flowers; some blue-tipped asters and iceberg superiors to use in floral arrangements around the school. But the administration didn't want to wait around for sprouts; they wanted showy color right now. They wanted pop. And who could blame them? Already families were mustering outside the new structure, trying to peer in through the foggy glass. By the afternoon we'd be crowded over, and if everything went to plan, the first impression people had when walking into the greenhouse would be of entering another world, steamy, rich, and bright. Parents would imagine their own young flowers blooming under the care of the Donne School masters, and students would picture themselves in a wild new jungle of possibility. The opening of the greenhouse should, I'd been informed, set the tone for the whole school year.

By lunchtime I was sweating, my hair tied up in a messy bun. I thought I heard my name called once or twice, but whenever I turned to wave hello I found myself alone, a pack of girls bustling away down the path with their heads pressed together and hands clasped tight. Giggling, punching one another in the arm. It always went that way on the first day, I told myself, with unions resumed and pacts re-sealed; and so if I felt a prickling on the back of my neck or an uncomfortable rumbling in my stomach whenever a set of eyes homed in on me only to divert sharply away, I ignored it. At noon I ran my hands under the greenhouse tap, wetting the blue bandanna John had given me to tie around my neck and wiping the dirt and sweat from my face. I had a year's pass to the dining hall, and although I'd also bought a hot plate and kettle with an advance on my salary, there was no time to cook for myself before the large exotics arrived. I'd need to be on hand to supervise where they were placed, how they were arranged; to make sure the watering system was correctly installed, and that there were fans angled around the room to provide proper airflow to every corner.

"Lunch?" I said to John. All summer we'd eaten together midday, choosing from the bare-bones selections the cafeteria provided for the year-round staff, and I knew that with students and parents present the food would be more carefully prepared, a table of fresh-baked pies—apple, cherry, peach, pecan—set out to accompany the beef stroganoff and chicken à la king. "Just a quick one."

"Oh, in there?" He frowned towards the dining hall. "No, hon. Siobhan packed me a sandwich. There's some to share, if you want."

I considered the offer. Eating in the greenhouse was faster and easier; we'd finish in time to double-check our staging plan before the first truck showed up, and make sure no interlopers snuck in before the unveiling. It made sense, and I knew I ought to say yes. But I couldn't help feeling the reflected glow of the new semester on my skin—an afterglow, really, in my case—and wanting to take part to whatever degree I could. The festival air was so familiar that I half expected Margaret to turn the corner and give me a perfunctory wave. Plus, I knew the limitations of my own cooking, and didn't look forward to the months of scrambled eggs and sardines on toast that stretched ahead of me. A mouthful of hot food would do me good, I was sure.

"Ok, I'll see you in half an hour, then," I said. John raised his eyebrows and dug around in the knapsack he'd thrown into a corner several hours ago, pulling out a pastrami on rye.

"Your funeral," he told me. A strange choice of words, or so I thought at the time.

20.

APPROACHING THE DINING HALL, MY toes and fingertips tingled with goodwill. So many people hugging hello and good-bye. Such a fever of affection. None of the girls remembered yet that they'd have course-work beginning the very next day, long afternoons with mimeographed articles and eight A.M. classes to pull themselves out of bed for. They saw only the intermezzo: timing things just right to hand off notes in the hall between Geometry and European History II; the late nights of punch-drunk study parties that made seven-thirty alarm clocks so impossible. Spying a cute boy in town and pretending to have business the same direction he was strolling, coming up with terrible excuses to walk past the public high school or the arcade—or, if their tastes ran a bit more to silver, past the Eagles Club. All summer the campus had felt empty and bleak, but now it was home again.

As I picked up my tray, one of the cooks spotted me from across the room and gestured furiously. John O'Brien and I often stayed to chat with the ladies over coffee, so I knew them all by name. This was Hilda, and running up behind her was a younger worker named Nadine. I waved back and flashed them a smile. Just then, someone knocked into my left elbow, sending my tray skittering onto the floor. "Oh!—" I said, as a group of students pushed ahead of me towards the entrée line. They didn't look my direction, just tossed their hair and kept on chatting— something about wanting to avoid the leftovers, which didn't make sense, since this was Welcome Day. I assumed they hadn't seen me, and grabbed a new tray, sliding behind the threesome and grabbing a plate of stroganoff on a fresh bed of noodles. Hilda shouldered her way through the hungry crowd and ran over to me. She grabbed my elbow and steered me away from the line, picking up a piece of strawberry rhubarb (*New flavor!* was still all I thought) on the way to a table in the far corner of the hall.

"Why are you here?" she hissed.

"Lunch?" The confusion must've shown on my face, though a dim glimmer of awareness was starting to break through. All around the room, groups of students and even a few parents were taking peeks at me from the corners of their eyes.

"But not *now*," Hilda said. "The vultures are out."

"Don't be ridiculous." I tucked a napkin—cloth, for today only—onto my lap and took a bite of pie. As a graduate I felt quite adult, and had decided I was allowed to eat dessert first if I wanted. "Who's a vulture?"

"Hmm," said Hilda. She watched me eat the pie, my face growing pinker with each mouthful. *Leftovers*, the girls to the right of us whispered. *So sad. So pathetic. It's putting me off my appetite.* I finished the pie and turned to my proper lunch, but before I could make much headway an entire table of third-years walked up and clattered their trays down next to me, a few scrapings left on each plate. My cheeks were now quite red and hot.

"The kitchen's right there," I said. The bus tubs, where you were supposed to place your dishes for washing, were still almost empty.

"Ohhhhh." One of the girls, who I thought was named Kay, stopped and looked over her shoulder at me. "We knoooooow, but we just thought you were looking for scraps." She smiled, her eyebrows aloft with innocence. "We wanted to help!"

I looked down at my food, and then over to Hilda. Her face was stern and set.

"Come on, you ninnies," she said. "Do your own dirty work."

Kay smiled wider, coming around to retrieve her tray. Her hair was yellow and tied back in a braid, which she flipped over her shoulder like a mink.

"You know," she said, "we thought we already did."

Hilda and I watched each girl flounce up and remove her tray, scraping the extra food carefully into a trashcan before placing their plates in the tubs. They *tsk*ed about the waste, but we didn't make another sound until all of them were done and gone. It was only then I realized they'd taken my tray, too. My eyes stung, but I blinked and kept my gaze steady.

"You know, Nadine used to be a Donne Girl." Hilda spoke with a casual air, as though the idea had popped into her head for no reason. She looked at Nadine, who was back in the kitchen, then nodded at me. "Scholarship, like you. Her people are from Appalachia."

"Really." I didn't know where Appalachia was, but I could guess its character. Barren. Blighted. Or anyway nothing like the glittering towns that gave birth to Kays and Margarets. Farm horses instead of dressage. Oatmeal by necessity instead of for improved digestion.

"Mmmhmm. She liked art history. Still does, as a matter of fact. Sometimes goes into the library museum after hours to look at the prints. But anyway," Hilda swatted aside the idea of the school's prize archival collection, "when she was done with her studies, she didn't have much in the way of options. Go home to her momma. Try and find some work. She always used to cook for her cousins, and that was how she ended up staying here."

We both watched Nadine in the kitchen for a moment, humming to herself as she dropped plate after plate into a sink of soapy water. Something must've told her she was being observed—a tickle behind the ear, or a twitch at the base of the spine, goose over the grave—because she looked up all of a sudden and caught my eye. Her expression was hard to read.

"Things can go ugly fast," Hilda mused. "People can be ugly." I thought she might say more, but she didn't. Just put a hand on my shoulder before standing up and retying her apron, then disappeared back through the kitchen's swinging door to help Nadine finish up the wash.

## 21.

THANK GOD MARGARET WASN'T THERE amidst the vultures—she'd never see me this way, through the eyes of these girls. As far as she knew I'd picked up my bag and left town at the same time as the rest of our classmates, landing days later in a whole new life. She and I had discussed our post-graduation plans just once, and she accepted my vague answers with disinterested poise, perhaps filling in the details for herself. That's what I hoped now. Her expectations of me naturally weren't too high, but maybe she pictured me doing something secretarial. Not in New York, but maybe Pittsburgh or Detroit—big, if not the biggest. Not the finest, but still fine. I knew she planned to spend the summer on Cape Cod helping her mother decorate their new beach house before heading to Sarah Lawrence in the fall. My name would be disappearing from her memory by now, reduced to a faint buzz in the back of her brain. But at least the buzz would be a pleasant one. *Oh, you,* she'd think. And then she'd turn to the next topic. Something with a little more zip.

I hurried back into the greenhouse, shutting the door behind me with a slam and leaning against it to catch my breath. John turned from the length of sprinkler pipe he was fiddling with, and gave me an assessing look.

"That bad?"

"Why," I asked, "didn't you tell me it would be like that?"

"I thought you knew." He shrugged. "You lived here for two years. You didn't notice they were all stuck up?"

I went over to the table of seedlings and ran my finger along a green bean vine curling up a thin stake in its terra-cotta pot. The stake, piked deep. The vine, slowly strangling the pike. Yes, I knew the Donne girls were snobs, but I didn't realize they were cruel. I'd never worked for them before. *I don't know if I can do this*, I almost said, but my thoughts were interrupted by a honk from outside, and the rumbling of an engine, cut short. My exotics. I took a breath and tied the bandanna back around my neck for protection from the afternoon sun.

The next few hours passed quickly. We organized the plants not just by color but by region, creating biomes in each corner. One full of palms and banyans and birds of paradise, African iris and beehive ginger. One for the American southwest desert with ocotillo and aloe and agave, and even a small saguaro, which would cause me endless stress. For the southern belles we had orchids, honeysuckle, and a few tobacco plants— plus a Venus flytrap, which I'd assumed was from somewhere with deep jungles, but I learned was actually from North Carolina, and simply couldn't resist. I was reminded of childhood summers, when heat and effort erased the very hours from the clock. Spot-checking the sugar beet leaves for insect eggs, turning the soil, beginning the harvest, my mother handing out jugs of cold water with a hint of lemon and a breath of vodka to encourage the blur of minutes into days.

John and I ran around, wrangling both citrus and rhizome. While we worked I had no time to think, though I wouldn't realize this until later, and wouldn't learn to cultivate it as an escape for longer still. My body, though, must've felt the relief and grabbed hold of it. By the time everything was in place I was breathless—from exertion, yes, but even more so from excitement. Snobs or not, the students and parents would have no choice but to be bowled over by our display. As the sun fell low, the greenhouse filled up with pink and orange light, burnishing the already rich colors and softening the edges of the leaves. I half expected to dissolve into the haze, leaving no trace behind but a pair of dirty shoes.

As the first visitors trickled in, drawn by the Welcome Day itinerary printed out for them by the school's planning committee, my expectations were more or less gratified. Mothers *oohe*d and *aahe*d at the flowers, and fathers poked the moist soil with an air of gardeners' camaraderie. The girls looked bored, or calm and sly. But they kept their mouths shut, which was enough. I began to think we'd achieved a coup, John and I. We'd set the tone for a year of mute appreciation.

The girls came in waves according to class, freshmen and their eager shepherds first, seniors last. And it was only with the latter of these groups that the tide in the room began to change. The air grew stuffier. I noticed more touching of the plants: girls tweaking stems and leaving half-moons in the leaves with their fingernails. My polite coughs gained nothing, but neither did my overt displays of authority: whenever I asked someone to refrain from shredding the foliage, I was met with a blank and ruthless stare. "Me?" the girl would say. "I didn't even realize." The greenhouse garden represented hundreds of hours of work, from research and selection to the careful setup of the past afternoon. But more than that, it was my livelihood. It was my life. Every plant, from the most familiar strawberry to the most outlandish vine, was a part of me. It was all I had. And they—who had so much more by comparison—knew it.

By the time we got down to the last few families, I was desperate. An entire ginger plant had been destroyed, and several roses had been snapped but left attached to their stems by a thread, beheadings as sadistic as they were incompetent. There would be an administrative inspection the next day, and it looked like I'd arranged the greenhouse by letting wild dogs run loose from door to door. I saw Kay, who'd hung around long past the rest of her classmates, say something to a fourth-year named Susan, who had occasionally quizzed Margaret in French. Susan nudged a planter with her toe, just a little, then just a little more, until it tipped over and spilled the barbed orbs of a teddy bear cholla across the floor. "Oops," she said.

I'd had enough. Paying no attention to John's quiet hand motion—a finger run, knifelike, along his neck—I walked over to Susan and Kay.

"What do you think you're doing?"

"Oooh," said Kay. "We're admiring all the beautiful work."

I turned to Susan. "And what about you? You know me. I'm friends with Margaret."

She looked at me with an expression approaching pity. "No you're not," she said, and shoved the spilled planter some more with her shoe, rubbing circles in the dirt. "You knew her, but that's not the same. Even you don't think it is." Kay giggled, and Susan rolled her eyes, then grabbed Kay's hand and pulled her towards the exit. I just watched. Kay's braid swishing back and forth across her spine, Susan walking with a graceful heel-toe twitch. I could feel the plants in the greenhouse throbbing, or maybe that was my own head. I thought of the ocean I had crossed, the beet field I'd pulled weeds in as a child while Susan and Kay drank glass after glass of sugared fruit juice and probably lounged by the side of a pool. They both had that look: expensive powder over a residual tan.

When they were gone, John told me, "Don't worry. We'll put it right." And indeed we worked into the night, restoring tilted plants and trimming back ragged edges until the greenhouse looked spic and span, ready for the early inspection. The next day, the administrators would be impressed, winking at me and hinting of a long and prosperous career. But that night I went to bed exhausted and spent, an orphan girl with dirt under her fingernails, too afraid to use the communal bathroom shower after creeping back into the dorm. An orphan girl hollow with the knowledge that she still had no home after all these years.

# Lev

23 June 1931
Airmail via [Redacted]

WHERE DID I LEAVE OFF BEFORE, VERA? Drunk on my first sight of you, I expect. Shivering in my shoes as you ran your fingertip over the rim of your wineglass at that doomed party in Leningrad, making it hum. We discussed literary ambition—"The key," you said, "is to see possibilities in the world that no one else has the bravery to face"—and I described my book to you. The same precious first I search for now, then the only. You said the ideas held promise, though I remember the look of mild displeasure on your face. Probably the very look you're wearing as you read this letter.

But still. That night. With each breath you drew closer to me, until I was inhaling almost directly from your mouth, my Lev-ly proboscis ever approaching your lovely lips. I asked if I could take you on a walk along the canal, and you said yes, then looked around for your father—not to ask him, but to be sure he wouldn't see. You were seventeen. I was twenty-three. At the doorway a towering butler blocked our path, but I distracted him with a cigarette, which he pinched from me with two thick fingers and sniffed in a vaguely obscene manner. *God bless all obscenity*, was my opinion. I wanted to toss you into a dark corner and tear you apart with kisses, but didn't dare. I suspected even then that you could swallow me whole without a second thought and go on your way, little Lev swimming around, hopeless in your belly. Yes, I was afraid of you, Vera. I was exhilarated. Outside you strode over a bridge, on the top of a wall, just high enough that I could see a hint of thigh beneath your uplifted skirt, and when I reached for your hand you gave me just the tips of your fingers, which I sucked. They tasted sweet.

"Naughty boy." You used your dress train to sock me on the cheek, and then climbed carefully back down.

"I have a page," I offered.

"A page?"

"Just one, from the manuscript. It's in my pocket." I'd been considering this ever since we left the party—it seemed dangerous, like an early proposal. We'd been speaking for only an hour, and already I knew that to give you any piece of my literary efforts would be to embark on a path from which, for good or ill, there'd be no return. But how could I resist the draw of your intelligent eyes, the flick of your clever fingers? "I could let you have a look."

"Alright." You stopped, and hopped back onto the wall to sit. Suddenly I was nervous. Sweat broke on my forehead, despite the chill of the night. Whereas you hadn't a care in the world; you swung your legs and whistled. Still wearing your black mask. "Well?"

The paper was folded into quarters, tucked in the inner pocket of my tailcoat right above my heart. I'd written it earlier in the day, smoking copiously. At that time in my life I had little else to do but sit at my desk and flick ash out the window onto the heads of passersby while I scribbled down my ideas, but even if I'd had teaching duties or—better still—a plan of escape, I was too intoxicated with the work to leave it for longer than a few hours. I'd gotten into the habit of carrying my latest pages around so I could reread them, or even just touch them to remind myself they were real—a sensation half verbal, half autoerotic. I knew no one else thought the way that I did, the way that I do. No one else would see our country for what it was: a land bearing thousands of counterfeit kings, with the legitimate ruler lost among them, having forgotten himself. That was my story. Amnesia, dislocation, masquerade. Peasant kings stealing from the rich before turning on one another, heads beaten in with wooden scepters. I handed you a page thick with script, hoping you wouldn't see my fingers shake.

You read. I watched, pacing back and forth in a wide arc, since the wall made it impossible to fully circumnavigate you. I could tell by looking at your eyes that you went through the whole thing twice, and could also see when you stopped and lost yourself in quiet thought. At last you turned to me. Your breath coming out as small puffs of cloud.

"Perhaps," you said.

"Perhaps?"

"Perhaps." You refolded the paper and held it up between middle finger and fore. "May I keep this?" Though it lasted only a second, you must've seen the hesitation in my face. "I see." You smiled a grim smile and handed back the page.

"What do you mean *perhaps*?" I was unable to stop myself from asking. I could feel something dark and meaningful spinning inside your chest, Vera. My polestar, my pet, my set of teeth.

"You can be great," you said in reply. "Perhaps."

At this you jumped down and took off down the street, your dress dragging on the ground and your hands folded in front of your chest for warmth, though it looked like benediction. I didn't know then the calculations you were making, considering not just you and me but your own place in history, guiding my hand. You must've felt your hold was tenuous. I scampered behind you, having restored my writing to its proper place, but just as I caught up you stopped and stamped your foot.

"What?" I asked. Panting, heartsick, hands on knees.

"It's ridiculous that I should be leaving tomorrow. Tomorrow! This idiotic country." Naturally I agreed. You and your father were scheduled to depart for the west the next morning in a trap pulled by a single skinny Vyatka mare, catching the train in a small-town station outside the city. I was still stuck at the Herzen Institute off Nevski Prospect, and hadn't yet put together the money to flee. When my parents were still wealthy (and, of course, alive), my role as a university student and tutor had carried a bit of chic. But now the family money was frittered away in land grants to the government of thugs, and the school was a shell of what it had been. Every course of study was restricted to the narrow regime-approved areas of focus: Death of the Individual; the Trigonometry of the Motherland; Comrades, Computations, Combinatorics. I felt daily more like a wastrel.

You said, "I will it not to be so," and snapped your fingers. When nothing happened, you repeated yourself more emphatically: "I will it!" Lifting your hands up towards the heavens as if to pull down God himself for a chat. And then. Do you remember? A dove fluttered into your waiting palms, cream white and still quite ruffled from his descent. It was as if a lump of snow had gotten confused and manifested; we looked up to see if we could find the strange cloud it had come from, or indeed the chagrined deity who had dropped this marvel on us. Instead there was a rather fat man on a balcony looking frantic and gesturing in our direction while a red-cheeked auntie blew her nose and shook out her handker-chief by his side. You pulled the dove close to your face and looked into its beady eyes. It cooed. You looked. It cooed again. And all at once you threw your arms skyward and the dove flew up, back to its corpulent and inattentive master. Who knows what kind of menagerie he had in there—he caught the bird in one hand like a tennis ball.

Vera, it was torture for me to let you go without me, but what choice did I have? You were safe in Paris, if not quite secure. And for my part, I spun into a tizzy of activity, writing, writing every hour—except when I had a letter from you. Soon enough I completed my manuscript, and tore back through it page by page. When I was satisfied I copied it out for you, and sent it to your father's place in a brown paper package, wrapped thrice-wise and hidden inside a hollowed-out copy of an early Party history book. Around this time there was an increase in search and seizure for all those leaving the city to avoid counterproductive ideas moving across the border, and with my own departure plans on the brink of readiness I knew I couldn't expect to get away with my book in hand. (You'll remember the hectic nature of my final escape plans, fraught until the moment I realized that, in my regimen of constant drafting and revision, I'd saved the last few rubles I needed for bribes by forgetting to eat.) So I tied the original manuscript with twine, shut it up in the most airtight box I could find, and buried it at the end of a trolleybus line. You were to be the safe-guard of my future—as indeed you'll insist you have been, if not in quite the way I initially imagined.

Some weeks of anguish followed, but at last I snuck out of Leningrad on a transport train, pretending to be a mute priest from Lithuania on my way to give counsel to the archbishop of Rome. You met me at the Gare du Nord in a skirt that brushed against your calves. I remember you'd gotten slenderer. Just a quarter inch lost around the waist, but I mourned every molecule. Right there, standing by the man selling crepes from a cart, smelling of burnt batter and hungry civilians, I took you in my arms and slipped the blouse off of your shoulder, biting you and leaving a mark with my teeth. You looked at me in much the way you'd looked at that daring Russian dove, and for a moment I was afraid you'd release me too. Into whose custody, Vera? Instead, you straightened your clothes and took my hand and said, "Well, I think we'd better get married."

It would be more than a week before I learned you'd burned my manu-script, for my "own good and protection." I didn't inquire about it sooner, as I was too busy proposing to you and proposing to you every hour, trying to make up for the fact that you had asked me first. Plus I trusted that the pages were safe in your charge—an idea you'd have anyway confirmed. Not quite acknowledging that your idea of safety was far broader than my own: that you thought safety for me and my words meant sometimes saving me from myself.

When I found out I might have screamed at you. I might have walked away. But by then we were quite officially engaged. Weren't we, Renka? And it was more than that. By then we were inextricably in love.

# Zoya

## 22.

DEAR READER, THIS CABIN IS TOO QUIET. That was never a complaint I thought I'd level, but here I am: no plant misters hissing on, no dehumidifier humming by the cacti, causing the tarpaulins to shift. Just a quiet room and the scratch of my pen, while outside the wind occasionally has the good grace to whistle through the pines. If I sit very still I can catch the breath of mice under the floorboards, or the crinkling footsteps of birds in the eaves. And I can remember a time when I'd have killed for this kind of peace. Back then, when I thought I was drowning in sounds.

Have you, has anyone else, ever been driven mad by the squeak of saddle shoes? What about the swish of hair being rearranged? Fingers combing out a knot, then dragging the strands back into place, to be set by a ribbon or clip. It sounds petty, I know, but what you have to understand is that these noises were also harbingers for me of greater unpleasantness oncoming. And they were omnipresent. I might walk into a hallway and hear six girls running to beat the bell, their shoes all squealing against the tile. (One or two would bash into me, if at all possible, though over the years I got better at dodging.) Or I'd duck into the cafeteria for an afternoon cup of coffee and hear sixteen, seventeen braids being redone. Nine buns being pinned. The locks of twenty heads brushed out next to the salad bar. There was a kind of music to it, which I occasionally allowed myself to enjoy: such rich youth, the fat of so much success in the shifting of hair and the snap of well-bleached bobby socks. I sometimes watched the waves of young women—pale or sunburned, auburn or blonde, round or rail-thin—voluminate over the campus lawns and felt a tug. Perhaps nostalgia? Or something more. But these tender moments only made the rest of the time more unbearable.

As my first year at the greenhouse wore on I curtailed my visits to Marie's café. They made me too sad. I remembered dragging in my school-books, working to diminish my accent and build up my classroom bluster—and couldn't bring myself to walk through the door. It was as if I feared seeing my past self at a table, and having to face the disappoint-ment in her eyes. Sometimes Marie waved to me from behind the counter when I walked by, but over time the gesture grew more confused, until at last it stopped.

Instead, I worked. I dug, aerated, primped, and pruned. I babied my seedlings, and sometimes when no one was looking I gave them little kisses. You have to be gentle with a young plant, when even the tenderest touch can knock it asunder or snap its weak spine. But I'm convinced they can feel love.

Girls streamed through the school, washing up and down its many shores giving me pinches or whispering nasty words. Often I felt the flash of their flesh on my flesh, the exquisite bloom of a bruise, and it got to the point where my heart quickened any time I heard a footstep. With reason. Once, I found myself alone in a corner with a fourth-year named Leah, uncertain how it had come to pass. She moved closer and closer, telling me terrible things about myself until her mouth was on my ear, her hand around my waist. One leg twined between my legs to hold me in place as she petted my hair and let me know in no uncertain terms that I was a beggar, a puppet, a ghost. All this was bearable only because I was able to consider the plants my protectorate. The greenhouse a kingdom with me standing guard. Kay and her friends stayed away, most of the time—even Leah cornered me on neutral ground, in the empty student union—and that was something to be proud of, no matter how many lips hissed against my neck.

That year, I also began making more trips to Maple Hill's small bookstore. During my schooling, I hadn't often read for pleasure—the bookstore carried only English-language texts, and besides costing too much money these struck me as a waste of leisure time. Now I found, to my delight, that reading came easy. Some language switch had flipped in my brain; I dreamed in English, I spoke it constantly, I corresponded in English with the phone company and various seed distributors. John invited me over for dinner with him and his wife, Siobhan, and we laughed through the night, even playing a board game now that I was confident enough to understand the instructions. Although I'd always enjoyed strolling through the aisles of Sugar Books, smelling the paper and running my thumb over cover cloth, life took on a new tone of satisfaction along with my ability to pick up a volume and skim a few lines before deciding whether or not to buy.

As you might expect, I gravitated especially to Russian writers, for the flavor of home. But none satisfied me half so much as Leo Orlov. He was like nothing else—impressionistic, yet voluptuous in his images. His work unfathomable yet steeped in the human and mundane. Perhaps what I liked best was how *strange* he was; I didn't know the term "science fiction," and even if I had, I'm not sure that's what I would have called him. (Of course this is a matter of much argument these days, with literary gatekeepers urgent to hold on to him and space/time aficionados praising his stories with nothing short of militant ecstasy.) But I knew that his work would take me on unbelievable journeys, and that was all I wanted. The comfort of a bolt-hole. A doorway appearing, cut into the very air.

You'll probably remember him from his first true sensation, *Felice*, the one in which a girl becomes a bird and forms a new army of starlings and crows to get her revenge on the men who betrayed her. But I knew him long before that. There was a small society of us, almost all expatriates, who started with his journal stories published in France and kept on through *Knife, Knave* and *Impresario* and *Sun Sort*. We were all a bit churlish about *Felice*, not because we found it less than brilliant, but because it let so many new readers suddenly reach out and claim our Orlov for their own. On the other hand, the book that broke him fully into my heart—that ran him, hot liquid, all through my blood—was a short novel called *Rothschild*, which not many people have read even now. I can't understand why, but of course this makes it all the more personal and delicious.

*Rothschild* showed up at Sugar Books in late winter, after an initial thaw had given way to the year's final deep freeze. I'd been spending nights in the greenhouse, tucking towels around the seams in the windows and readjusting the vents as needed. Suffice it to say, I got little sleep. Once the Donne girls figured out what I was doing, they threw snowballs at the windowpanes on their way home from midnight study sessions, sometimes knocking at the door and running away, leaving poppets on the step with pins stuck in their eyes. God knows where they found the time to make poppets.

The days were bleary with exhaustion, and as one such afternoon smeared over into evening I walked to the bookstore, hoping to cheer myself up. I'd been in recently, and didn't really think there'd be much new stock, but it was all I could think of. Indeed, the New Arrivals shelf was sparse: just a small shipment of obscure philosophical texts and an unsealed box addressed to a publisher sitting at the foot of the checkout counter. The register girl saw me trying to peer inside.

"Oh, we're sending those back," she said. "They packed too many by mistake."

"Can I look?" Everything else was picked through, and I was too tired to walk through the aisles and try to get excited about some romance or mystery I'd passed over several times before. The counter girl shrugged.

"Knock yourself out. Just try not to muss them up too much or the publisher won't take 'em."

I pulled the cardboard edges out from where they'd been tucked underneath one another, and they gave a squeak—then I gave a yelp. "Is this a new Orlov?"

"Who?"

"Leo Orlov. He's a writer?"

"I figured." The register girl leaned over the counter for a better look. "Hmm. Search me. I guess it's new. We didn't think we could sell that many books by a guy no one has heard of."

"I have."

"Well that makes one."

Lev already lived in New York then, but he was still obscure in America. I pulled a copy out of the box and looked regretfully at the rest. No way I could buy all of them, and anyway what would I do with them if I did? The book seemed to shiver in my hand, the sole survivor of a shipwreck. I was reluctant to hand it over to the register girl even long enough to let her wrap it.

"What's it about?" she asked.

"I don't know yet. I have to read it."

"You're not even going to check before you buy it?" She wrote out a receipt for me and placed everything in a brown paper bag. "That's devotion. Not a lot of readers like you out there anymore."

"I know," I said. Though I knew nothing of the kind, the idea made me proud.

"Let me know how you like it," the girl called out as I left the store. "Maybe if it's good I can convince the owner to re-order them."

I had planned to walk to the store for a loaf of bread and a bit of cheese, but I decided that Orlov trumped my aversion to the cafeteria. I'd slip in late and hope that Hilda or Nadine would be there and let me eat with them in the kitchen. A few students would be sure to see me, and no one would applaud me for eating with the cooks, but what did I care? *Orlov*, I chanted to myself. *Orlov, Orlov, Orlov.* When I reached the edge of campus I broke into a run, clutching the paper bag in my hand. Buildings blurred by, along with trees and faces. I was almost at the dorm. I was almost free. Most likely it was this excitement that kept me from noticing Kay's foot stuck out in front of me—a rookie move, really; she tried it every time we crossed paths—and I tripped over her toe, skidding to the ground.

"Whoops!" A yellow braid loomed above me, the rest of her hair covered up with a knit cap. "Must've hit a patch of ice. Want a hand?"

My knees were skinned, a hole scraped into the left leg of my pants. Most likely they would've worn through soon anyway, with me on my hands and knees at all hours checking heaters and watering hard-to-reach plants. But it wasn't as though I could easily replace them; a book was one thing, but proper clothes were another. Knowing I'd probably have to make a visit to the charity shop, I batted Kay aside with stinging palms.

"Get away from me."

"Temper, temper. And here I was just trying to help."

I pushed myself up, grabbing the book from where it had skittered across the paved path and shoving it back into the bag. "You help like a hole in the head, Kay." Spending time with John O'Brien had improved my idiomatic language immensely.

"Such a bitter leftover," she told me. "Someone should really put you out with the trash."

"Well, someone should really teach you some manners."

"What did you say?" Kay smiled, her eyes cool. I almost never parried her attacks. "Say it again."

She was in my way. I was so close—my bed, unslept-in for days, was half a minute's walk from where we stood. In my hands I crumpled the Orlov bag, its paper already colored with a streak of blood. I stepped towards Kay and took a breath.

"I said you were a little bitch."

The silence that followed was a beautiful thing. I suppose I can savor, here in this lonesome cottage, the similarity between that moment and this one. For once, Kay was at a loss for words—indeed, in her surprise, she seemed unable to move at all. It wouldn't last long, I knew, and taking advantage of the momentary calm, I walked around her into the dorm, locking the door to my room behind me.

## 23.

I CAN STILL RECITE BY MEMORY THE description on the back of the book:

> *Rothschild*: a new novel from the critically acclaimed foreign
> writer Leo Orlov. PICTURE yourself on a world far away, but not
> so different from our own. IMAGINE a terrible illness overtaking
> every woman and girl, be she Missy or Mrs., Ooh-la-la or

Oh-no-thanks. First, a green line winds up her leg—yikes! Is it a varicose vein, or something more sinister? Ladies don't take any chances, slicing the new arrivals off with razors and nail scissors, burning them off with cigarette lighters. But no matter what they do, the illness continues, the growths return, and women become slaves to it—until one brave girl decides to take an unlikely stand.

It was rare for me to read the jacket copy of an Orlov book—I preferred to let the story wash over me, in all its twists and thrills. Plus, whoever wrote the jacket descriptions was a dunce. Not once, until after the success of *Felice*, did the description come close to reflecting what the novel contained. The basic details of the plot were there, but none of the depth, almost as if the publishing house didn't want people to realize what they had until it was too late.

But in the case of *Rothschild,* for some reason, I skimmed the summary and then set the book down with shaking hands. There was a sink in my room—a luxury the rest of the dorms did not contain, because my room was really intended for floor monitors and other adult visitors. I turned the water on, hot, and cleaned the gravel out of my palms, snipping away bits of dead skin and wrapping my wounds in clean white bandages. After inspecting my pants, I decided they might still be mended, and set them aside in a laundry basket before dabbing my knee with iodine. Then, with a shuddering sigh, I sat down on my bed wearing nothing but my camisole and underwear.

I began to read. The night was predicted to be another cold one, and eventually I'd have to go out to the greenhouse to take up my watch. I could bring a flashlight and continue on with the book from there, but the beam would draw more girls to the glass, and I was worried an icy snowball might eventually smash through a window. *Just an hour or so,* I told myself. If I didn't eat dinner, the time wouldn't matter much. *Just a few more pages. Just a chapter. Or two.*

A world full of invaded women opened up before me, with gentle passengers that clung to their legs. Not just green veins, but green *vines,* giving way to rich green pods and eventually small creatures with warm, sticky fingers. When the first afflicted woman saw her passenger emerge she was horrified, until the creature opened its eyes. They were—how to describe it? Very dear. *A woman alone was just a woman, but now she was chemistry, a valence of heart and hope,* Orlov wrote. *The beings triggered bonds so elemental that they seemed like natural law.* Most of the time they kept their eyes pinched shut to conserve energy, but occasionally they blinked at their women so tenderly that none could bear to do them harm. Some even took on the illness intentionally, fostering their passengers with pride. Legislation was written to protect the creatures, making it illegal to try and snip them free, as many had done in the early days. Because how did they survive? They sucked the energy from their women like milk through a straw.

One girl tried to fight this, arguing that children, at least, should be allowed to get the creatures removed and try to live their lives unencumbered. But she was shouted down over and over again, until at last she died of a gunshot wound on the floor of the senate, her purple blood leaking out across the white tile. When I closed the book after reading the last page, the whole world was winking out—once the women all succumbed, life became impossible. Babies couldn't be born. Men died out, lonely. And at last the only sentient beings left were the passengers. They'd never intended to do harm, but now they were starving to death on an empty planet, tugging at one another's arms and wailing as they realized there was no one left to love.

Lights winked out across campus, too. In my room, I hugged the book to my chest and tucked up my knees, turning my whole body into a knot and closing my eyes, just for a moment. I remembered my old life, its sweetness and annihilation. A pan of *piroshky* baking in the next room, the mist of yeast and meat and broth filling up our whole apartment. My father waving to me across a field in the summer, the light burning out my view until all I could see was his silhouette. My mother, brushing aside a strand of hair before leaning down to kiss my forehead. And then, too, my face, crushed against the pavement, a cacophony of ordnance exploding above me.

My blood was warm and thick, my eyes heavy. I fell asleep still clutching the novel, and eventually it migrated between my thighs. When I woke with a start in the middle of the night it was still there, hot where my skin pressed into it. Outside the wind made a sound like an animal. I threw on some clothes and rushed to the greenhouse, bringing the book with me. Not to read, just for company. So I could remember for a little while longer the feeling of opening it for the first time.

*Lev*

26 June 1931
Airmail via [Redacted]

THERE ISN'T MUCH TIME TODAY, VERA. The days seem to be shorter, here, where the west meets the east. And I'm not talking about loss of light, I'm talking about actual hours. The practical tock of the clock, tick-less. Sudden jumps. I pick up a cup of wretched coffee in the morning, and before I set it down the day's gone, and I've accomplished nothing. Time is always different without you, but this feels new. Were you previously winding something in my heart that I wasn't aware of? Is there a wifely duty you never bothered to outline? Please reply and help your liminal Lev.

The good news is I've got a lead on a courier at last. As you know, I can't very well stroll across the Soviet border and hand them my passport. People have been killed for less. The courier and I are supposed to meet and discuss terms at a quarter to four, dead of night—which I thought was twelve hours hence, but I just glanced out the window and saw a sky of inky blue, so maybe it's sooner. I've probably lost time just scratching out this paragraph. And me with so many things left to do: I need to count half the man's fee upfront, in small bills. I need to clean my little Galesi pistol, which is essential on the streets, and such a pretty thing. Mother-of-pearl handle, dark snub nose. It's almost alarming how fond I've become of it.

But we were talking about my manuscript, weren't we? (Or anyway I was, but considering your correspondence habits lately, that's more or less the same thing. Me, with a pen in hand, imagining the look on your face, which comes so clear I know in an instant everything you would have said after making it.) I still remember the reeling of my senses, a feeling not unlike vertigo which overtook me when you said you'd burned it in the kitchen fire to keep me from debuting with a story below my worth. Too concerned with politics, you told me, too insular, just not good. Your face was calm, perhaps a bit of fret about the lips. I put my hand on the table, to steady myself. You said I looked green, and I broke out in so much sweat it seemed I'd been washed over by an ocean wave. I walked out of the apartment onto the streets of Paris and didn't return for a night and a day.

I have no recollection of that interim. My first time jump? Or a simpler answer: a mind frosted over for its own protection. Erase what should, by all measures, be lost. When at last I showed up in your building's vestibule, I was stubble-grown and raw of throat. Still wet all over, though you said there'd been no rain.

Even then, back in your arms, I dreamed for a time of your murder. Many scenarios presented themselves: a sympathetic fleshly fire, a bullet, a pair of hands around your throat. But you know this, don't you? You were there, after all. You peeled my fingers off your neck, face calm as evening. You pressed me backwards, away from you—not a shove, just a suggestion—and picked up a cigarette, licking the tip to check for stale tobacco before lighting a match. Your father had gone out for a bottle of champagne, the better to celebrate our upcoming nuptials. I looked at you and quivered, Vera, because you seemed to know everything I didn't know.

But. We don't need to dwell. Do we need to dwell? I just saw a star fall across the velvet sky. Red sparks in black night—so, not a star, but a shell, exploding in what looks like celebration. I feel I'm back in that close apartment, watching you smoke. Drawing deep breaths, sucking in your cheeks. Exhalations more magnificent, coils undulating through the air. After which, you drew me forward, understanding that I would forgive everything. An explosion is a pleasure, Vera. An explosion means release.

Do you know that the word *grenade* comes from *pomegranate*? So many seeds, spilled. So many chances, lost—or perhaps you could say honed, winnowing life to its essential pieces.

I wanted you dead. You put flame to paper. We both had our reasons, didn't we?

# *Zoya*

24.

FOR A WHILE I WAS SURE THAT KAY would do something awful. She'd run to the administration and claim I'd perverted her vocabulary. She'd accuse me of aural assault, or battery of the brain. I thought she'd try to get me fired, just from spite. It would've been, in some ways, a relief.

Instead, days passed and—nothing. At first I waited for the early class bells to ring before venturing outside my greenhouse. I finished all my morning chores, weeding or watering, spritzing a mixture of hydrogen peroxide to decrease the chances of mildew and mold. No biology students were due that week, on account of the weather, and so I was able to creep away unmolested and go into town for breakfast. When I returned, I reluctantly opened the greenhouse for viewings (a simple matter of turning over the WELCOME sign, since I couldn't leave the door ajar), and day after day no one came to visit except a first-year named Daphne who liked the hydrangeas.

I confided to John O'Brien about what had happened, and he laughed before turning serious. We were replanting some of our first seedlings into their mature pots, and he stuck his spade upright in the dirt, brushing off his hands and giving me his full attention.

"Zoe, have you ever considered going on a date or something?"

"What?" I must've looked shocked, because he quickly shook his head.

"No. Oh, no. Not with me." John went a bit pale with embarrassment. A few months before, after a couple of beers and a dinner with Siobhan, he had pulled me into an embrace while walking me home. I hadn't even needed to protest—he drew away of his own accord and apologized profusely, saying he just felt like we were family, and had gotten confused. I never brought it up again. "With a young man. Someone your age?"

"Oh," I said.

"It's not that I think you did anything wrong, honey," he added. "I just wonder sometimes if you don't need another place to turn your attention. So those girls won't get under your skin so much."

I promised him I'd think about it. There wasn't, in truth, a lot of extra time in my days, though of course I'd structured them that way on purpose. The greenhouse was my life, and I kept a mental calendar of which sections needed pruning or fertilizer, how often a major cleaning was required to keep the window glass pristine. Before I left in the evenings—provided there was no freeze in effect, and thus that I was able to leave at all—I whispered good night to many of my favorite plants individually, thanking them for their hard work and telling them how beautiful they'd become. In my time off, I often had to wash or mend my clothes, or else clean out my room, and was always surprised by how much of my time cooking and shopping took up every week. I was in the process of looking for an apartment, as well. It seemed likely that unless Kay ratted me out for vulgarity, I'd be offered an extended contract at the greenhouse, and I didn't want to stay on campus over the summer, or ever again. There were several small houses being let in the area, and I'd been making my way through them with help from Nadine, who enjoyed circling rental notices in the newspaper. When all that was through, I liked to read, or take quiet walks by myself. It seemed a full life.

But there was something about John's suggestion that struck a chord with me, nevertheless. My body had always been serviceable: long enough limbs, strong enough hands, good teeth, decent digestion. I'd been so young when I began working with my parents in the Lipetsk field that it felt natural to consider my legs primarily in terms of locomotion, and my fingers as diligent pincers for plucking weeds or removing pests. In school I changed focus, but still, there were things I needed. Eyes for reading, the ability to sit without growing stiff. I hadn't given much thought to the fact of my body, its very existence. There'd been no call to.

Lately, though, things were different. It would start like this: a morning walk around campus with the clouds grading down into fog and then mist and then rain, moisture stuck to the fibers of my sweater, heat inside my clothes. I'd breathe in, and the air would have a scent like chopped ice, though it wasn't quite cold enough anymore to snow. Bits of too-big gravel would trouble my feet beneath my shoes, and I'd kick them off the path, turning just in time to see a swallow sweep down over the lawn. And then came the girls.

You might think that a year would be long enough to get used to constant touch, but in my experience the longer it goes on the more you simply become attuned to it. On the same quiet walk, I might see two second-years approaching on the path, and they'd knock their shoulders into mine, tossing my body first one way and then the next. Two would become four would become six would become ten: neat shoes crushing down on my toes, an unlikely heel kicking my Achilles tendon and leaving a bruise that would persist for days. Girls seeming to run for their first class, but slowing to a walk once they'd swatted my thighs with the books they were carrying. Pinches in the lunch line, pinches in the greenhouse. A hand reaching for my cheek and then snatching at my ear, giving it a tug.

When I wore my hair back it was always pulled. When I tucked in my shirts they were always yanked free, and objects were inevitably knocked out of my grasp. After Kay tripped me my palms scabbed over, and the scabs were so large I could feel them bend. And this—this is the part I could not tell John, or anyone—my body buzzed with the sensation, and I didn't want it to stop.

Here's what a bruise can do: ache and ache. You press your thumb to it and there it goes again. Purple pain, morning pain, private pain to explore in one's own bedroom. Tear a piece of skin off like you're breaking the peel of an orange. Snap a rubber band on your wrist until the flesh gets vivid.

On the whole I did not want to hurt myself. But I kept walking into the cafeteria, didn't I? I kept letting myself stray into the part of the campus where I knew girls took smoke breaks, noting the uptick in heartbeats per minute that felt like fear but also desire. My system was nervous, sympathetic. The more blood in the room—but let's not get macabre; I mean swimming in veins, beneath skin, blushing lungs—the more blood in my cheeks. A senior let her cigarette fall onto my bare knee, and I gasped at the burn with an interest that covered more ground than just pain or surprise. They still infuriated me, these girls with their dads and their cars and their beaus, their sweater sets and tennis whites and ski vacations and beautiful, terrible smiles. I hated them because they were so cruel to me. But I needed the cruelty, because it was the only way I felt hands on my shoulders, fingers down my spine. Pull my hair, push me over, grab my wrist and draw me close.

My body: I knew it, all of a sudden. And if I didn't love the life I was living, at least I knew I was alive.

## 25.

JOHN KEPT PESTERING ME, AND OVER THE course of that spring I did agree to several dates with boys from town. "Young men," as John called them, who had jobs at the soda shop or the local factory, packing spring coils into boxes to be shipped to another factory and used in who knows what contraption. One of my dates was a veterinarian's assistant, and I enjoyed meeting him at his clinic: he took me to the back where there was a wall of cats in tight cages and a row of kennels full of dogs experiencing various degrees of distress. It was like a more boisterous version of the greenhouse, and I told the boy this. His name was Colin.

"It's like what?" he said.

"You know, they're all separated by type, and you have to do tasks to keep them healthy. Trim parts back, give them a drink . . ."

I trailed off, seeing Colin's frown. I was reasonably certain John had told Colin what my job entailed, so I wasn't sure what he found so strange in this comparison.

"It's an entirely different thing," he told me. "Plants can't think."

"I know that. I'm just saying there's a likeness—"

"Hey, uh, the movie's soon."

Colin put his hands in his pockets and looked towards the exit. I followed him out, and we hurried to some ridiculous matinee, having rushed to make the cheaper show so Colin could also afford to buy me a popcorn. He kept trying to put his arm around me, and though I wasn't opposed to the idea, it made walking to the theatre difficult and watching the movie impossible. Every time I shifted in my seat he tightened his grip, so whatever new position I worked myself into was made uncomfortable in a different way. Popcorn kernels got stuck between my teeth, but I didn't want to pick them out while he was so near to my face. There they remained, and when he tried to kiss me at the theatre's exit—I'd refused to be walked home, not wanting to bring a boy to campus—I turned my head aside, and Colin never asked me out again.

We did run into one another a few weeks later, though. Colin was coming out of a bar, and I was walking home from Sugar Books, where I'd been disappointed. Nothing special, nothing new.

"Hey Zoooeeeeee," he shouted, half a block away. "Hey Zoe, you know me, we went to a moooovieeee."

I stopped and let him catch up; Colin's friends laughed and kept walking in the opposite direction, so when he reached me we were alone.

"Zoe," he breathed, reaching out and tucking a strand of hair behind my ear. During our entire date he hadn't said my name half so many times. "Why were you so mean to me?"

"I was—what?" Colin smelled sweet and like sweat. He hummed and fizzed. "How was I mean?"

"You said the animals were plants. You wouldn't let me kiss you good night."

"Oh." He was now fiddling with a button on my green jacket, so the fabric pulled against my shoulders and chest. I looked down, suddenly shy. "I guess I was afraid you wouldn't like it."

"Come here."

Colin stepped away, and walked into an alley behind the tailor's shop. They appeared to have abandoned the process of changing their window display, and several dummies languished there, headless and half-dressed. The alley was full of sickly brown puddles from the spring melt, but I went anyway. Colin took me by the shoulders and pushed my back against the brick wall, and there he kissed me. His breath muggy. His thumb resting on the place between my bottom lip and chin. He pushed his legs against mine, and let his free hand move down to my waist, and I kissed him back, little knowing what else to do, and also—wanting to. With each breath, I seemed to be taking air right out of his lungs, and this puffed me up until I grew light-headed. For a second I was sure my feet had lifted off the ground. That my skirt had lifted from my knees.

"Hey!" A voice called out from somewhere around the corner. "Lover boy! Come out, come out!"

"Ah—" Colin drew back with a look of fleeting regret. But then the wolf whistles started, and he seemed to remember something. "Well," he said. "Fair's fair, now. Done is done."

"Done?" I repeated. I was not done.

"See you around." Colin touched my chin one more time. Then he jogged out of the alley and shouted something I didn't quite catch, which was met with hoots and more whistling—the sound of which diminished down the block. I leaned against the wall and listened to their footsteps disappear, and when it was perfectly quiet again I straightened my skirt and went home and put myself to bed.

## 26.

IN THE END, KAY DIDN'T DO ANYTHING. That is, if you don't count telling the other girls to be increasingly nasty without ever telling them why. More vile names were whispered to me when I walked across the commons, and a gutsy squad of seniors broke into the kitchen to steal a dozen eggs, which they waited half a week to use, ratcheting up my anxiety by the hour. I kept waking up and running to the greenhouse, expecting to find a smear of yolk and shell on every pane. But at last they threw a few each at my back, making two hits and several near misses which smashed on the sidewalk and were washed clean by the rain. I didn't tell anyone, though it meant dry-cleaning my coat mid-season.

I never told about anything, really, except in confidence to John and Hilda. I carried on. What else was I supposed to do? At the end of the year I got the extended contract, and John took me out for a glass of celebratory wine. I signed a lease on a furnished house five blocks away from campus—one bedroom, a study that was attached to the living room, and an eat-in kitchen. My own bathroom, at last. In the greenhouse my orchids were thriving, and a well-traveled parent sent me a bonsai tree, which I dutifully pruned into contorted proportions.

The staff were expected to attend graduation, mostly standing around the edges of seats filled by students and proud family members. Seniors were placed up front, and the other girls sat in order behind them—I could see my own spot from the previous year, now occupied by one of the egg girls. Her hair curled and pinned back neatly beneath her cap, a smile of self-satisfaction quivering on her lips. I listened to the speeches about greatness and empathy and moving into the world to do good in our dark times—America wasn't at war, but I suppose all times feel dark in their own way. Certainly the day felt different from my own grad ceremony had, more bittersweet and ominous. Afterwards I accepted a piece of white cake with yellow frosting, buttercream.

"Hi, Zo!" Kay called from a nearby table. An eating area had been erected outside to help celebrants enjoy the weak spring sun. "I so look forward to seeing you again next year."

She beamed, and I tried to smile back with some measure of aggression, enthusiasm. But it was as if all my emotions were on mute; even Kay couldn't get a rise out of me. She seemed distant and almost dear. Already parents were lugging boxes into cars while girls signed yearbooks and blubbered over their good-byes. I could feel the shift. A floodgate, open. A tide, receding.

When the proceedings were over, I went back to my little house and lay down on top of the bedclothes. I still hadn't quite gotten used to the idea of relaxing in the living room, sitting on a couch or chair. But the house was mine. I rubbed the edge of the blanket against my cheek, calling up the faint memory of a blue bunny, many years before. Lost now. I felt a bit sad, and reminded myself that I had work to do all summer. Good work. We'd planned a total inventory of the species in the greenhouse, reorganizing and cutting back as necessary, making room for the new year of biological science students and their Mendelian experiments on radish seedlings. I was going to help John choose new border flowers for the campus walkways. The weather would grow hot, and I would take one of the wooden kitchen chairs out onto the porch and sip iced tea. There would be fireflies.

I feel so keenly for that girl now. Her terror of being alone. I know the rooms of the house creaked and echoed, and that the pilot light in the stove soon developed a habit of going out just when circumstances called for a cup of strong tea. I know she cried herself to sleep, sometimes. That memories of her parents and the smell of bullets burning through flesh would come to her at the strangest moments. She'd look at walls and imagine them crumbling, falling on top of her, weakened by mortars or booby-trapped with wire. A friend, reaching out with soot-blackened fingers from beneath a stone too heavy to lift.

But I also know that the summer would end without calamity, as would the year following, and the year after that. Three years gone in a blink. I know that the girl had pleasures in her future she couldn't yet dream of. Troubles too. But pleasure first, for once. Lev first.

# VOLUME TWO

# *Lev*

28 June 1931
Airmail via [Redacted]

I'M IMAGINING YOU, MY DARLING, ON THE first day of our new life in Maple Hill, which didn't go quite the way we expected. You wore a blue dress—wool, despite the warm fall weather—and your hair was cut so severely I thought I might slice my hand if I brushed a strand off your shoulders. After the years we spent in Paris and the years we spent in that absurdly small apartment in New York, we needed a change and you had found it.

A pair of children ran by outside. Young girl with a knapsack, following a boy who seemed to be her brother. They cast long shadows and laughed as they ran, and through the window you watched them, waiting for me to meet you by the door. One hand on your hip, purse at the ready. Really devilish shoes, I must say. I stood at the top of the stairs and watched you, your eyes tracking the children and then tracking their absence. Small-town life. I had a momentary impulse to lift you off your feet and throw you onto whatever surface was available, taking torrid liberties. Making you as round as an onion, so I could peel you back and see what was inside. Your little white face, replicated. But I restrained myself, knowing as I do your delight in keeping a schedule.

Neither of us wanted to be in New Jersey, though you wouldn't admit it out loud. It was an afterthought of a place, a backcountry charm school.

That was certainly my first reaction when the letter arrived, offering me a tenured post—we'd been in New York long enough to consider all land beyond the Hudson provincial. But the provost at the Donne School was a fan of my writing, and willing to overlook what many more prestigious administrators had called the "childish philosophical wish-making of a pseudo-biologist" (among other plum summaries of my work). Not to mention the money was surprisingly good: wealthy parents, rich tuition. And so you insisted this was what we needed. A place to rest, after all our wandering. Until the day my books could support us I would have to teach, and I could teach here. Little girls. Little women. I was surprised you didn't protest on this point. Instead, before walking me to campus for the first time, you smoothed my lapel and re-knotted my tie, running the length of it through your fist with a flourish.

"There," you said. "Dashing."

By then I was used to having you dress me. Everything I once owned had been thrown away by the date of our wedding, or else pressed and brushed, nipped in with a tailor's unfailing eye. I'd never cared about my wardrobe, and found it relaxing to have you take the reins. One less thing to occupy my mind while writing. Sort "clothes" with "food" and "friends" and "mail." The postman handed you our stack of letters, and you cut them open with a nifty switchblade from one of the more roguish Parisian flea markets. When something merited my attention—like the offer from George Round in Maple Hill—you let me know. The rest you dispatched yourself.

Our true partnership—it started with my manuscript, didn't it? A single, cleansing fire. After that I gave myself over to you. Not a statement of regret, my love, just a dispassionate review: our lives as a slide show, leading up to the Donne School steps. Once we made up, there were conversations held late into the night, ideas I scribbled down on napkins and scraps to show you in the morning. The wrinkle in your forehead when you were scratching something out. You found all the pieces of me that I wanted to deny, and excised them with neat precision. Extraneous phrases, characters who could be combined into one better man, lopsided philosophies. Nothing escaped you, and I grew to rely on it.

That morning, I watched you apply lipstick in the hallway mirror. Our house was still half empty then, though your embellishments were beginning to show. A few tasteful portraits hung in the sitting room, plus one wedding photo. Coffee cups with blue limning stacked in the cabinet at rakish angles. Your bedroom bureau an airplane console with powder compacts and brooches for buttons. I sometimes had the sense that I was looking at fragments of your mind left out in plain view, the larger picture still obscured. But of course—I reminded myself—I knew the larger picture. Our success, toasted. Our happiness, secure. You pressed your lips together to smudge the red more evenly around your mouth, then used a pinky nail to scrape away an imperfection that was, to me, invisible.

Looking up, your reflection caught mine studying you. It smiled.

"I know you're not sure about this," you said.

"I'm sure about you."

"It will all come right."

"I trust you."

You nodded, and I thought back to the weeks we spent discussing *Knife, Knave* before I sent it off to the Parisian editor your father introduced me to. How whenever you made a good point your cells would swell with certainty, a celestial sarcoma to which you are particularly inclined. The book made a small wave, as did the next one, and the next. My writing, but somehow also your brilliance. You knew which dotted lines to sign and which to notate for a new round of negotiations. Never take the first offer. Never let them see your fear. Good advice for a teacher, too, it turned out.

At the school we met George to sign the contracts, and then walked round the grounds, getting what he called the "five-dollar tour." ("What about the ten-dollar tour?" you asked, and he laughed. Stick bug of a man with a bristle of a mustache. I should really be kinder to George.) It included, of course, a look at the underground steam tunnels where industrious girls brought their boyfriends to neck, in addition to the more broadly advertised clock tower and library. I also met my first-semester pupils, a hundred little Tabithas rasa peering up at me from their seats. Slender ankles, of course. Wrists switching back and forth, fingers pinching pencils. *There, you see*, I told myself. *There may be some fun in this after all.* But that day I mostly introduced you around, and shook hands with the fathers, nodding gravely at their schoolboy interest in Rilke and Freud. They all wanted their daughters to recite poetry because their mothers had recited poetry. No strange stirrings there.

By the afternoon you were at home again, and I was ruffled, taking a solo stroll to clear my head. Trees everywhere, and bright green lawns. A glint in the distance: light off the greenhouse. But let's rewind for a moment. Back to that morning, before we opened the door. Your lips were plumped with conviction, and your hand lay so light on my arm that I could have forgotten it was there had you not given my elbow a squeeze. How much did you know? Enough, I suppose, to keep me from any distraction that might have compromised your plan, which was to give us some stability at last. The telephone rang as we walked out the door for our meeting with George, and you turned me away from the sound.

"Ignore it," you said. "They'll call again."

So we carried on, me reluctant, you cocksure. I saw what I saw, I met who I met. And it wasn't until after the sun had set that I learned *Felice* had gone into an unexpected second printing. Surprise bestseller. Five-star reviews. An instant classic. By then the contracts had been signed for the year, and it was too late for us to leave New Jersey—exactly as you intended, I suppose. You took the call. I came back to our house after my walk and slouched into a chair, where you ran a hand through my hair and—did I imagine it?—gave a quick tug. A shadow passed over your face when you told me the news, having first made sure I was equipped with a glass of scotch. Triumph, Vera, at steering me just as you'd planned? Or remorse? I never knew. Perhaps first one, and then—much later—the other.

*Zoya*

27.

THERE IS SUCH A THING AS TOO MUCH foreplay. I learned that while
waiting for the administration to decide about giving me a raise, early in
my fourth year as a Donne School employee. I admit I didn't need it—I
had my house, some serviceable work clothes, and enough money to keep
me in books and sardines. I usually cultivated a few extra plants to make
sure I had fresh food all winter, a couple of tomatoes and a huge pot of
basil, the exotic purple swell of an eggplant, which I liked to put in soup.
Tweak free a lemon or two for tea, which I took with local honey that I
got in trade from a nice older woman named Maureen Finnegan who
lived on the edge of town and wore Wellington boots on every occasion
that we met.

But my tastes had changed. After a few months of fixing scrambled eggs
for every meal, I lost my appetite for them entirely. Sometimes I'd pick
up an egg and start to cry: because of the blank slate of it, and because I
was so very tired of cracking them, mixing them, eating them. On a budget,
eggs are the perfect food, until they're not.

I'd also become more selective about who I let John O'Brien fix me up
with: now I made him run the boys past Siobhan, who picked slightly older
fellows. There weren't as many of them available, so I had maybe two
or three dates a year, but they took me out in earnest. Movies, yes, but
dinner too, and sometimes dancing. Instead of a diner or a small café,
we went to proper restaurants with cloth napkins and dim lighting.

Chandeliers. Like the men, there weren't many such restaurants in town, and I quickly developed favorites. There was in particular a dish of stewed rabbit with mushrooms and wine that I sometimes dreamed about. That I dream about, even now. I thought it would've been nice to take myself there, without the feeling I was offering anything in exchange for the meal, and to go whenever I wanted instead of waiting to be asked.

Still, I would never have considered asking for more money if John hadn't given me the idea. It happened one day while I was inspecting a tray of herbs that had been seeded by students the previous year, and the pot holding a sprig of parsley came apart in my hand. I cradled the small root ball and blew a lock of hair out of my eyes, biting back a yelp of frustration. John was with me, taking inventory as part of a larger effort to catalogue the current growth on campus, and he noticed.

"Penny for your thoughts?" he said.

"It's just stupid." More hair fell across my face, and I had to spit it out of my mouth as I spoke. "Those girls pay how much in tuition every year and the school can't afford a few dollars for new pots and spades?"

"Not to mention, well, have you looked at your clothes lately?"

I glanced up. "What about my clothes?"

"Nothing! Nothing. Just," he puffed his cheeks and shrugged, as if changing his mind. All the while staring pointedly at the tear in the knee of my pants, which I'd patched up years ago, after Kay tripped me.

"So nice that you noticed," I said. "Girls like that sort of thing."

"All I'm saying is, you deserve more for yourself, too. You've been here long enough. Proved yourself, so to speak."

"That's—true. I guess." It was hard for me to place a particular value on myself, but he had a point. Above me stretched a canopy of greens, yellows, reds. Things were trimmed back at the moment, to encourage new growth for Welcome Day. But the greenhouse was thriving, and clearly so.

Later that afternoon I talked to Peggy in the Office of Human Resources, and she helped me submit a formal letter requesting a salary adjustment for cost of living and performance excellence. John had already walked me through the appeal for an increased project budget; that money, it turned out, was in the bag. He'd been planning to ask for it himself if I hadn't brought it up, and the arbiter of the funds was a friend of his.

The raise, on the other hand, required a catalogue of all the tasks I performed on a regular basis, broken down by category and expertise. I had to show growth and improvement and flexibility. *Too bad*, I thought, *that I can't list my new talent at putting awful little girls in their places.* Since Kay graduated, my relationship with the student body had improved, though each new generation seemed to inherit at least a modicum of her spunk and spite. The difference was that now, when I was taunted, I was able to pull a mask over my face, porcelain and still. When they pinched me, if there was no one around, I jabbed them with my finger and walked off looking innocent as a flower. Nothing that would impress the administration, unfortunately. But it made me feel better.

After making my request, the school scheduled a series of meetings for me: a walk-through of the greenhouse, a conversation with my immediate supervisors, and a final decision to be reached and relayed to me by the office of the provost, a Mr. George Round. By the time the last meeting came up, I'd been circling the prospect of new money—my new money—for weeks, and it had crept beneath my skin. I found myself looking critically at things like dish towels and tea cups, thinking about color schemes and bookends that might improve the atmosphere of my home. It wasn't as though I'd be swimming in gold if the raise went through, but I would be able to take myself out to eat now and then. I could, as John so kindly pointed out, replace my torn jeans. There was, deep within me, still some trace of that undernourished girl who clung to the rail of a ship and dreamed of America, and I wanted so badly to impress her. To show myself how far I'd come.

Sitting outside Mr. Round's office, I smoothed my skirt over my knees and tried to keep from hyperventilating. A secretary perched nearby, typing. Her method was peculiar—she'd stare at the paper, taking measured breaths, fingers poised—and then with no warning burst into motion. Then she'd stop to think again. It was difficult to listen to, in my condition; I spent the silent periods in tense anticipation of a new surge of keystrokes, and when they came each one resonated in my head like the blow from a hammer. I had no idea what the provost was likely to say. My initial bluster had worn off, but in the meantime I'd grown attached to the idea of being comfortable—something I couldn't remember ever having been before. I clasped my hands tight, and looked at my shoes. Scuffed, of course.

The telephone rang.

"Yes? Yes. Alright." The secretary looked up at me and smiled. "You can go in now."

This, then, was it. I walked through the large oak doorway into a corner office, brightly lit by two enormous windows. Another desk, bigger than the secretary's, was stationed ten paces away in the rear, and behind it sat a frowning gentleman in a perfectly pressed suit. I smiled to myself—George Round was not *round*. He was slender, and had a nice lavender tie. There were, I noted, three separate houseplants in the room, an African violet, a philodendron, and some type of fern. Obvious choices, probably selected for him by the secretary or some unseen wife, but still—well cared for. Positioned for sufficient sun. George Round looked up from the paper in his hands, and motioned for me to sit down.

"Miss—"

"Andropov," I supplied, unnecessarily.

"Yes, of course. Well." He cleared his throat. "Tell me—" I leaned forward into his pause, prepared to defend my understanding of soil types and inflation rates and educational horticulture. My significance as a human being. "Do you have lilies in your greenhouse?"

"I'm sorry?" The simplicity and directness of his question caught me off guard.

"Lilies," George Round repeated. "Do you have any?"

"I do."

We both waited for the other to continue. George Round twitched his moustache.

"And what—"

"I have several—"

We laughed.

"Well, that's lovely." His glasses must've fogged, because he took them off and cleaned them, using the underside of his pretty tie. "I care a great deal for lilies. Such an elegant flower."

"I agree," I said. "Most people prefer roses. Which—I like them well enough, but there's something ordinary about the shape of them, I think. People are familiar with roses. Whereas lilies—"

"A simpler profile, but somehow more elusive."

"Yes."

There was a brief silence. George Round picked up the stack of papers in front of him, and straightened them out, clearing his throat again. A tick, I wondered, or the precursor to our real conversation? Perhaps now he'd question my core competencies, or bring up my behavior towards Kay. As far as I knew she'd never ratted me out, but I couldn't be sure what was written there. Dark marks in the file cabinet.

"This all seems to be in order," he said.

"Excuse me?"

"I mean, I think I have everything I need. It's been a pleasure meeting you, Miss Andropov."

"Sir." Not knowing what else to do, I stood up. "And my salary increase?"

"Oh! Approved. Heartily approved." He beamed. "Unless you're unhappy with the amount?"

"Not at all," I said quickly. Later, I would wonder if this was a mistake, if I could've asked for more. A skill I'm still learning. "Thank you."

"It will be reflected in your next paycheck."

I nodded and thanked Mr. Round again, and when I walked out into the antechamber I gave the secretary a dazed smile. That was all? That was all. I'd thought of nothing else for weeks, prepared my arguments for days, and now it was over. I had done well. The sun was shining; early fall. Practically still summertime.

As I pushed out of the building, I wondered if George Round knew to water the African violets from the bottom, and whether he remembered to spritz them when the furnace dried out the office air. Probably so. And if not, what did it matter to me?

It was hot, I realized. The good pair of stockings I'd worn to look chic were now sticky with sweat, so I ducked behind a tree and peeled them off, rolling them up into my purse. I walked to the ice cream parlor and got myself a scoop of strawberry, then wandered around until the cream melted down onto my fingers, and threw the half-eaten cone away. Despite being happy, there was a strange feeling in my fingertips, toetips, the top layer of my skin. Unresolved energy, sparking. I thought about wandering until I found Colin, my unfortunate old flame, and throwing him against the side of a building to see how he liked it. Probably he would, probably too much.

What had I hoped would happen? Perhaps that my life would change. But people walked by and no one congratulated or admired me. My body just kept going, like a well-wound clock. I took a taxi to the department store and picked out a new blouse and new dress and new pair of work pants—reinforced duck cloth instead of denim. In the dressing room I paused to feel the weight of the fabric against my skin, slightly different with each garment. I took another taxi home and tipped the driver well. We passed a moving truck at one point, which of course I gave no thought to at all. In the pivotal moments of your life, how often are you really paying attention to what matters? I'd like to ask Vera that: I suspect her answer would be different from most people's. Different from mine, absolutely. She'd probably wrapped every item on that truck herself, with cleverness and care. Her own innovative solutions. And perhaps what I felt was not just the glow of a job well done, but some subconscious glimmer of anticipation.

The next day, all our lives would change, every one. In a couple of brief sightings: a man peering into a greenhouse, hat in hand. A girl, breathing against the glass to clean it, startled by the closeness of his face. I know it was Vera's idea to bring them to Maple Hill, and so now, looking back, I wonder how much of the future she might have expected. Reason suggests: almost none. But when did Vera stoop to reason?

# Lev

28 June 1931, later
Airmail via [Redacted]

ONE MORE THING. I'LL SEND THESE LETTERS together, and hopefully you'll feel the tug of time between them, how I set down my pen and folded the paper, and then was bowled over by the sense of you, present. I often get this feeling at home, when we're separated by a wall or a few city blocks; some whiff of you walks into the room behind me, brushes its fingertips over my shoulders, reaches a hand down the top of my shirt to caress the tough nub of my breastbone. I never want you more, Vera, than in those moments. When the distance between us is but a clarion cry, a note on our closeness. Tonight you crawled up onto my knees, pushing my chair back several inches and nearly toppling both of us over. I could feel the weight of you, could almost make out your outline. Your fingers scattering themselves over my skin, as if setting spells from some private grimoire, a book of incantations built to my exact specifications. Bring in the clear and cloudless wife. Her invisibility irresistible, my brain all woolen with desire.

Were those hands my hands? The ones that pulled at me, put me in my place. Was it my hips that pitched and rolled until the inevitable cataclysm? Hull of a ship, breached. Cheek of a woman, brushed by cheek. I know what most people would say about lonely Lev in his lightless cottage at the end of the land. Lantern kicked over, fire brewing in the dirt of the floor before fizzling out. Self abuse, heavy use. But I have more faith than most people. In you, especially.

Tomorrow night I'm meeting again with the courier, Vlad, so he can secret me across the heavily patrolled border back to the home of my birth. Our births. From there I'll have twenty-four hours, along with my own sense of momentum and the hand spade I picked up—an ingenious contraption that can be folded in two so as to look less like a knife if one's possessions are tossed by suspicious soldiers. Today I found a small hillock and practiced shooting into it, getting used to the kick of the Italian pistol and fumbling my fingers through the process of a quick reload. I won't write you again until I'm homeward bound, or perhaps I won't write again at all. Whether due to hasty retreat or an untimely bullet in an unlikely place (forehead, home of dreams, kaput, et cetera), this may be the last missive you receive from my misadventure. I pray that fate not let those Marxist thugs derail me—I could not stand the *sovietskii sabor* on my tongue forever, flavor of a lost country. You know they'd keep me if they could, writing incompetent manifestos or moldering in an early grave. With any luck you'll see me soon, manuscript in hand, all triumph.

But if not, at least I had one last taste of you this evening, and I wanted you to know it, that your distant body was as nourishing as any meal. Salted radishes. Stewed pear. White wine. Red blood. I bit your unseen lip and into my mouth there came an iron tang. Back in our house, in our bed, by your candle, I'm sure you cried out and then reached for a tissue to wipe away the stain. Touched a finger to your newly bruised mouth. Settled back into the pillows, content.

# *Zoya*

## *28.*

THE NEXT DAY I WAS FLUSH WITH my financial success, reorganizing
succulents to make room for a new display—a small pond for water lilies,
which seemed an appropriate homage to the tastes of my new benefactor. When I heard something scuffling at the building's rear, I thought,
*Already?* It was early for the girls to be harassing me on my home ground.
Most weren't even moved into their dorms, so where had they found the
time to come creeping? *What eager devils*, I thought. *What pretty witches.
Let's get started, if you wish.*

Taking care not to crush the water lines or kick over any vital terra-cotta,
I picked my way to the sound's point of origin. A window, tapping. A stick
outside, giving up with a snap. I thought I might give them a bit of a scare,
these interlopers, but even after pushing aside several jungle plants I
couldn't see a soul. The glass was fogged up and lightly mildewed—
annoying after the deep clean John and I had done, but this particular
pane stood behind a bushy palm, and the fronds hid the worst of the mold.
Since my shirt was already filthy, I breathed onto the stain and wiped it
away with my sleeve.

Then I screamed.

In that scream: terror, surprise, embarrassment, and then—a tiny trill of
pleasure. For there was no pert girl waiting to wiggle her fingers at me
in some impertinent hello. Just a long nose, a raised eyebrow. A man bent
over and trying every bit as hard to see my face as I was trying to see his.

And what's more, I knew this man's name. It was Leo Orlov, beyond a shadow of a doubt, though his hair was combed differently from as was usual in his photographs. *Lev Pavlovich*, I would come to call him.

He stood up and gave me a genial nod, then walked off across the campus lawn as if he did so every day. And, in time, of course he would. I put a hand up to my heart, then touched the cold glass. Not a hallucination. Thirty paces away he stopped and wiped something off his shoe on the grass.

But what did it mean? An imagined Orlov could have been chalked up to the same bout of magical thinking that had led me to strip off my stockings while standing a stone's throw from the Hall of Science the day before. Dreamy lust, bodily volition. But a real Orlov, a flesh-and-blood incarnation? Perhaps he was just passing through. A road trip with some fellow expatriate, on the run from an agent of the Soviet secret police, the dreaded NKVD. A book tour with a signing at the local shop. I knew vaguely that he was married; perhaps his wife liked maple trees. Perhaps they were visiting someone, an old shut-in astronomer who was helping Lev map the rules of a new star system. Two planets orbiting the same sun in an infinite double ellipse. That kind of thing.

It was lunchtime. Taking a moment to wash my hands and de-smear the green matter from my clothing, I went to the cafeteria in search of answers. Hilda and Nadine both waved from the kitchen; they looked more and more alike these days. Returning students bubbled around me, *oohing* and *aahing* at the new ice cream freezer and pulling their parents away from the salad. It was nice to go unrecognized; I had been right before, it was too early for the girls to pay me any mind. Glancing behind myself to make sure I wasn't followed, I slipped into the kitchen and stage whispered.

"*Psst!*"

Nadine appeared from nowhere and whapped my head with a dish towel.

"*Psst* yourself, private eye. Long time, no see."

"Don't be grouchy," I said. "I've been busy."

"I know, Miss Moneybags. John told us. So is that why you're here? To show off some new gold rings? Silk shirts? What's going on?"

I tried to look casual, downplaying my interest by inspecting a bowl of fruit salad, moving the grapes around with a set of tongs. Then, as an afterthought, "Is there a new teacher this year?"

Nadine shrugged, and looked to Hilda, who did the same. "There's always one or two. Someone gets sick, retires. Someone finds a better post. Why?"

"Nothing," I said, picking up a slice of apple and nibbling the end.

"Malarkey."

"No, really. I just thought I saw someone I knew."

"You?" Now Hilda was interested. "Like, another graduate? Or something else. You mean a *Soviet*?" She looked perturbed.

"It's probably nothing. Just a writer I like."

"Oh, him." Hilda laughed. "Well, then I was sort of right, wasn't I?"

"You've met him?"

"He came through with Mr. Round, he and his wife. She's pretty, if you like 'em mean."

"Should fit right in around here," I suggested. At the time, I didn't know we were talking about Vera, though I'm not sure it would have changed what I had to say.

Nadine made a *hmm* sound in the back of her throat and handed me another piece of apple. "So. You like his . . . writing? His . . . big ideas?" I turned immediately red.

"Yes, I do. And what's your point?"

"No point." She smiled. "Just trying to make sure we're on the same page."

I popped the last bit of apple into my mouth and tried to swallow without really chewing, then coughed. Hilda had to slap my back. "Well, I think it's time for me to get out of here."

"You do that. We'll keep an eye out for your Mr. Writer."

I left with the sound of laughter following me—a friendly sort of humiliation. I would never have admitted to them that I was intrigued by Leo

Orlov, but I was pleased anyhow that they were on the case, ready to share any news they came up with.

That night at home I pulled all my Orlov books off the shelf and piled them around me, curious to see if they gave off any new energy now, my body having approached so close to their maker. I flipped through my favorites, pausing on the pages I'd folded down at the corner and rereading passages I'd underlined with pencil. In my hurry, I got a paper cut on my index finger and sucked the blood away until it dried, then went on checking the biographies printed on the rear flaps of the novels hoping to note any changes in them over the years, however small. I wanted to know when he'd moved to the United States, when he won his first award. I wanted to know everything about him.

## 29.

I LEARNED SOON ENOUGH: LEO ORLOV was a flirt. A burning flirt. I didn't need Nadine to tell me, either; I heard it straight from the Donne girls, who'd begun using the warm corners of the greenhouse to gossip while pressing red petals between their fingers. Plucking those petals from the flower and bringing them idly to their lips. Girls spilling over with them-selves and their enthusiasms.

"He sat on Katie's desk," one said, "and asked her to recite from Byron."

"Oh yeah? Well, he said he wanted to measure the hem of my skirt, and the ruler was touching my leg the whole time." A swoon sound.

"I heard he brought a bag of candies to class and threw one right into Nora's mouth. She almost choked, but she said it was worth it. Right from his fingertips onto her tongue."

During these confessionals I made sure to carry out minute tasks, things requiring the appearance of my full concentration. I wound vines up stakes, searched for and eliminated caterpillar eggs, trimmed dead branches off the flower bushes. In my state of pathological attention, the girls soon forgot about me; it was a convenient camouflage. But often I heard more than I cared to.

"He told Sophia how short to cut her hair."

*Leo Orlov wouldn't do that.*

"He graded Bridget's paper B for Buxom."

*Leo Orlov is respectable. Leo Orlov is married to a beautiful wife.* It didn't matter that I had the same designs as everyone; the idea that he would stoop to flirting with children insulted me. I wanted to give all these girls a talking-to, shake Orlov's books in front of their noses and tell them— what? That great men didn't stray? Even I wasn't that naïve.

One afternoon, about a month into the semester, I was sitting outside taking a break and enjoying the last of the waning fall sun when I heard a screech coming from a stand of laurels. Flashes of color whipped through the branches, too quick to make sense of. Then a girl jumped around a nearby tree and leaned against the trunk, grinning. Panting. It was Daphne, the onetime freshman—now senior—who used to haunt my greenhouse during finals week, trying to relax among the green. She looked insane.

"Come out, come out," a voice called. Daphne pressed herself tighter against the bark, nearly melting into the tree despite her giggles. If you squinted, her arms were branches, her hair the bloom.

"Oh for god's sake," I muttered. Except, not wanting Daphne to overhear me, what I really said was *Bozhe moi.* Russian still found its way to my tongue now and then, for secret keeping. Useful, as it turned out.

A hand reached around and tapped Daphne on the shoulder, and she squealed.

"Now, my dear," said the droll voice attached to the hand. "Run away to class, I know you're late. You've made a quick study in the art of escapism, brava."

I watched. She scampered off across the lawn, her little slippers so light she seemed to be dancing a ballet. Spring fawn, *grand jeté, grand jeté, grand jeté.* In retrospect I always imagine myself, in this moment, smoking a cigarette in furious protest, but that wasn't yet my vice. I'd learn it from Lev soon enough.

"*Nu, chto zdes est'?*" What have we here? A man—my man, the same fellow who had peered into my greenhouse, the same pair of eyes that first dreamed up the words in *Felice*, which I'd just finished devouring that

morning—walked over, wiping his hands on a pocket square, which he
then deftly re-tucked. "*Prostitye*, kto *est'*." Forgive me, *who*.

"Who, what, where," I replied. Hoping to sound cool. "It doesn't matter
what I am, because you don't *have* me."

"Oh, very nice. I like that very much. But really, I need to sit for a
moment. These infants are exhausting."

Just like that I was sharing a patch of grass with Leo Orlov, hero of my
reading life, current delicious villain of the rest. I tried to ignore the fact
that he'd said exactly what I wanted him to say, and that he smelled like
umber—the color, I mean. I wasn't sure how he did it, but was too afraid
to sound foolish asking. It crept up on me, invading my sinuses and my
good sense.

"You seem to enjoy them well enough," I told him.

"Well, one enjoys young creatures. The enthusiasm of the barely born.
Don't you think?" He asked me the way one asks a fellow traveler. A
connoisseur. Then he leaned back against the greenhouse, glass creaking
slightly beneath his weight. From the corner of my eye, I noted his mussed
hair. The long hollow of his smooth-shaven cheek.

"I think they're terrible."

"*T'i stishesh*," he said: You're joking. He moved so easily into the familiar
*t'i* that I hardly had time to register it. "How can something so naïve be
terrible? They don't have the strength."

Without speaking I held out my arm, showing off a dime-sized burn
on the inner curve of my elbow. Just a scar, now, but still a standout. Its
twin itched on my leg, though that one had at least appeared accidental
when it happened.

"No," he said. "Them?"

"The very same. Baby animals. Sharp teeth."

He corrected: "Sharp fangs."

At last I turned to regard him straight on. "I'm Zoya," I said. "Zoya
Ivanovna Andropova." I laughed. "You have no idea what a relief it is to
say my whole name for once."

"Lev Pavlovich Orlov." He held out a hand, which I shook. "And I think
I might." Lev switched back into Russian without missing a beat. "There

are days I can't stand talking to anyone at all here. I just want to crawl into my bedroom and lock the door. Leave all those dreadful *Hey Misters* outside and take a sleeping pill with a glass of vodka." He employed a dreadful American drawl to say *Hey Meeester*.

"You don't really drink vodka."

"Oh, of course I do, it's medicinal."

"For a cold."

"Not for pleasure."

"Never pleasure."

"Never, no." Lev picked up my hand—I'm ashamed to say I jumped, but his touch was so welcome and warm it shocked my system. He inspected my fingernails. "So let me guess. A working girl."

"That's right, Comrade. What else could I hope to be, as a functioning member of society?"

"Then you lost everything, too."

I shook my head. His home, I thought, must've been magnificent, with gold woven into the curtains for texture and window lintels of dustless mahogany. It was tempting to pretend I was indeed the kind of girl he imagined, wealthy and fallen, with my own fond memories of angora rabbits kept as pets and a taste for expensive, peppery wine. But I didn't want to lie. Whether I thought it would've been an insult to him or to my parents I'm still not certain. "Never had anything to lose," I said.

"Hmm." Lev moved his fingers down my own; they traveled light. A drop of water. Spray of rain. I could see my hand, beneath his, as almost delicate, though his nails were buffed and mine were not. He lacked calluses, but still. It was in the way he handled me. "I can't say I entirely agree."

I felt—my tongue grew very warm. I wanted to touch his neck, to smell his hair. I wanted him to reach into my mouth and count my teeth and see what the years had done to me. It was sex, but it was also the rest, unspoken: that we'd lost more than money when we lost our homes. That we didn't just escape a bad situation when we snuck across the border, we'd allowed our whole world to be washed away. Grammar, subject, object, tense. And that somehow together we could tally up those losses more completely. Already I wanted to press my tongue against his ear and see if I tasted a Russian fall. Watermelon. Jam. Smog. My mother and father. But here we were, two people in a school for girls where *propriety* was the watchword. I sat perfectly still, hoping he wouldn't drop my hand. His eyes flicked to the watch on his left wrist.

"Forgive me again, Zoya. I think I have somewhere to be." He stood, and I remained where I was. Couldn't have moved. Wouldn't have. Wanted to imprint the moment more permanently on my mind. "But I'll be seeing you again, won't I?"

There was no need for me to agree.


## 30.

THERE WAS A PERIOD, FOLLOWING, THAT passed like a dream, when every-thing I did was augmented with the fluttering, light-headed quality of sleep. I would find myself sitting at the table at home and not quite remember getting there, only to put a spoon into my mouth with no notion of what was on it. I'd close my eyes and wait for the flavor to break on my tongue: cranberry preserves or chicken stock, wild rice with butter or, one time, chocolate sauce, as if I personally had no power over what I ate or where I went, subject perpetually to a series of dramatic reveals. I worked with purpose in the greenhouse, but even there I was dozy and occasionally daft: John found me once putting rose petals in my mouth and chewing them up, a line of pink spittle dripping from the corner of my lips. When he asked me what I was doing I got flustered and made something up about how, in the old country, we tested for spider mites by taste.

"What if you've put on insecticide?" he said. And I had to tell him that no, those methods didn't usually go together. He frowned.

"But don't you treat your plants with it sometimes? Here, I mean?"

Of course he was quite right, but I wasn't about to discuss it. I waved a hand and distracted his attention with some other matter, a plugged drain near the rear sink that I'd been struggling to unclog, and when he wasn't looking I spat out the flower pulp and dropped it into a pile of mulch.

I had never been in love before. Never even really had a crush that I could give the name. When Lev and I waved to each other across the courtyard my heart would beat in my ears for half an hour, making me so dizzy that Hilda started threatening to give me pills, though I took pains to hide the depth of my feelings. In free moments I stared at the changing fall color, electric reds and yellows sending signals to my brain like live wires. The leaves in the United States had a different quality from the ones I'd known in Russia—not brighter, but more insistent somehow; less a part of the landscape and more of a treasured commodity, painted onto plates and mugs and stitched onto shirt cuffs and advertised in magazines as a local attraction. They were just as priceless here, but still felt somehow for sale, and I stored that idea away as a possible topic of conversation with Lev, as I did at that time with everything that passed through my mind. I thought of him constantly, repeated his qualities to myself incessantly. He was always clean and smelled of something new and alive, but had ink on his fingers like a dirty little pilgrim. If we passed on the grounds close enough to talk we would share a brief joke or observation, always in Russian, always quick as a flash. *Christos Voskres,* he might say, watching me stand up after tying my shoe. Christ is Risen. Holy, holy. When he caught me on the roof of the science building helping John trim ivy and laughing at my own clumsiness when I dropped the clippers, Lev called up *Pochemu t'i vesyolaya takaya?* Meaning both, why are you so high up, and why are you so happy?

I couldn't find the words to tell him, but I didn't have to. He knew. One day I stood under a covered walkway on my lunch hour, reading a concert poster someone had tacked up for a quartet in town that night playing Bach, when a hand slid into mine. I jumped, assuming it was one of the Donne girls planning something mean. But when I spun around Lev grabbed my shoulder and held me in place. "*Tolko ya,*" he said. It's only me. "*Tvoy dobry dryug.*" Your gentle companion. Your dear friend. The first time he'd touched me since the day we met, and he made it seem so natural. It hadn't been completely clear to me that he'd ever touch me again.

I flushed, expecting to be distracted any minute by a student running up with a question, or a pair of teachers in deep conversation. A man shaping hedges or sweeping the stairs who would want a word with me, and would be shocked by what he saw. But instead of letting go of my hand, Lev brought it to his lips and kissed it just below the knuckle, holding my eye the entire time. We were alone. As if fate had deserted us there, in that hour, to do what we wanted and go where we wished.

"Shall we?" he said. And I followed, without bothering to ask what he meant.

## 31.

HE TOOK ME FIRST IN HIS LOCKED OFFICE, hands down the front of my pants, looking directly into my eyes. He proceeded to repeat our earliest meeting back to me, but not how it happened, a whole other way. In this version a flock of birds made pinwheels above our heads—the birds weightless, atomic mist, scattered in the losing blue of the sky. *You didn't know anything about me,* I said to myself, pleasure flooding my unexplored places. *Why didn't you tell me there was more?* He kissed my hands again, he kissed my wrists, my ribs. As if to take one out of me and build something new.

"It's like I sensed you," he whispered. "Not just here, but everywhere. Like everyone I've ever loved was leading up to this, to you, to us."

He turned me around and my stomach rubbed raw against the edge of his desk, but I had no breath to protest. I wanted him to fling me, to pound me into powder. And I wanted to return the favor. The room was dim, but on the top of his desk I saw a stack of typing paper, covered with notes in feminine handwriting. I touched the edge of a page, a scratched-in signature—just a hash mark followed by a *V*—but then he turned me again and put his mouth to mine, and everything else was lost in sensation, friction, and the sounds of his still quite eloquent diction.

"A farm girl," he said. "And yet your body speaks in volumes, your mind, your mind—" He kept repeating this, until I realized he was actually saying *You're mine*.

## 32.

AFTERWARDS, I PULLED MY WORK PANTS back up, pausing to straighten even the cuffs, because attention to detail seemed important. Lev came over and buttoned my shirt for me, caressing my breast through a gap in the fabric before pulling back to inspect his work. I wanted to ask: And the others? All those girls? Have they been here with you, have you undressed and then dressed them after the act, taking so much innocence as if it was your due? But jealousy seemed cheeky. After all, the writing on those pieces of paper almost certainly belonged to his wife.

"What are you thinking?" he asked, a critical look on his face. Already he knew me too well.

"Nothing."

"Well that's not true."

"Isn't it?"

"No." He didn't seem disappointed by the lie, though. "Listen. I have to get home now—it's past six o'clock. But I want you to meet me tomorrow at my house." He tore an edge off one of the pages, making sure to leave the typescript intact but taking away a bit of notation; nothing legible. *In the case of* and then below that *visi–* and below that *–ly askew*. Lev wrote down his home address, which I tucked into my pocket. A part of me wanted to secure it in my bra, next to the skin, but one can only do so much to change their essential nature in a single day.

"Alright," I said.

"Three thirty." He buttoned his shirt cuffs. "Don't make me wait. I'll be miserable every moment till then." In a second, he was gone.

The next day I would walk into his house and be met by the portraits of Vera on the wall. I would know then; alone in the hallway outside Lev's office, I did not. But still something drew me to the scribbles on

Lev's note—not just his, but the mysterious others. *Askew, askew.* I traced the word with the tip of my thumb.

A few girls came into the hall and brushed by me, slipping something into a nearby mail slot. Then they turned to face me—but interested, for once. Bristled, but not overly aggressive. I was a different kind of creature there, stinking of my own body, flushed to the teeth. And we faced each other as animals in the dark, neither predator nor prey.

Some sort of kin. Wicked, sated beasts.

# An Oral History of Vera Orlov, née Volkov

*Recorded by the Maple Hill Police Department*

### WILL ELLIOTT, ASSOCIATE PROFESSOR OF ENGLISH, DONNE SCHOOL

"Yes, his wife's another funny wicket. Not a problem, exactly, just not quite what any of us expected. When Orlov got hired, Sophie and I hoped the two of them would make a bridge pair, or keep us company at faculty dinners, at least—you see, Sophie's always looking for another lady to conspire with. We'd heard the wife was an émigrée, like her husband, and that she helped with his work—gossip had it she did *every-thing*, actually, from grading term papers to licking stamps, but we didn't believe that. Sophie's a heavy lifter too, and she's been snubbed for it. Not everyone can hold their own in sophisticated situations.

"Anyway, we thought, how can she resist Soph? She's really well read, my wife is, see. Trollope, Brecht, Pound. Even a little Cervantes in the orig-inal! Took Spanish in boarding school, and of course we've traveled to Madrid. We figured they'd be thick as thieves. But Mrs. Orlov—I never have gotten comfortable calling her by her first name; she always twitches when you do it—she doesn't exactly *engage*. First time we met them for cocktails at George's house, Sophie mentioned that Mrs. Orlov might want to join her book club. I think they were reading Willa Cather or

Pearl Buck, one of those bestseller types, and Sophie was all in a tizzy about it. Mrs. Orlov stood there for a while and listened to her describe the club—which is, admittedly, a bit more pugnacious than suits my own tastes—twirling the cocktail onion in her martini around and around and around. And then, when Sophie finished and said, 'So, can we expect you on Friday?' Mrs. Orlov just said, 'No,' and she left. Not left the conversation, left the *party*. Set her martini down on the table without taking a drink and walked out the door. George told us later that she'd taken ill, but there wasn't any indication of it that I saw. He's a real diplomat, George is. Oh well. A pity for Soph.

"I've taken an interest in watching Mrs. Orlov since then, when we run across one another in social situations. And it's always the same. Absolutely *magnetic* when she wants to be, and not just because she's a beauty. I've seen entire rooms turn to listen to what she has to say, especially if it's in support of her husband. Can't fault her there, certainly. Holds his arm, steers him around the room, aims him like a gun, you know! Just has no interest in chatting. More of a looker out of windows. Likes to read the labels on wine bottles. And with a husband like Orlov, she can afford to be that way. No one on the faculty was going to touch him, after that book of his made such a splash."

GEORGE ROUND, DONNE SCHOOL PROVOST

"A lovely woman, and unique. Sharp as a tack. Cold as a Frigidaire. Every ounce admirable. Are we done here?"

BRIDEY LEE MAY, WAITRESS, THE MAPLE HILL CAFÉ DE PRINTEMPS

"Oh, that lady? Yeah, she comes in sometimes in the afternoons. Not sure why you'd go all the way to a restaurant just for coffee and a cookie, but whatever, she leaves tips. Picky, sure, but I can handle picky. What else do you want to know? She always wears, uh, I don't know, nice clothes, with these little details you can't help but notice, like a piece of ivy embroidered on the seam of her jacket, or her buttons are shaped like dried flowers. Things like that. She has a kind of mean expression a lot of the time, but really, compared to some of the jerks who come in here she's sunshine and roses. I think she scares a lot of the older men at the counter, which suits me fine. I always liked her. [*Notes indicate that Bridey shrugs and goes back to wiping down tables, but then calls the officers back over.*] Hey, I just remembered something. This one time? That lady came in for coffee like normal, only this time she brought in a stack of mail, you know? Letters and things. And at first I thought, ok, she's just stopped at the post office and now she's getting ready to pay bills or write back to whoever. But she takes some of the letters and starts blacking out half the words. That's weird, right? So I got a little closer, because I was curious, and it looked like all the letters she was blacking out had two people writing them—like, vacation postcards, you know? Where you write hi and your mom writes hi and your brother writes hi? Like that. And she was crossing out everything that one of them wrote. I came over with a coffee pot to offer a warm-up and asked her what she was doing. And she said, 'Privacy,' which, come to think of it, doesn't really answer my question. But anyway.

"When she was done she folded most of the letters back up, and then she asked for a match, and she burned two of them into an ashtray. Not the blacked-out ones, a different set, I think. I must've looked surprised, because she made sure to tell me they were her own letters that she'd written to her husband, as if that made it alright. I said I don't care *what* they are, you still can't do that here, and she just looked at me and smiled. And then left a real whopper of a tip, so I didn't complain."

# *Zoya*

## 33.

TIME IS A FUNNY THING, DEAR READER. For instance, you have been tracking great swaths of it on my behalf. Decades gone, in a flash. Little me, in my crib or cradle clutching a bunny, then suddenly sprouting long limbs and leaping over oceans and mountains and calendar years. Not a layman's task, as such, going forward and back, forward and back. Stopping stock-still on occasion to think through a remark or linger on the lover (Lev)'s face. The second time I met him, he took a piece of my hair and twirled it round his finger, so tight it hurt my scalp. I sometimes stay in that moment for days at a time. The intake of breath, how I moved slightly away to pull the strands even tighter.

Not much (true) time has passed since I began writing, though. (And even less, I suppose, has elapsed for you. You can sink my days of work into a half hour's leisure reading, the years of my life, thus, double-sunk.) I'm still in this cabin, alone, with far too many hours each day to think about what's happened, memories escaping along with the whorls of milk in every cup of tea. I got a splinter from one of the cabinets near the stove while rummaging around and looking for an adequate biscuit, and it took ages to pick it out with a needle, but when it was done I wished I had another, just to occupy my mind. The emptiness here is really starting to irk me, you see. I thought I'd made friends with a cat who came skulking for supper two days in a row, but it's been three now with no scant tabby. Loyalties are not so easily bought here. Perhaps if I had cream.

Perhaps if I could cleanse myself of the whole past, and start anew. Walk outside and find a river to dunk myself in. Kerplunk and done. Water so cold it boils over the rocks. Fish reaching out with teeth translucent to pick off my skin and leave white bones. There's something hideously erotic about the skeleton, is what I've come to think. How it lacks gender, identity, individual distinction. The dead bones of a beloved are not the beloved. I'm starting to lose my grip.

Let me just rewind, rewind. Let nothing barrel towards its inevitable conclusion. Let me pretend that nothing has ever happened, nothing but Lev's fingers on my scalp. Reader, do you have that power? Unlikely, impossible. But I do sometimes wish.

## 34.

THE FIRST TIME I STEPPED INTO LEV's home I was so busy fiddling with my clothes that I almost missed the momentousness of the occasion. Stupid, I know, but I just wanted for once to look trim and neat, and my shirt kept riding up at the waistline, tempted by the heavy static in my fall skirt. Now I know better than to think he'd care, or to think the clothes would last long on my body, but I was hoping to make a good impression. He always seemed so cool, compared to me. Lev was already there when I arrived—at three thirty, an in-between kind of hour—and when I got up the nerve to knock he opened the door with the casual air of a man who's done something a thousand times. Relaxed, almost businesslike. I stumbled when the heel of my shoe caught the doorstop, but he graciously failed to notice.

"Yes, come in, my dear." He hurried me across the threshold and into the living room, where I was happy to feel his hand slide a bit lower down my back than was strictly polite. Then it went lower still and I—I'm embarrassed to say I giggled. I was still getting used to the idea that pleasure could, and would, repeat, that there might be a rhythm to it that I could step into and stay inside, rocking back and forth, back and forth, into eternity. The sound of my laugh was like a hiccup. "You need a drink," Lev said, with a smile, and I was grateful.

While he was in the kitchen fixing us cocktails, I walked around the room admiring the furniture, the art, the geometry of the décor. It's funny now to think how much I read Lev into every flourish, from the arrangement of the books to the color of the rugs. He probably didn't choose a single thing. Any echo of him had been placed there by another hand, and some part of me must've known it, because I carefully avoided looking at any photographs. I wasn't yet ready to gaze into his wife's face, and superstitiously enough, I didn't want her gazing into mine.

(Did I really think she could? I always wonder what Vera knows, and how. Does she make plans and carry them out, like anyone, or does she actually see the future? Are she and Lev lovers, worldly man and worldly wife, or are they actually stitched together at the base of the soul, as each of them would have me believe? Though Lev, of course, says the same thing about me. His lovemaking bears troublingly telltale marks no matter who it's aimed to please, and I wonder if this is as true of his body as it is of his mind, his heart, his affectionate phrases. If his fingers find the same clever crevices, if my gasps sound like hers, or like another's. Like every other's. I sometimes wish I could test this question out on another body, re-creating his passage up and down my spine, between my thighs, to see if I can get the same results.)

Lev came back in with two small glasses in his hands, which we sipped from and then promptly abandoned in our hurry to get upstairs, where the time—evaporated.

Afterwards, we sat in our underwear and talked for an hour or more. I felt the intimacy of that: not touching, just looking. Calm and exposed. Like I was a baby and my mother had just been bathing me, was now patting me down with a towel. The light came through the window in flashes when the trees bent in the wind, and it reminded me of a time in Lipetsk when the birds had been doing wonderful things above the fields, their sense of gravity bothered by the rising thermals and their bodies casting small snatches of shadow along the ground. I must've been six or seven then, but I could call it to mind clear as day, and I told Lev about it, a memory I'd never shared with another soul. How the birds swooped and rose, never stuttering in their path. How even when you ran at them—as

I, a child, often did—they frightened with choreography, streaming up in two directions like a disintegrating vee.

"I'd have liked to see that," he said. "If only I'd ever in my life been allowed to choose where and when to go anywhere."

I laughed, and was surprised when he didn't laugh with me. "Really?" I asked. I couldn't imagine him feeling deprived. But he was serious, and I found myself in the strange position of having to explain that my life had not been easy either, that I had suffered. *Look at that girl with her smart little jacket,* my mother had said, pointing to the landlord's daughter in Lipetsk. *Someday, if you follow her example, people will think you're just as elegant and fine.* Was this what she meant?

"Listen," I protested, "it wasn't some field trip. It was—we had no choice." But Lev said it all still sounded pretty. He always saw a charming, Tolstoyan simplicity in the peasant world, an innocent bliss which the Soviets had cruelly destroyed. My father would've lost his mind to hear his struggles co-opted this way by a member of the aristocracy. But I didn't try very hard to dissuade him. You see, I benefited from Lev's illusion: if the peasant world was charming, that made me charming, too. And what did it mean to me, anymore, the truth of that life? It was gone.

"You know," he said a little while later, after we had gotten up and fumbled some more around the room. "I thought that when we arrived in New York, everything would be different for me. It was such a naïve idea, I'm almost embarrassed to admit it."

"What do you mean?" I asked. And he shrugged. Lifting a casual, bare shoulder and then using it to scratch his ear.

"There was this party," he started, pausing once more, maddeningly, to light a fresh cigarette. And then told me all about it, how he and his wife had been invited to a benefit for some publishing giant, and she hadn't wanted to go because the man had ties to a house that brought out Marxist literature sometimes—general-interest stuff, he assured me, purely educational. They had declined the invitation, but it bothered Lev. Losing the opportunity to mingle, missing out on connections with the members of the literary press who would undoubtedly be present. He thought he'd forget about it, as he usually forgot about their disagreements—"She's always right, you see," he said, with no small amount of irony in his voice—but the night of the party it was still on his mind, and he decided to slip out without her. What she didn't know about, he reasoned, couldn't hurt her.

So he told his wife he'd be meeting a friend for drinks, and dressed himself in a suit that was as close as he could get to black tie without raising suspicion, and then walked a few blocks before hailing a taxi to the hotel where the event was being held. He was, he told me, proud of himself for taking a stand, however secret. Had a glass of champagne at the hotel bar before taking the elevator up, to celebrate his good mood. "I must've turned my back for a few minutes," he said. "Just a few, you know. Maybe I talked to the bartender for a little while, lost track of time." When he'd paid for his drink he went upstairs and threw his coat at the first man he saw who appeared to be a butler. The host of the party walked over immediately, and said he was delighted they'd changed their minds. Lev laughed as he replayed the conversation: "'Hmm?' I asked the man, and he told me, 'Well, your wife is right over there, she said you'd be up in a minute from the bar.' And there she was, in the corner, making some old country-club type lean in too close to hear what she was saying. She caught my eye and that was that—she knew me better than I knew myself. There was no escaping."

I expected him to frown or something at the end of the story, but he looked, if anything, impressed.


## 35.

AT SOME POINT I WENT DOWNSTAIRS to fetch our drinks from the coffee table where we'd abandoned them, padding through the empty rooms in bare feet. This time, I walked right up to the photographs on the wall, curious to see who this woman was that had so disarmed Lev for so many years, who could find him at a party in the biggest city in the world, sensing him as if by radar across the boroughs. I think back to this moment, now, with a rising anticipation. Was my heart in my throat? Was my skin abuzz? Did I know that something was about to change? And, well. I most certainly did not.

## 36.

I REMEMBER, ALSO, THAT MORNING IN the library with Caroline, Cindy, and Adeline years before. How convinced I was that they were afraid of me in a supernatural sense, that they really looked at me and perceived something spectral, malign. Smoke rising off me, maybe. I have to stop myself, often enough, from thinking of Vera in that same way. When I spotted her picture on Lev's wall, I was certain that she could see me, her portraits sending messages back to the source. Wedding dress white as cream. Helmet of hair shining beneath her stark wedding veil, eyes glittering with private wisdom. Not evil, necessarily, just powerful as a boogeyman. Vera, Vera, on the wall. It didn't occur to me that she found him at that New York party simply because she read his mood, or that they had friends in common whom she might have called for information. Even now it's hard for me to believe she'd need to bother with something so mundane as that.

Did she feel my presence that afternoon when I walked into her house? When I strolled through the rooms in a man's shirt, her man's, with the cuffs rolled up. My hair loose around my shoulders. I wonder if she got, at least, some sense of the surprised recognition that made me reach out to touch the picture's lips and see if it was really there. Perhaps she heard the disbelief in my voice as I whispered her name—her original name, her father's name, not the one she took from her husband. "*Volkova*," I said under my breath, remembering the girl who walked out of our scout group and never came back. After so many years, here she was again at last, that strange creature lost in the wilderness of time. My opposite in every sense: dark where I was light. Wild where I was tame. At least, where I had been tame.

*Volkova.* The wolf.

## 37.

FALL HARDENED INTO WINTER, AND Lev went out of town on occasion, sometimes with Vera, sometimes not. When they were together, my mind was a flurry of imagined scenarios: her leaning over to sniff his jacket and smelling me, the echo of our past encounters. Lev kissing Vera's ear, so that she sighed into him, her hair falling across one eye. Vera convincing him to leave the city, the state, the country—which was of course ridiculous, since she was the reason they'd come to Maple Hill at all, her insistence that Lev needed stability and quiet after a lifetime of wandering and war. I wore my old green coat, which I still took religiously to the dry cleaners at the start of each season and scoured with a lint brush every night when I got home. It remained bright and lovely, if a bit young for me now, and several years less fashionable than it had been. I cooked for myself, and once or twice for Lev as well. *Steak au poivre*, green salads with lemon in the dressing, pasta with fresh greenhouse tomatoes and so much garlic it made me embarrassed of my breath. The day after I made that dish I woke up sweating garlic in my bed, the entire room stinking with it. My tongue furred, my hair emanating a flavor aura.

That year the snows were heavy and slumberous as Christmas came over Maple Hill, then passed. I never much cared for the holiday, myself: my sites of worship were more private. Bundled up inside my house, or in the greenhouse surrounded by the fumes of greenery, I reread *Felice* to fill the hours when Lev was not available—I wanted to be with him every minute, and this way I could. It struck me as odd, and somehow enchanting, that the same man who could write such extraordinary violence against a girl, and in such careful detail, could also grant her redemption and revenge. Justice, let's call it. It made his hands look dangerous and fair to me, which was a combination I enjoyed. The women in Lev's books tended to live traumatic lives, but he was always trying to save them.

I've never been able to forget this passage, for instance, about Felice and her husband, Peter, who drove her both to her death and her rebirth:

*This was their love: his hands on her face, smudging it into some semblance of a smile. Fingers pushing between her teeth, scraping the roof of her mouth and pressing her tongue back until she gagged on it. He shook her until her head came undone, brain rattling around like eggs in a basket. Cracking, leaking all over itself. She remembered one day in particular, crawling across the floor while Peter stomped on the hem of her dress. "You're so pretty when I look at you from above," he told her. That night he took her out to dinner, after brushing her hair and helping her apply lipstick. And she did look pretty, just as he said. Pink in the cheeks, with her hair arranged just so. He tied her belt for her, fitted tight around her waist, and kissed her so hard it brought tears to her eyes.*

*She had tried to leave him before, and when she came home, he was the one who always cried.*

I thought: *yes, he would cry.* Not because he was sorry, but because each return would prove that Felice hadn't understood him yet, that he hadn't gone far enough. For Lev, I thought, the pain of her returns must have been equally acute. Making a monster being, after all, not so different from becoming one. Perhaps he embraced his monstrousness just so Felice could be a hero. Maybe all those Donne girls froze their fingers so I could be proud of protecting the greenhouse glass from balls of ice.

When I had fifteen minutes to spare, I'd go find Lev, or he would find me. We were careful not to be spotted together anymore, but the logistics of that care sometimes meant dropping everything and running as fast as I could through the snow. I ruined more than one pair of shoes that way, and my fingers kept getting cold, losing feeling at the very tips, beneath the nails. Once, late morning, I came back to the greenhouse and found several flower bushes depleted of their blooms; for the next few days, girls all over campus wore corsages pinned to their shirts, smirking when they caught my eye. I'd thought I was safe because we were nearing midterm exams, but I miscalculated, or one of them just got bored and saw her chance. After that I always locked the door when I left, even to use the restroom. John got stuck outside a few times this way, since he always forgot to carry his keys.

"What's with the extra security?" he asked me, when I returned to find him shivering there, hands stuck under his arms for warmth. It was February then.

"I'm just taking precautions," I said. "Protecting our work."

"Well, that's fine, honey." John breathed into his palms as I turned the key and let us inside, heat hitting our cheeks all muggy and strong, like the warm sigh of a horse. "Just try not to outsmart yourself, ok?"

And I did try. I did.

## 38.

IT TOOK ME MONTHS TO ADMIT TO Lev what I knew about his wife. Namely, her maiden name, her patronymic, the way she wore her hair as a girl. I didn't want to risk losing his attention by bringing anyone else inside our stolen moments together, when I could keep his focus secure. Mouth to thigh, wrist bound to bed. Then I was just afraid he wouldn't believe me, as indeed Vera later didn't—"You're mistaken," she said. "I was never a Pioneer." And when I insisted she got stern and asked, "Do I really look like a cultist?"

But with Lev, there was no need for concern. It was spring by the time I got up the nerve, and we were both somewhat giddy with the turn in the weather. He laughed at my description of her twisted mouth and scout uniform, the way she dropped the yarn and fled. We were sprawled in my bedroom, limbs akimbo, with afternoon sun filtering in through the curtains. He reached across the mattress and pulled me on top of him. Murmured sweetly into my neck.

"Of course," he said. "I always sensed a connection between you."

You may be surprised to learn I took this as a compliment. Most women—or let me be clearer: most mistresses—want to distinguish them-selves from their lover's wives. Dye their hair the opposite hue, go vamp where she's virtue or vice versa. Say the things she never says, agree to whatever she's withholding. But I knew better than to play that game with Lev. For one thing, he adored me for just who I was, and said so. When he slipped into the greenhouse and walked up behind me, pressing himself onto the small of my back, he would say, "Hello, working girl." He took me on dates out of town, driving a recently acquired Mercedes-Benz with enough aplomb to make up for his lack of expertise, and took special pleasure in buying me things I couldn't otherwise afford. We had many fine wines under these auspices. Cassoulet and filet mignon. And there was something more—his genuine shiver of pleasure when he touched my skin. Which I felt too. The kind of awe you can't fake, or fully articulate. Our only fit vocabulary being touch, taste, smell.

But he didn't hate Vera. God no, he loved her. Couldn't get enough, and was terrified of her. Quick wit, pale skin, infinity as expressed through human flesh. There was some electric current that went between them, replenishing itself only when it was passed back and forth. The sex was good. He spoke of his work and I could tell he was picturing her face, the tics that let him know what was affecting and what was weak. Tics he had internalized, so he had an inner Vera, driving him by the sticky shift. When I climbed on top of him and rolled my hips, he was there, and he was gone. He was with her, too. A parallelism I know pained him, more and more as time went on. But, at least in the beginning, I was more flattered than distressed to be the grand exception to their perfect union.

"What do you mean," I asked, "by a connection?"

He turned away, moving me gently off of him and then lying on his back, rubbing his eyes with the heels of his hands. Lev, who fate had brought to me. "How else could I possibly love you both?" he asked.

"The human heart—?" It was a weak suggestion, but still. Surely he knew he wasn't the first man to find a second bed, a second comforting womanly form. Though I winced to think of myself that way. Always wondering: *what about those girls?* Leo Orlov chasing fawns across the grass.

"Don't be ridiculous. It's not a matter of being fickle. Maybe when I was young." He sighed, and I knew: he had been fickle then. A spritz of envious fireworks went up in my head and in that moment I stopped being able to contain my curiosity. Not ten minutes earlier, he'd bitten my inner thighs so hard there were marks.

"But what about your students?"

"My—?" He laughed. "Well, I suppose I love them in a certain way."

"Which way." I reached over and grabbed him. Caressing with just enough force to make him open his mouth but not enough to elicit a gasp. "Tell me. Be honest."

"Oh—my dear. I always am."

"Are you?"

"You draw the truth out of me like a venom. The girls. What are you asking me?"

I kept moving my hand, and I said, "You know." His face flexed painfully, and I wanted to kiss him hard and shut him up. Keep him mine. But I wanted him to answer my question even more.

"Oh no. No. They—I never. Never touched them."

"That's not what they say."

He licked his lips. "Children."

"Yes."

"They lie."

I stopped. My eyes filled up with tears. The same eyes with which I'd seen him running after Daphne, stalking her amidst the laurels.

"It doesn't look like a lie."

Lev sat up and regarded me. His face touchingly flushed. He didn't reach out for my shoulder, didn't take my hand and nibble my fingers, as he often did for a distraction. In fact he looked as serious as I'd ever seen him, no less so for his obvious arousal, his body alert for action.

"You noticed. Of course. You were supposed to—or anyway, people were." I turned away to wipe a tear, and now he did touch me, taking my chin in his hand and swiveling me back to face him. "I thought maybe in time you'd guess it."

"Well, I haven't."

"Try."

"You love me." He nodded his encouragement. "But it started before we even met." Another nod, raised brow. I crumpled. "I don't know."

"Think, darling. You know how Vera is—a part of my professional life."
Now it was my turn to nod. "You know, then, that she is in charge of every
move. I don't mean to say I didn't let it happen," he gestured to nothing,
an irritated flick of the wrist. The memory of a party, or two or three, that
he tried to escape to, only to find her already there. His manuscripts, all
covered with her writing. A blessing first, and then more of a trap. "But
now it seems unstoppable. When we came here—well, I didn't want to be
here at all. No, don't protest, of course that's all different now. But I mean,
she has always been able to change things for me." A haunted look. "Out
from under me, even. And I started to wonder, once we settled in, what it
would be like if she couldn't anymore."

## 39.

HE TOLD ME ABOUT HIS PLAN, WHICH had been cooking underneath his
hood for who knows how long. Less a plan than a feeling. If lowly, loving
Lev gave in to his baser impulses, who could blame his wife for being
upset? He might let it slip over drinks with a fellow prof, or over scotch
with George Round: things not exactly rosy at the homestead. And yes,
he'd say with a little *mea culpa* wink, perhaps he had been seeking
succor, though a gentleman would never tell.

They wouldn't ask. The provost? He wouldn't want, exactly, to know if
his new star faculty member was dipping into the company ink. They
would just assume, and over time it would become the face Lev wore in
public. Rapscallion. Dashing bastard. Brilliant enough that no one would
protest, least of all the conquered coquettes, picking up a bit of color before
going co-ed. No need to actually touch a single hand when the story was
so likely, and had so much of its own steam.

Over time things would heat up—he'd mention lipstick on a collar, you
know, theoretically, and how wives—plural, imprecise, unnamed—might
not like it. Might throw a fit, or even a lamp, straight for the head. Though
a well-timed duck meant the object smashed against a wall instead. And
at home he'd elbow one over, so if any breezy questions were put to Vera

she'd be forced to corroborate, in a manner that made her look complicit in the lie. "Oh yes, he's terribly clumsy, isn't he? I can't let him near any of our finer china." Meanwhile she would still be signing off on every move, shifting the chess pieces in whatever order she pleased, and he'd make sure she sent every letter, attended every important meeting, made most of the phone calls. Her grip visible on every part of his life except one.

He was a writer. He could come up with the right set of circumstances to forestall any serious suspicion. A woman pushed over the edge, maybe to a sanatorium, maybe something more, when she found out her control was less than total. She would do the work for him, anyway. He just needed to set the stage.

"You really want her gone?" I asked. I'll admit I was surprised.

"I want to be free of her," he told me. "I thought it would just be for a while."

But now, he said, there was me to consider, and I'd changed everything. (A thrill I can still feel, remembering how he said it. Everything?) I'd reminded him that his work was his own, as I'd reminded him that his body was. A stint away, having her mental health called into permanent question, no longer seemed enough. We were too alike, she and I, he said. We were the same soul, a twin soul, in two different women— because of course how else could he fall for us both, how else could he need us both so completely, when his heart was so terribly true?—and the laws of nature would not let us abide for too long side by side.

"We have to get rid of her once and for all," he said. For his books, for my safety, for our happiness. So all of them could flourish unchecked. I would help him push her to it, he said. Learn her habits. Find a time.

And like a fool, I let him convince me.

# *Lev*

5 July 1931
Airmail via Berlin

MY GOD, VERA. A SHORT NOTE TO LET you know I've survived. Recuperating in Berlin, under false name, natch. Will be home within the week. Alert the school to resume my courses in the fall. Prepare yourself to hear the story of my failure.

As a side note, I hope you've had a lovely time on the coast. I was glad to know you decided to take the trip, after all. Your letter reached me just before Vlad and I were set to depart, and it cheered me infinitely to learn you'd be traveling with Zoya and taking the waters side by side. She strikes me as a virtuous girl. Entirely your cup of tea.

## Zoya

40.

THAT FIRST NIGHT, AFTER HE TOLD ME about his plan for Vera, I cried into Lev's lap. Face scratching against the thick hair on his legs, tears soaking the skin and then, later, staining his pant leg while he petted my head and told me it would be alright.

I asked: "But don't you love her?" and he said, "Of course." And that was all. Terse. Determined. He had lived for too many years under her ingenious thumb, and had finally decided to break free. He looked like a man making a terrible choice, which I suppose he was, and it made me wonder what my face revealed to him. Did I look like a weapon? A *femme fatale* with a knife held casually between her fingers? I told him I didn't have it in me to kill someone, and he said, "No, darling, we need her to more or less do it herself anyway." Which I had to admit, with Vera, seemed like the only plausible way. I imagined her stopping a bullet with her hand, just lifting a palm and batting it to the ground. Smelling poison in a glass, or wrestling her way free from a strangling. She was, Lev told me, surprisingly fit. That's why I was only to watch her for now, and figure out the right time to act.

He didn't let me dress when he did. Said he was going to tuck me in bed like a good little girl, so I could sleep away my sorrow and wake up the next morning to examine our options with a critical eye. He kissed me, all across my face and down my neck, paying special attention to the flat expanse where my breastbone gave way to my breasts. We had been

meeting for months, and he knew what I liked. How I loved him. Most of
all when he broke my skin with his teeth, or pinched my thighs so hard
they bruised. When he marked me, changed me, made me his. That night
he slipped out the door and whispered, "Sweet dreams." And I lay in bed,
blanket up to my chin, shining with the tender lesions he left all up and
down my arms and legs. The darkest spot a bruise on my heart, a thought
in my head I could not escape.

I loved Lev, but still, my first instinct was to shield Vera. Perhaps out of
fidelity to our shared past, the things we had both survived so far. I imagined her shivering alone at home, maybe lighting a cigarette on the
front porch with a shawl wrapped around her shoulders, waiting for her
husband to come up the walk. Our town in spring was a haven for bats,
who came screeching through the sky to decimate the insect population.
We all found them rather heroic, but the total saturation was unnerving,
as was the way they'd swoop and turn, bending their arcs of flight errati-
cally in the darkness. In my mind's eye, one came close to the imagined
Vera and she gave a cry, dropping her still-lit cigarette on the wood slats
and stamping it out madly before running inside. I wanted to knock the
bat away and comfort her. Run the back of my hand gently across her
cheek until she'd cried herself to sleep.

But that was a peasant's response: protect the ruling class, protect the
status quo. Well, and I was a perfect peasant. During my last years in
Moscow suspicion was general throughout the city—everyone informing
on everyone else, everyone condemning the informants behind closed
doors. I used to have tea with our next-door neighbor Albina, a pleasantly
stout *babushka* who had the unfortunate habit of smacking her gums—
the result of bad teeth, which predated state medical care. I'd been visiting
her for several months when she pulled out a scrapbook one afternoon
and began paging through it with me. Not family photographs or pieces
of baby hair cut from her children's balmy heads, but a bunch of newspaper clippings. They were, I realized, from underground papers, of the
sort people passed from hand to hand in dark alleys or printed on T-shirts
so they could be couriered without suspicion. But these didn't contain any
vital information from a resistance party, they were just—jokes. Bad

jokes, mostly, at the state's expense. "Where has Comrade Stalin's mustache been lately?" and "Who disappears faster: a man whose wife has found him cheating or a loyal Party member?" Half of them didn't even make sense, but there was a hysterical earnestness that made it hard to look away. Albina must've thought I'd find them funny. Instead they chilled me to the bone.

I'd like to say I didn't tell on her, but it was a dark time. At that point all I knew was that the Party was in charge, and that I was meant to respect authority the way I loved my own father and mother. More than, actually, since by then my father was gone, taken away for the protection of our household values. With a young person's paranoia, I became convinced that the NKVD would somehow know what I'd seen at Albina's, and track me by the counter-revolutionary phrases burned into my retinas. True, I didn't denounce her to the police—I was a child, not a monster. But I did let slip to another neighbor who shared our court-yard that Albina had something she should not. There were rewards for denunciation, and we were all so hungry. Within a week Albina was gone, and I never saw her again.

I wanted to believe I'd grown since then, but was that true? Once again I found myself choosing between happiness and good, as my father had insisted I must, and choosing wrong. Vera had always had everything— me, nothing. I knew this. But it was one thing to borrow, and another to steal. One thing to run my fingers over her throat, and another to pinch them closed and squeeze. I would have preferred to absorb her instead, drinking her essence up through a straw. But I didn't have that option. I had Lev, and he had his opinions.

## 41.

AND SO I BECAME A SPY. EVERY MORNING I set my alarm for a half hour earlier than I was used to, and instead of turning left at the end of my street I turned right. My new path to the Donne School campus was round-about, but it took me past Lev and Vera's house in a neighborhood two ticks more upscale than my own. Their street was beautifully leafy, green in the summer, then golden, then bare; now it was springtime, and the ground was pocked with the pale, bent figures of emerging crocuses. There was a particular mother who, in that period, sometimes walked the street with her infant girl at six A.M., hushing the child on her shoulder or else pointing out bluebirds in the trees; it reminded me of the walks I used to take through Maple Hill during my first winter, when everything was limned with ice. An innocence, I suppose, shared between both.

Over time, I got good at pretending to be casual, checking my lipstick in a pocket mirror or stooping down to tie my shoe. Buying myself a minute or two to dawdle without calling attention to myself. I watched Vera carry a coffee cup—or was it tea?—through a doorway (I presumed from the kitchen) and up to the bay window in the front of the house. She rarely lingered long, but I enjoyed seeing how her hair changed from day to day. Loose waves, low chignon; visible static or perfectly smooth. In the mornings she always wore a kimono-style dressing gown of purple and white, which made her look a bit like a magician.

After she disappeared from my view I'd walk on and arrive at the greenhouse by six forty-five, unlocking it with my black metal key and breathing deep the sweet wet mix of mineral and vegetable, oxygen pulsing from the space's veins. Sometimes I'd stop and gag for a moment, trying to force out the sickness that settled, more and more often, in the pit of my stomach. Work was the only place I could feel normal.

And work I did. I checked for insect infestations with a level of attention normally reserved (or so I assume) for technicians monitoring dials at the making of a bomb. I coddled my favorites. The small saguaro cactus I'd acquired at the beginning of my tenure had gone gangrenous— it was too hard to keep it dry, especially since I'd made the mistake of potting it first with a mixture of peat soil, which "absolutely invited mites" as John so helpfully put it. The bottom shriveled up like a raisin, and the top looked pale all the time, with weak spots. But instead of giving up I checked on it every day, repotting it with a great deal of sand and moving it around the greenhouse to make sure it never got sunburned or spent too long languishing in the shade. I helped Donne girls sprout pea pods, and grew a new variety of tomato for the cafeteria on Hilda's request: a fussy plant we started from seeds her mother sent over from their home garden in Nebraska. John and I added goldfish to the lily pond, and occasionally they splashed startlingly in the quiet.

What I wanted to know was whatever marinated in Vera's core. The small and secret preferences. Did she like tea biscuits brought over from England? Did she sneeze when she cracked too much pepper on her food? When she saw the color yellow, did she hear bells, and when she hummed to herself were the notes blue and green and melancholic? Was there pity in her marrow? I often returned to the house at lunchtime and saw her sweeping away on foot to who knows where; Lev always took the car, although he readily admitted that she was the better driver, and wherever she went she had no interest in taxis or buses or limousines. Her purses always matched her shoes, and both were sensible but stylish: a low heel that still somehow managed to make her legs look longer, her ankles slim. She had perfected that purposeful stride which generates gyrational speed from a sexual wobble at the hips. In May she stepped on a robin's eggshell, crushing it beneath her toe. I don't know why I thought any of this would help me.

I tried to follow her once when she left the house, but without turning around or even—to my knowledge—realizing I was there, she took evasive maneuvers involving a flower garden and a row of parked mail trucks, each identical. She always did have a habit of disappearing at the trickier moments. Nonetheless, there is no level, I found, of cruelty or savvy in a victim that makes you feel better about contemplating her murder. Not better, no, but perhaps more accustomed. I wondered if maybe she was unhappy in her marriage, if anyone had ever felt sorry for her, in all her life. I wondered if she was doing wicked things to Lev's manuscripts, remembering that word she'd scrawled: *askew.* The longer I spent around Vera and my plants, the more the tenor and tone of the projects bled into one another. If Lev was right, and she and I were like two roses from one bush, then we were just dead-heading old flowers to allow for new growth. In this case: her head, my growth. A fairly painless and ordinary process for most gardeners that grew more and more difficult for me, until I found myself sobbing down the front of my shirt, staring at the pruning shears in my hand like an absolute imbecile.

## 42.

POINT OF INTEREST: WHEN YOU PRUNE a plant, a certain number of them actually bleed. Take the rubber plant, or ficus, common to office desks and dusty shelves. If you cut a bit away with a knife—making sure to cut towards your thumb, to maintain control and avoid slicing open your hand; there are tendons in there that can roll back all the way to the elbow—a thick white syrup will pour out down the stem. Eventually the wound will callus and the plant will heal, not only growing in a more attractive or convenient direction but often sprouting two to four new stems, getting bushier and bushier for all you cut away. Which sounds, from a certain angle, like a threat: it hemorrhages as you plunge in the knife, but after that gets stronger and fitter, shedding limbs like so many shirts and stockings, lingerie dangled off the end of a finger before dropping, drifting to the ground.

# An Oral History of Vera Orlov, née Volkov, cont'd

*Recorded by the Maple Hill Police Department*

ROBERT HORNE, PUBLISHER OF HORNE BOOKS

"Yes, it's absolutely uncommon for one of my authors to have a wife so involved in the process. Most of them keep their family life well out of it—distracts from the artistic method, you see. Not easy to dip into the well of inspiration when there's a toddler running around your feet, or a woman asking for pocket money so she can pick up milk at the corner store. But Vera's not that type of woman.

"Yes, of course I call her Vera. We're on excellent terms. She was the one who initially contacted me and said they were interested in bringing Lev's books to American audiences. Of course I was excited as soon as I saw the first translated manuscript for *Knife, Knave*. His French editor's a friend of mine, so I'd been hearing good things, but you see, gossip is no substitute for the feeling of holding a bit of genius in your hands, and responding to it in your own individual way. That's something people don't understand about the editorial process, I think: how much of it's intuitive, almost mystical. Sometimes you can tell, intellectually, that you're reading a great piece of writing, and still not want to come near it with a ten-foot pole.

"Anyway, no, I haven't spoken to her in several months. Lev had a big plan that he'd sworn me to secrecy on—exciting, but really hush-hush, you know writers. They always think someone's going to steal their ideas. It's not uncommon for the pair of them to go dark when he's working on something. When she has something to say, she'll say it. And of course, I'll let you know, if that would be helpful."

[*Notes indicate Mr. Horne was polite overall, but spoke in a rather tart manner and hurried the officers out after making his statement, claiming business obligations. Officers were then stopped by an associate of Mr. Horne's down the hall, one James Tipton.*]

JAMES TIPTON, PUBLICIST, HORNE BOOKS

"I'm not supposed to say this, but I really despise her. Nothing is ever good enough for that woman. And my god, can she not take a compliment."

OCTOBER REDFORD, EDITOR, *STORIES OF ASTOUNDING WONDER* MAGAZINE

"She tried to up-sell me on the price for a story in my own magazine. [*chuckles*] Called me up and said, 'I know you pay twenty-five dollars for an ordinary piece of fiction, but wouldn't you pay more if someone could guarantee you were buying an early work of brilliance?' Gave her husband forty, just on moxie. Can't say she was wrong, either—we still get notices about that story. It has shades of *Felice* in it, like an artist's sketch before they make a painting, see? That's really the only time I ever talked to her, though. What exactly are you looking for?"

# *Zoya*

## 43.

JOHN CAME INTO THE GREENHOUSE one morning in spring, holding a coffee for me.

"Knock, knock." He rapped his knuckles on my head and handed me the cup.

"Well, look at you," I said. "Almost polite. So close."

He shrugged, but couldn't mask his pleasure at the compliment. We'd seen less of one another lately, and I knew John worried he'd done something wrong. But what could I say to ease his mind? Every afternoon I raced home and waited for Lev in the kitchen with a pot of tea, shedding clothes on the way to the table. Or else found a note in my satchel that named just a time and a place—the town library, the local park, by the rhododendrons—where I was to arrive alone, and wait. Sometimes I waited for close to an hour, until the loneliness was overwhelming, the quiet screaming in my ears and telling me to *Get out, get out.* But before I could, I'd feel a hand on my shoulder, pressing me gently to some half-secret place and then reaching up under my skirt, pulling aside my underwear. The rule being, I must never look around.

For years, John had been bothering me to make more friends, saying there were better things for a young lady to do than spend her Friday nights playing board games with a middle-aged man and his wife. A fine sentiment, certainly. But now that I was occupied, he didn't seem to like it. I suppose he thought I'd meet some girls in town, or bother Nadine into the occasional movie. Something we could talk about after. (Dear John, I realize I've been out of touch, but a man's been investigating my hip bones with his teeth.)

"There's a flower show happening, you know." He was examining the banana tree, pinching a still-green fruit between thumb and forefinger. "Couple of towns over. We should go and see if there's anything worth picking up."

"Alright," I said. "That sounds fun."

"Really?"

"Sure. I'll make a thermos of hot chocolate."

John laughed. "It's seventy degrees outside."

"At home, my grandmother always said you should drink hot things when it's hot and cold things when it's cold, so your inside temperature doesn't get confused and conflict with the air."

"Really?"

I nodded, and knocked his hand away from the tree. I wasn't thinking, really. It was a nice day, the warm air after the final cold snap that turns people cheerful and goofy. Anyway, she did say that.

"That might be the first time you ever mentioned your family to me," John said. I froze for a moment, but managed to make it look like I was just inspecting the bruise he'd left on the banana leaf.

"Well, I only knew her when I was really young."

"What about your parents? I mean, I know the story: orphan boat." He winced. "But you must've had some time together with them."

My parents, who protected me and ferried me between country and town. They were poor, but hard workers. Isn't that what people said? Papa, with his dark beard, *mamochka* with her hair tied back. The last time I saw my mother, she was begging me to stay with her, even though we could hear the boots of agents walking door to door, looking for dissidents. She held me back by the arm, by my dress, by my hair, telling me to be quiet and save us. But I still believed in the revolution, then.

"Maybe," I said, "there's a reason I don't talk about it."

John held up his hands in surrender.

"I'll pull around the truck," he said.

## 44.

MY MOTHER USED TO TAKE ME TO THE market to pretend we were looking for dressmaking cloth, though in fact we got all of my clothes second-hand, and she wasn't adept enough to take in sewing work; her fingers, thick and callused from digging, made it hard for her to stitch with any precision. Still, for some reason we both enjoyed walking past the stands of pickled cabbage and the large cages full of watermelon, ending up among the rolls of fabric that hung from wagons and got propped up in stalls. Many old *babushki* lay out crocheting there, which I was not allowed to touch. Lacework, wool work. My mother was on a perpetual hunt for cloth the deepest shade of blue.

"Probably have to look at silks," she'd say. "Because of the way the cloth takes the color. Looks too black on cotton. What we want is the night sky before it's really night, see?" Together we stretched out bolt after bolt, sometimes asking for a tiny swatch to take home and "think about," which we usually received, even though the shopkeepers knew we'd never buy. My mother kept these swatches sewn together in a tiny booklet, and if you flipped through you could start to see the blue she was imagining, with elements of darkness and elements of flash and glow.

The market, chaotic and jumbled as the best of them are, was also a good place to find back-alley action if you knew where to look. You might see, for instance, people trading secrets, people handing off illegal goods or evading tariffs, a whispered conversation followed by a man reaching into a pile of potatoes and pulling out a bottle of scotch. Illicit texts sewn into the spines of Party histories, photographic proof of murders tucked into the pocket of a tailored coat. American cigarettes and chocolate bars hidden beneath piles of beads. Often, old women stood on top of their quarry and spread their skirts out to protect it from prying eyes. The secret police knew about this, of course, but mostly let things be. They had to get candy for their sweethearts too, after all.

Sometimes, though, the air changed. We'd walk up for a closer look at a pile of apples and see a man shoulder through the crowd pushing a clip into his gun. My mother would grab me by the back of my shirt and pull me close, out of danger; she had a way of disappearing into the background of a scene that I've never been able to replicate. Once we saw a whole building come down, the wall in front of us crumbling to its knees and catching a girl who'd been about to offer us a mouthful of cider. I swear in an instant my mother turned us both to smoke, that we floated above the rubble and I couldn't breathe, couldn't cry, as men kicked through the market's husk and shot survivors in the face so no one would be left to remember. Some of these men we'd seen before, laughing, ruffling the same girl's hair. But this was also my mother's wisdom: she knew that even the nicest person could turn a nastier cheek.

My father had disappeared the year before, and we would never know where. Though we could guess. (A memory: One day I came home from school and he was missing, his absence somehow a presence in the rooms. My mother sat at the kitchen table with a lock of hair between her lips, which she wouldn't move to brush aside. She sucked on her hair and I crept to the bed I made each evening on our sofa to hide myself beneath the blanket.) Our house became more cramped in his absence, and watchful, though I would still not admit that the Party had done or could do wrong. So, I thought, she must be the one who was.

Before the agents reached our door I sprinted out to meet them, closing my mother in behind me. What happened to her when the men kicked their way into our home? I don't know. I didn't see. I imagine her flickering between forms, now the wooden grain of a chair, now the filament in a bulb. I imagine the agents hauling her up by the arms as she disappeared into the fabric of her dress, so it fell empty in their fingers. Perhaps she became the waxed thread in a cross-stitch, or the brass button on my father's shirt, which she'd kept and worn like a sweater. The stain on the rug from when I had the flu as a child and threw up before she could get me to the sink. My birthing blood. Any putrid element, mouse shit or exposed wire, which the men might overlook or drop with disgust. Maybe she escaped somehow, melting into that deep and glorious blue, which I hadn't known before was the color of despair at its most unutterable.

But even if she did manage to transform—into an elixir, a miracle—I know the men would've just barged in and soaked my mother up in sponges, then wrung her out on the floor of a prison so cold she froze. Into a puddle of ice. Into the purple body of a woman left for dead. Later I saw pictures of such bodies, printed in newspapers as evidence of the horrors of war. But who was I to judge people, to judge war, when I had run into the arms of my captors with a grateful cry at being rescued by the Party faithful? Later letting myself be smuggled out of the home for girls and onto a boat when I realized there was no fidelity except to life. No creed of truth, no heart that's home.

I'm beginning to change my mind about this, but it's taken an awfully long time.

## 45.

THE FLOWER SHOW WAS HELD IN A BIG pavilion—a series of tents connected by muslin walkways, which was also used for state fair exhibitions and smelled of pigs and hay. John and I enjoyed the birds of paradise, each shaped like a Technicolor blade, and picked one up that was orange and magenta just to make the Donne girls squeal with glee. The local plants were mostly mundane, but several farmers had lugged in prize gourds from the previous fall, dried out and hollow but still impressive. When you held your ear up to the larger ones, they made a sound like the ocean, akin to a seashell. We ate popcorn cooked in a kettle and drank the chocolate I insisted on dragging around; too warm, perhaps, but delicious all the same.

"What about this?" John asked, looking at an Italian grapevine, which offered itself as low-maintenance fruit.

"I don't know," I said. "What about a coffee bush?" We each popped a red coffee cherry into our mouths, and though I understood John's aversion after biting too hard and almost cracking a tooth on the bean, I thought it tasted sweet and good. We dragged a wagon behind us, filling it up with flowers and shrubs, and John occasionally patted my shoulder, as if he were my proud old dad.

Near the end of the show, I saw a man and woman crouching around a yellow rosebush, holding hands. She was leaning into the flowers, sniffing each one as if they were telling different stories. The man was laughing, and picked up the pot with obvious pleasure, despite miming shock at the cost. A decoration, perhaps, for a new home. You saw couples like this often at the spring shows, looking to restock their gardens, and I don't know why these particular people made me catch my breath, but I stopped mid-step, leaning on a nearby table and pretending to inspect a very ordinary blueberry bush. John paused with me.

"Nice looking couple," he said.

"Hmm?" I checked the price on the blueberry. Outrageous.

"Well, sure, isn't that what a girl wants?"

"Is it?" Was it? I realized I was no longer certain. Though they did make me want *something*. The rose woman, as it happened, looked a bit like Margaret, five or ten years on. Same bouncy hair, same nose. She would make little Margarets and send them to nice schools too, outfitted with pressed wool skirts and a sense of exhaustion at the idea of dealing with the housekeeping staff. "It isn't that I don't like them," Margaret had always said when required to ask maintenance to fix something, or beg a favor from the maids. "It's just that I'm so tired by everything I already have to do, it seems like, why should I have to do this?"

I understood her fatigue, now, because I felt it too. About—everything. Lev had become insistent that I was the only one who could rid us of Vera. That my hand must push her towards the cliff, even if she took herself over. It had to be me, and it had to be soon, because he was leaving in early summer to rescue a book he'd hidden years before in what was now the USSR. He'd secured help sneaking in from the U.S. military, having charmed a pilot into adding him to an overseas flight manifest by implying he'd model a character off the man in his next story, and he needed Vera to be gone before he got back. She would destroy the book, he was sure, and that was something he couldn't abide. The plan was so magnificently ill advised that I almost wondered if he'd dreamed it up as an excuse just to get out of town—or I would have, that is, if he didn't speak with such moving tenderness about the book, which he really thought would save his life. It, and me. First thing he ever wrote, and (his words) the last woman he would ever love. He was aiming to depart sometime in June, which didn't give me much time to decide.

"When I have that book," he said, "then I'm really free. But I need you to stay here and make sure things go on as planned. Have you talked to her? You'll have to talk to her. I think I've come up with a way."

Men and women met; they married. I'd always thought that was important. Lev still spoke of his passion for his wife, her spectacular galactic beauty; before him, I'd had nothing, and if I lost him, things would go back to the way they'd been. The rose couple at the flower show tugged at some part of my heart, but when I followed Vera I felt a different pull. A tightening in me, a rumble of power. And I wondered: was that so bad?

"Let's go," I said to John, who seemed, in spite of my best efforts, to see something unsettling behind my careful expression.

"Are you sure?"

"Things to do, people to see," I said.

"Alright then." One more time he frowned towards the man and wife, who were now looking at a young dogwood. "I guess it's up to you."

# *Lev*

7 July 1931
Airmail via Berlin

RENKA, NOT SURE YOU GOT MY LAST LETTER (was notified it was forwarded home from your hotel?), but if you receive this (God, I hope you receive this), can you take care of a few things for me while I'm still in Berlin? Just want to make sure I'm ready to look my best in classes this year; now that my course load has been reduced "as befits my national reputation," I'll need to make an impression.

Black suit, pressed (not by the tailor on the corner who put a burn on the lapel of my Parisian grey wool; you know I despise him).

A few new shirts from New York; whatever you think. You know my size. Though I may have dropped a few pounds in the past wretched weeks, I plan on fattening back up as quick as can be.

Attendant to this: clotted cream, to go on all the summer fruit. A variety of wine, red and white—it would be particularly lovely if you could get Léon to dig up another bottle or two of that 1901 Château Mouton Rothschild. (I think he's been hoarding them for himself, but you know that man; he always has a price.) Steak, best cut. Slender asparagus. Now I'm just making myself hungry, so suffice it to say I trust you to do the shopping.

I'll need a new pair of eyeglasses, so please make an appointment with the optician. The old ones were crushed in an unfortunate brawl, the details of which I'll fill in for you in person, as it would be unwise to commit them to paper.

If there's a metalsmith you trust, I'd like to get my new pistol cleaned, too, at the earliest convenience.

That's all for now. *À toi ma vie, à toi mon sang,* my love. When we meet again it will be Heaven, or something like that, so I hope.

# Zoya

## 46.

LEV BOUGHT ME CIGARETTES, MOSTLY because he wanted to smoke in my house, and taught me how to hold them. To take one and tap it on the table, packing the sweet tobacco in, and then light the faraway end with the close side perched between your lips. Mostly I made him light them for me, not because I couldn't but because I liked to watch him puff and puff, and then to put in my mouth what had been in his. I watched him like a child watches an older child, slyly, and from the corner of my eye. Always hoping for him to approve of me in some way, since he was my life's first coup, the first thing truly wanted and procured.

On those languid afternoons at the end of the spring semester, when Vera had been told he was running an extra seminar, Lev would sometimes let slip his ideas for new books, stories set in the cold black of space, which he said was not really cold at all but just so low in pressure as to boil liquid into a gas. I imagined this lack of pressure as an embrace, no temperature at all but still so intense as to turn your very blood to steam. Only if you had a cut, Lev corrected. The blood in your body is a closed system. The liquid on your eyeballs, though, would evaporate right away.

We talked about Vera too, which always made me very tense. By the end of May Lev had finalized his plans for the rescue of his manuscript, which he said was doubtless just where he'd left it, and which would change the course of his career.

"I gave her a copy, you know, a long time ago. She didn't like it."

"I'm sure it's wonderful." I pet his cheek and he batted my hand away with a vexed flinch. It wasn't always easy to tell what he'd find maudlin.

"You'll like it," he went on. "That's the difference between the two of you. You know how to love what I love." He lit another cigarette for me and I took it.

He would be leaving the third week of June, not long now. Gone for who knows how much time. "It's impossible to plan, darling. I'm toppling governments here. Well. Circumventing, anyway." He told me that, at any rate, I needed as much time as I could get. He had casually dropped my name to Vera as a possible companion, someone to help her pass the time while he was away. She'd spat on the street and kept walking, without seeming to hear, though he'd referred to me as a person he'd met only once or twice on campus. And here I was supposed to convince her to go on a trip with me, somewhere discreet, where I could do away with her in total privacy. "She's just angry that I'm going after the book," he said. "She doesn't like to have her plans tampered with." And in her plan, the book was long dead.

"What was it," I ventured carefully, "that she didn't like about it?"

"You think I know?" He blew a cloud of smoke towards the ceiling. "She burned the thing without a warning, and just insisted she was trying to help me. Didn't feel the need to be specific. Would've driven me mad if"— here, a wry, sexual twinkle—"well, you know we have a passionate marriage."

"Yes," I agreed. Still, the question bothered me. Vera seemed always to be with us, a shadow on the wall, a hum in my ear. I imagined her sitting on her front porch directing flies orchestrally, or seeing a stray dog pick through her trash and nudging it out into traffic with pure mental noise. What had she seen in that book? Would I, in spite of Lev's insistence to the contrary, see it too, once he brought the thing home? He said she and I were the same person, in a certain sense, and though I knew this was mostly a lie he told himself to feel better about sleeping with me, it was also starting to feel true. In *Rothschild*, the infected women fell in love with the passengers wound round their legs. They let the creatures' vines crawl up the back of their knees and inculcate themselves into their blood vessels, thickening between their ribs and eating away at their bones like ivy taken root on brick. Vera had become my passenger—or had I become hers?—and I sometimes felt her eyes opening up behind my own, just slightly, blinking as if tired. I wanted to prod her awake—less, now, for safekeeping, and more to hear what she might say about the book and see whether it pinged anything within me. Though this seemed a terrible thing to admit. After all, the reason Lev loved me was my ability to be completely on his side.

That night we smoked in bed until the sun went down and the sheets reeked. When Lev left I walked across the room naked, with a very formal bearing, and looked at myself in the mirror, smudging my face to the left and the right, lifting the skin on my forehead to change the angle of my eyes. Did I look like Vera, in any part? I didn't see it, but maybe there was something in the underlayer. Maybe there was something oncoming, already too far along to stop. I cooked dinner naked, too, positioning myself as far away as I could from the pan where my chicken leg was frying, holding the tongs with only the tips of my fingers and extending my arm till it clicked in the socket. After a minute I stepped closer—losing my nerve and shrieking when the fat popped, but then taking another step, and another. The hot oil glistened in the pan and sizzled onto my skin in a light mist; it hurt, but there was a certain interest for me in how much of it I could stand. After a while the red spots on my stomach and thighs began to look beautiful in their way. Pointillism. Abstract expressionism. Something I had done to myself on purpose.

## 47.

DESPITE HOW MUCH I THOUGHT ABOUT her, I didn't speak to Vera until a week after Lev left for Europe. I saw him the morning of his departure—he'd promised me a visit since he'd be gone for weeks at minimum. Maybe months. He came over while on the pretence of a walk, stretching his legs before the long flight and jittering out a few of his nerves with a brisk lap round the neighborhood. It wasn't entirely a ruse. After

knocking, twice, he waited for me on the porch instead of slipping inside
with the key I always left for him under a flowerpot, and when I emerged
he grabbed my hand and pulled me into his pace. A stiff-legged, energetic
shuffle.

"Here." He thrust a manila envelope into my hand, a medium-sized
mailer sealed up and folded over twice.

"What's this?"

"When she takes her tea," he said, going on as if he hadn't heard me,
"she's very particular about getting the sugar loose from a bowl, and never
in lumps or cubes. I couldn't get anything in the form of a powder because
it would've looked too odd, but you can crack these open, I think, and
just mix it in." A green look crept in around the edges of his face. "God,
just make it seem like you don't ever take sugar in your tea, or coffee. Just
to be safe, so you don't eat any by accident."

"I don't take sugar."

"Well," he said. "All the better."

A child laughed on a nearby lawn, jumping through a sprinkler in an
orange and yellow swimsuit. School was out. I hefted the envelope in
my hand, trying to count the pills through the paper. Six, seven, eight—at
least nine, and I had no idea what they were, though I supposed it didn't
really matter.

"I thought the idea was for me to convince her to do it herself?"

Lev twitched his shoulder, almost imperceptibly.

"I thought about it. That would never work. Can you imagine her
swallowing a handful of pills, downing a glass of something stiff? How
could she ever get so hopeless, so fast?" His face was pained, almost as
if his question was sincere, his wife suicidal. As if I had the answers he
needed to pull her back from the brink. "It'll still look that way on the
blood work. And no one will ask too many questions. I kissed that girl
Daphne behind the library before she left for the summer. There will be
rumors."

The world, a pinpoint. "Excuse me?"

"Oh, don't be difficult. You know we're in this together. It's all for us."

We kept on with our frenetic stroll, and Lev began to calm down, take deeper breaths; I stuffed the envelope out of sight in my pocket and he cheered further. Now he held my hand lightly, rubbing my forefinger with his thumb. "I've thought about it," he said again. "I thought about it a lot. An awful lot." That was probably true. He thought a great deal about everything, from the rotation of planets around different types of sun to the question of whether all self-aware creatures (hypothetical ones; he had no great affection for cats and dogs and wouldn't have given them that much credit) counted as human and deserved the same societal place. (Mostly this was an issue of robots.) His wife, well. Certainly she weighed on his mind. I had seen it: how in the middle of a sentence his jaw might drop as she swept in and settled down. Her fingers tightening invisibly on his wrist. But I couldn't help feeling that the weight of this particular situation had just been transferred onto me. A yellow envelope, creasing in my pocket. Lev was hours from boarding an airplane that would take him far away.

We made our way onto campus, and though I assumed we'd head to his office, Lev pointed me towards the greenhouse instead.

"People will be able to see."

"There's no one here," he pointed out. "It's summer. And anyway, this is where we first met."

Reluctantly, I let myself be drawn inside. It was Saturday, so John was unlikely to come by, and the only real danger was from townspeople using the campus as a shortcut now that the students were gone for the year. It was, I told myself, romantic that he remembered. Lev brought me to a table at the back of the greenhouse, one covered in orchids. The plants steamed and fogged. He embraced me from behind and began to kiss my neck, placing one hand on my shoulder and snaking the other around to the front of my body. I sighed into his touch, trying not to look out the window. In a couple of hours he would be gone.

"Vera," he whispered into my ear, pressing himself against me and reaching around to undo my trousers. "Remember, Vera." I couldn't quite tell if he was instructing me or mistaking me, but now I could feel his skin against my skin. Hot, needful. He pushed inside of me, grabbing my hair in one fist. "Vera," he said again, and then he didn't say anything more. Pressed his forehead into my neck, gasped and sighed. *There will always be a Vera,* I remember thinking. *One way or another.*

## 48.

As we cleaned ourselves up with a packet of tissues, a rock hit the window of the greenhouse right near my head. I jumped.

"What the hell?" Lev said. He ran outside to see if he could catch whoever'd thrown it, but I was more concerned with the glass. Even a hair-line fracture could affect the greenhouse's temperature, and though I could cover it up with paper and beg Facilities to rush in a replacement, we'd risk losing several of the more delicate plants. I ran my hands all over the pane: nothing. Maybe a scratch. I slid down to the floor and rested my head on my knees. *It's ok,* I told myself. *Nothing happened.* But I was still rattled. Who would do such a thing? It seemed too providential to ignore.

Lev puffed back through the door. "I didn't see anyone," he said. "Probably just boys." In his exerted state he looked a bit ridiculous, mopping his forehead with a handkerchief and straightening his collar as if getting ready for another round of polo at an afternoon fairground. I tried to smile, but couldn't muster anything very convincing, and Lev offered a hand to help me up and pulled me into a tight squeeze. He wiped some dust from my rump. "Don't worry about it, darling. Come give me a kiss good-bye."

A sob broke from between my lips, surprising me. I'd known for weeks that he was leaving, but now it was real; now it was now. I clutched him to me and pressed my nose to the front of his shirt, mindful not to grab his jacket with enough force to leave wrinkles. I tried to inhale him in short, inelegant gasps. *He's going to rescue the novel,* I told myself. *And you're going to rescue him.* Lev laughed and tilted my face up to his, and kissed me. I felt like I would never see him again. Or he would never see me.

"Good-bye, little working girl," he said. "Little hero. You'll just have to bear the silence. You have a job to do, after all." By silence he meant: he would not write me. Too much of a risk, and too unlikely to find a reliable postman.

I refused to watch him walk away, as I knew he would be whistling, a spring to his step. Man on an adventure. The sky was a painful blue, and there were fledglings swooping round the lawns. Everyone believes themselves to be the exception to unflattering natural laws, but I knew then I was not immune to envy, self-pity, fear in the face of certain danger. Forcing myself to breathe, four seconds in, four seconds out, I took the pills from my pocket and rattled them in their envelope. Each full of poison and bound for the gullet of a woman I'd seen a hundred times in my dreams, and often enough through her own front window. As I listened to the shift of capsules against paper, I began to calm down.

I was a peasant girl, after all, hardy and strong. I had lived through worse trials than this: there was work ahead, but at the end the future would belong to me. And now it was time to get started.

## 49.

THE DAY I WENT TO VISIT VERA I WOKE up early and drew a hot bath, sipping tea while it filled and then lowering myself in slowly, savoring the light burn. For half an hour I scrubbed and soaked, shampooing my hair and taking a pumice stone to my heels until I was clean and smooth and red as a tomato. After drying off with a fluffy white towel (one of my first indulgences after winning my raise; growing up our towels were threadbare and rough, holes nibbling away at the edges, and the one I'd been using since my arrival in Maple Hill wasn't much better) I painted my nails red and sat still for half an hour to let them dry, hazarding the lacquer just enough to turn the pages of a magazine. My hair was set in curlers, and with my nails done I blew it dry into a cumulus halo.

Lev didn't much care for the looks of me done up. He accepted it when we went out to restaurants or on other special occasions, but he preferred me in what he called my natural state, with dirt riming every ridge and my hair tied up in a bun. You have to understand, I didn't let him keep me from proper hygiene, but I took special pleasure in getting ready now, knowing he wouldn't be around to pout or moan about my hairspray. Anyhow, one always dresses with more care for a woman.

The momentum from my bath carried me all the way to Lev and Vera's house before I started to get nervous. By now he'd be in London, or huddled on the back of a transport truck as it trundled through Alsace; I'd calculated carefully to make sure I seemed casual when I finally showed up. It needed to look like I was just in the neighborhood, unaware of Lev's precise date and time of departure. A friendly girl, perhaps a bit dim. Red nails, red dress. Behind the door, Vera was going about her day, scratching out a note to Lev's editor or planning a week of supper menus. I pictured her doing something mundane with just—a little ripple in the air, some machination still unseen.

The pills were tucked away in my purse, not to use, but more as a talisman. They helped me keep heart, you see. I couldn't wear anything Lev had given me, lest Vera recognize a familiar bracelet or pin; I didn't entirely trust Lev to be original in his gift-giving. *Vera*, I thought. Little girl, black hair, long nose. I reached into my mind and rearranged the Pioneer scarf around her neck to its proper dashing angle. There was something so comfortingly familiar about her, something so like going home. I had to remind myself that we hadn't been friendly back in Moscow. She hadn't even known my name.

After a couple of minutes I decided that my skulking behind a tree at the corner was becoming conspicuous, and gathered myself up to walk to the door and knock. A shuffle and bustle somewhere unseen, and then the door swung open to reveal a stocky girl wearing vivid green earrings.

"Yeah?" she said.

"Oh." I took a tiny step backwards, which I hoped looked casual. "Who are you?"

"Excuse me? You knocked. Who are *you?*" On second inspection, the girl was older than I'd thought—at least my age—and her clothes were rather slapdash, considering her jewelry. She saw me looking at the earrings and reached a protective hand up to touch one. "Mrs. was letting me try them on."

"Oh, I see. Mrs.? You mean Vera? Is she home?"

"Why would you come if you thought she wasn't?"

"I didn't. I mean, I didn't think. Didn't, um, know."

"Ok." The girl twisted her mouth up untrustingly, but couldn't find any further reason to object. She disappeared into the house, leaving the door cracked open, and when I was sure she was gone I pushed it wider with my toe. Everything was as I remembered it. There was Lev's suit jacket folded over the banister. Somewhere inside there were stacks of his shirts, and buffed shoes lined up in neat rows. The scent of him drifted out towards me, and I parted my lips to let it in, poking my head just past the door frame to get a closer look.

Just then, Vera turned the corner. She saw me and stopped short, raising an eyebrow—not quite enough to look angry, but enough to let me know I was not especially welcome. There was a moment of silent comparison between us, though perhaps this was only in my head. Vera, a few years older than me and a century more powerful, somehow. I can only imagine how wanting she found me, but, well, she was supposed to. That was the plan. Glancing over her shoulder at the girl, who was in the process of removing the green earrings, she nodded that she was alright. Then she stood in the doorway, blocking it.

"You must be the girl Lev is trying to foist on me. Took you long enough to show up."

"Vera." I couldn't help myself. "You're Vera Petrovna." She was slim and sharp and so light-skinned she appeared to be glowing. As if her bones were tubes of neon.

"Pardon me?"

I held out a hand, conscious of a thumbprint marring one of my newly painted nails. It hadn't been part of the plan to tell Vera that we knew one another or get her thinking about connections. But I remembered her so clearly, and it seemed impossible she wouldn't know me too. "Zoya

Ivanovna Andropova. We've met. You were Vera Volkova, back in Moscow?"

She stared at me, and then—took my hand. Looking less like she planned to shake it and more like she wanted to make a close canine inspection. Indeed I thought she might lick my fingers to see where I'd been.

"Zoya. *V'ui otkuda?*"

"Like I said, Moscow."

She frowned. "I don't think so."

"Well, we spent most summers in Lipetsk, but I was born in the city."

"I mean you don't know me. We've never met." Her voice was softer than I thought it would be. Fewer hard edges than her face implied.

"Well," I said, "as you like." There would be time to pursue our shared history later. (Though, as you know, dear reader, Vera never gave an inch.) For now, the future was more important. "May I come in?"

Vera leaned closer, and when she did I could smell the talcum she'd applied after her bath. And—apples. And something both sweet and sour, like yogurt. She put her face near enough to mine that I saw her lips part from her teeth when she spoke, which she did very quietly.

"Little bee. Buzzing around my nest. I've seen you hovering, you know, on the streets and at that silly school. What are you looking for?"

"Excuse me?" My voice, too, came out in a whisper. The best thing to do, I knew, was to feign ignorance and stick to my story: a silly girl, just looking for a friend. But it made me nervous to think she'd spotted me, when I'd been so careful.

"You want to come inside? Why couldn't you find your way before? On your own."

"I don't know what you're talking about."

Vera stepped back and straightened up. Her voice dropped and became casual, almost loud.

"Zoya Andropova. You must have a cup of tea with me. But not today, I'm afraid. As you must be aware, my husband left on a trip recently, and I've been overtired. Can you come back? Say, Tuesday?"

"Alright," I agreed. Wary, now. "What time?"

"Two o'clock, precisely. The right time for tea. I'll have something to eat, too. Do you like *pastila?*"

This was, in fact, my favorite dessert—a gelée of fruit and sugar reduced over days of heat and pressed into a delicate square—which Lev sometimes bought for me at a European bakery in New York. My mother had made her own version when we worked in Lipetsk, to give me something to look forward to during those interminable summers. I nodded, mute, and Vera smiled.

"Wonderful. We will see each other then. Now, I'm afraid you must buzz along, little bee."

Behind her the short girl, who I decided must be the maid, giggled, but Vera made no sign she'd heard. Instead she watched me walk away—I could feel her eyes on my back, her attention swarming over me, urging me on until I turned the corner and moved out of sight. At which point I broke into a run, not caring if they heard the sound of my heels clicking against the concrete.

## 50.

BACK AT THE VERY BEGINNING, I WOULD sometimes—not so often, but occasionally—see Margaret tucked up in her bed under mountains of quilting and electric roastery and consider crawling in beside her to avoid walking out into the cold and snow. It will sound mad to you, reader, I know, and even I, in my delirium of exhaustion and homesick ennui, realized that to cross this threshold would mean a sweet death at the very best. To hunker under all that heat, where surely there was sweat between Margaret's shoulder blades, a waft of salty bread yeasting out from underneath her arms. She would kick once or twice in her slumber and I'd curl up in the shadow of her back to evaporate, evaporate, evaporate. Melting, husking, fading to a vapor, which would, when she threw back the sheets, simply disperse into the air. *Fine,* I thought. *Fine.*

"What are you doing?" she asked once, turning to see me standing beside her, all kitted up in my green coat.

"Nothing. Just checking"—I grasped at straws—"whether you needed another blanket."

She, gruff. Half-sleeping. Her hair all chestnut disarray. "I'm fine."

"If you're sure."

"Mmmhmm." She turned away from me and lay her glowing cheek back on the pillow. Gone before I closed the door behind me. She never needed to study much to make her grades. She got up in the morning at half past eight unless she had an early class, and ate a slow breakfast in the caf, sometimes flipping through the newspaper that her father had subscribed her to against her will. She liked the science column, the society column, the reviews of books and plays. I read her a passage, once, from Lev's first book, *Knife, Knave*, thinking we might share the pleasure of his words, his turn and flick of felicitous phrasing. She wrinkled her nose.

"God, too much," she said. "Can't he just say anything plain?"

She was the sweetest when she was sleeping, air coming through her lips all a-flutter. A different person from the girl who stood in the lunch line as shiny as brass, laughing with her friends and maybe waving to me from across the room with the understanding I'd never try to join her. In her sleep she softened, unthreaded. She was susceptible to whispers, and would sometimes talk to me from deep within a dream. I never told this to her waking self, because she wouldn't have understood. She knew only the back of my head as I walked into the hall, the quiet lifting of my hand from the other side of a long corridor. And never mind. Never mind all that. A fever of the past, long since broken. Mystifying Margaret, gone entirely her own way.

## 51.

A FEW BLOCKS FROM VERA'S HOUSE MY toes began to pinch and I slowed down to a walk. My feet were sweaty, and I felt every sickening slide they made against the leather of my shoes. The few people I passed on the street shot worried glances my direction, and it was hard to blame them. I needed someplace peaceful, someplace cool to clear my head. What had just happened? The glinting emeralds, Vera's chalky scent. Her accusation. I supposed it wasn't a loss. She had agreed to see me again, after all.

Downtown, I found the bookstore closed, which was disappointing. I didn't want to eat a hamburger (in fact I never quite got my head around this as a form of food), didn't want to sit through a movie and let my thoughts get overwhelmed. I mooned around outside the hardware store counting the loose screws in the window display, and letting the June sun beat down on my head. A pigeon hopped along the sidewalk, cooing, and I had the urge to kick it. But I couldn't. And wasn't that the point? Not much of a murderer, me, for all the bloodred dresses in the world.

A bell chimed from a nearby doorway. *Of course*, I thought. Marie's café. In the years since I'd been a regular there, the shop had stayed open and practically unchanged. The flaking paint on the door frame had been replaced by a pristine coat of blue, but otherwise, nothing. Through the window you could see the same old tablecloths, littered with coffee stains and frayed at the trim. I walked in and was greeted by three familiar paintings hung in dusty frames with yellowing price placards perched hopefully beside them. The work of a local artist, whom I'd never known to come by and check on her wares. In the air, butter and spice.

"Hello?" I said at the counter, to no one. Marie popped up from the floor, her face covered in flour and loose bits of scone.

"Whoops, had a little mishap. Just a tick."

She ducked back down and then hustled into the kitchen, arms full of something. I heard the back door open and momentarily wondered if she was running away—there was the dim memory of Marie as a refugee, perhaps escaping a brute husband or leaving a baby on some doorstep, all wrapped up in a blanket—but then came the slam of a lid on a trash can.

"Alright, inspector," she declared upon reentering. "Nothing to worry about here."

"Oh no, I'm not—"

She waved her hand. "Bad joke. Sorry. What's your pleasure?"

"I think—" I looked at her and welled with hope, waiting to see some flicker of recognition. "A coffee? Do you still do free refills?"

"Up to two." She frowned. "We never did more than that."

"Oh," I said. "Alright."

I took my cup to the window seat and sipped, though the pot had obviously been sitting on the warmer for hours.

"Want anything else?" Marie called. I was the only customer in the store. "Food? Baked goods? Scattered crumbs?"

"No, thanks." I rested my chin on my fist, elbow on the table, and watched her sweep cookies off the display plates only to replace them with fresh, identical versions. Her hair had streaks of grey now. New dangly earrings, a touch more eyebrow pencil. Her fingers, moving with quick assessment over her wares, had developed a permanent curl, bulging out at one or two of the joints. She seemed happy enough, though. I wished I'd brought a book, some small reminder. Marie had been—how to describe it? A balm. When I had little else to make me feel safe.

At last I got up the nerve to flag her down, lifting my hand as if I had decided on a bite to eat, after all. When she came over I asked, "Do you remember a girl, who used to study here?"

"You'd have to be a bit more specific, honey. There's a school nearby. And the junior college."

"Right, sure, but someone in particular? Came here a lot?"

There it was: just a faint shine across her vision, an unmistakable fond gleam. "Well, I guess there was a girl. Few years ago now. Long time, really."

"Yes," I said. "You gave her biscotti."

"Mmm. She liked almond. Sure, I remember. But why?"

Wasn't it obvious? "She's me. I'm her."

"Oh, honey, no. I told you, a lot of girls come in here."

"No, I—" I wasn't sure what to say. "Really, I used to sit here all the time, for hours."

"Moved away, though?"

"Well, not quite." I flushed. "I just got busy."

Marie looked doubtful. "Listen, the girl I'm thinking of—" She tilted her head to the side, giving me a thorough once-over. "Maybe there's something similar in the hair. But it wasn't you. Much younger."

"You said yourself, it was years ago."

"In the eyes, I mean. You don't age so much in the eyes. Not that fast."

"Marie," I said. "It's me."

She shook her head. "I'd remember. But I mean, don't worry about it. It's just that I'm thinking of someone else."

"Ok," I said. "Well. Ok."

Marie looked at my cup. "Need a warm-up?"

"No thank you." I pushed it away from myself with two fingers, and stood. I wasn't sweating anymore, but my limbs still felt sticky, and now all abuzz. "Got to get going."

"Sure, hon. Keep those home fires burning."

I left, and the bell chased me out to the street. Marie, I saw, had moved back behind the counter, scouring something unseen. I rested my forehead on a wall a few steps away, knocked it gently against the bricks. A little boy walking by with his mother looked at me with great seriousness.

"What," I said to him. "*What.*"

But his frown only deepened as he moved farther on.

# Excerpt of a letter from Vera Orlov to Robert Horne of Horne Publishing

(provided to the Maple Hill Police Department by Mr. Horne, with some reluctance)

SITTING ON THE TRAIN HOME WITH THE contracts in hand for the re-release of *Knight, Knave*, making corrections (as I'm sure you assumed I would, Bobby). How many times must I tell you all that a delivery date for the next book is impossible? No addendums. Just buy what's on hand. If anyone tells Lev he *must* work by such and such day he'll hole up in his study reading *Oblomov* for half a week and then disappear in that terrible car. Let him be, and he'll sit at the desk. The words come unasked for. Things that matter always do.

Meanwhile this train is impossible. What is it about Americans that makes you all want things to be new and disposable? Tea in a paper cup. I don't understand. It seeps through at the seams. And you. You keep buying ghost stories, Bobby—yes, I look through your catalogues—but what do Americans know about ghosts? I could tell you a thing or two about spectrality that would curl your hair.

In Leningrad we knew our spooks on a personal level, to the point where a party at the end of the world looked just like a party at the height of one's power. Candles, tables, buildings, liquor. Bloodlines, necklines, age lines, ambitions. Fingertips gone orange from tobacco and white hair swept at just such an angle to hide where it's thinned. Terrifically civilized. All the while, everyone was on the verge of dying. That's the trick, you see. True horror is when the worst possibility wears the face of ordinary life, but no Americans consider themselves ordinary, do they? It's your prerogative to transform overnight, and people act like this is some kind of virtue. This attitude is rubbing off on Lev, and I don't like it.

But listen to me, going on. I'm sure you have better things to do.

Don't bother sending the next round of contracts to Lev, just courier them straight to me. And please get rid of this letter, Bobby, you know I find it morbid and distressing when you keep them.

*Editor's note: This letter was undated, but police records indicate that Mr. Horne, when pressed, estimated its vintage as late 1930.*

# Zoya

## 52.

MY PLAN, IN ITS BASIC FORM, INVOLVED earning Vera's trust and getting her to take me on a vacation (Lev's idea: get her out of town and away from prying eyes. Now that I'd met their maid, I understood this requirement much better). A trip to the ocean seemed like the thing—quiet seaside hamlet, a rented cottage. Plus, New Jersey is lousy with beaches, so we wouldn't have to go very far. Once we arrived I would give her the poison, and make an anonymous call from the road so her body would be discovered without much delay. Neither Lev nor I was interested in putrescence.

It wouldn't be easy. She was, Lev assured me, a naturally suspicious woman, and I was coming out of nowhere, more or less. ("Less" Lev's introduction, but that clearly hadn't won me any favor.) In her position, I wondered, would I agree to such a thing? A sudden vacation with an ardent stranger, conspiratorial whispers over sherry. I considered my empty apartment, teapot whistling into space, and then thought about strolling down a boardwalk or sidewalk, brushing Vera's shoulder with my own. Without being proud to admit it, I knew I'd jump at the chance; I was not exactly choking on friendship. And that was the point; neither was Vera. Though she gave off an air of self-sufficiency, surely it couldn't erase the natural human need for love. Why else lend her earrings to the maid?

On Tuesday I went home early and tidied myself up, though not nearly to the same degree as I had for my first visit. I washed my face and put on a clean blouse without bothering to change my pants or shoes. Didn't curl my hair, just ran a brush through. Added a touch of lipstick, and left it at that. Vera wouldn't be expecting fireworks and I thought perhaps she'd appreciate the fact that I worked for a living; after all, Lev did. My fingernails were chipped and rough from where I'd torn at the dirt, pulling up weeds by stalk and root.

This time when I knocked, Vera answered the door herself, wearing a light cotton skirt and a shirt so crisply white it seemed to be made of sun on snow. The color—or lack thereof, I suppose—suited her. She looked like a weather event. Or perhaps like something more peaceful and self-satisfied. A young scout, say.

"Come in, my dear," she said.

It felt strange to walk around the living room without Lev. The same, but not. His clothes had been removed from around the ground floor; no more jackets slung on the backs of chairs or errant cuff links on the windowsill. Just as I could feel his presence in every detail before, I could feel his absence now. A tea tray had been set out with a gleaming silver service and a platter of *pastila*.

"Did you make them yourself?" I asked, indicating the sweets.

"God, no." Vera laughed. "You think I have time for that?"

I thought: *I don't know how you use your time.* But that wasn't quite true. I knew when she got up, knew the side of the house where her bedroom lay. I knew that she attacked Lev's work with the loving axe of a firefighter saving a child. I knew she scratched and sniffled, curled her hair occasionally, bothered to wear different shades of lipstick to suit her skirt or shoes.

"But did you learn to cook as a girl?"

She gave me a hard look. One of many questions she would never answer about her past. For instance: whether she hoped Lev's greatness would save her from it, or from some dark future. Or something else. "Let's sit."

Vera positioned herself beside me on the sofa, so near that our knees almost touched, though there were several open chairs. She poured, making sure to include a dash of milk in my cup just as I prefer, and the *pastila* came from the store Lev frequented, or so I judged based on the taste. I bit into one and was flooded with a sense of well-being, warmth that spread from sternum to shoulder blades, and from there down. It was not lost on me that Vera guessed without asking how I took my tea.

"Now," she said, once we both had our cups and plates. "I have something for you."

"Oh?" I tried to think how I might take control of the conversation, but all the tricks I'd learned in school—the sudden topical swerves and bold declarations—seemed impossible under the circumstances. My body recognized a dominant creature and grew sleepy. Passive. "That's . . . nice. You shouldn't have."

Vera pulled an envelope from under the tray; manila, like the one Lev gave me filled with pills. I realized they must have often wandered into one another's offices, and would naturally share the same supplies. She handed the envelope to me, and inside I found round-trip train tickets to the coastal town of Twisted Branch. Vera watched me, waiting for some kind of reaction, but even in my half-drunk kitten state, I was at least able to keep my face blank. Finally she spoke, with a false brightness.

"My husband mentioned that he met you on the Donne School campus. I'm not sure how well you know him, but I imagine if you've spoken even once you'll understand that his whims are often ridiculous." I said nothing, and still refused to frown or smile. The longer I was quiet, the more Vera would have to say—something. Talk into the white space of me. "Well, I admit I wasn't happy with the idea of being blind-matched with a companion this summer, but he was quite insistent. 'You'll love her,' he told me. 'She's a gem,' and so on. Not in those words, you understand, but that was the general bent of it."

"So?" I prompted.

"I'm giving in. Let's be friends, take a trip. Visit those . . . deep waters." She made it sound like drowning.

"Well, that's wonderful, of course." I said. "But you didn't have to buy my ticket. You're supposed to be my friend"—I offered a shy smile—"not my benefactor."

"Nonsense. The one is the other. And I'm not sure if Lev told you about my reluctance," (*She spat on the ground when I said your name*, he'd said) "but I want to make up for it. On a spiritual level. So we can start our relationship on an even emotional footing."

"Spirit, emotion. That's rather heady."

"Well." Vera smiled. "That's the first thing you'll learn about me. I'm a rather heady person."

## 53·

WAS I APPREHENSIVE, READER? NATURALLY I was. I'd expected an unwilling participant, a Vera of cold and ice pushing me away with both hands. I'd found instead a bosom buddy, ready-made. Too easy. Too neat. I hadn't thought Lev was going to tell her about our trip to the seaside— that was to be my suggestion, once we started getting along. And so when she handed me the tickets it felt very much like a dare.

Still, there was something intoxicating in what she offered. No Donne girl had ever done so much to win my favor: not Cindy and Adeline with their sweet blackmail, nor Caroline with her sad, dead friend. Not even Margaret. Just Vera, here and now. That she had designs on me, reasons of her own—I had no doubt. But she found my favorite tea cake. Praised the simplicity of my hairdo and leaned in to embrace me when I departed. I couldn't get the scent of her off me all day, and found myself smiling whenever it surprised me, looking around with a pang of regret when she didn't appear alongside it. Putting her hand over my hand. I went back to the greenhouse and pruned rose bushes for the rest of the afternoon, pricking myself several times on the thorns. My arms, when I left, were streaked with blood. Lev had prepared me for Vera resisting, but not for Vera playing our game.

And, well. There is a special pleasure to be found in having one's expectations subverted. Opening a well-loved novel and finding the dead dog resurrected, the hero turning course at the moment of his doom and retiring as a beloved medical doctor in a village *sur la rivière*. I thought Vera would be distant until the moment of her death, a (temporarily) living embodiment of the vast space between memory (mine) and fact. But instead she was fully present, physical. Ready to wound me, or so it seemed. Her face recalled Kay's healthy malice; I could almost imagine her hair into a braid.

Sitting at home with a glass of wine, I spread the pills before me and fidgeted with them, sticking my fingernail into the seal and seeing if I could pull them apart. One almost split right there in front of me, and it was tempting to open them all and spill them into my cup. What would Vera do then? If I called her in the middle of the night with stomach cramps, and had her rush me to the hospital? If I called, and she found me stiff and dead, and suddenly her problem? I didn't want to die, but I was inspired to make big moves in order to impress my opponent, to show her she was not the only one who could expand the field of play. Our train departed in two days. I had to arrange for John to keep an eye on the plants, had to scour the kitchen of perishables, pack.

I expected Vera to be stern, not sportive. But wasn't that just because Lev had told me she would be? He left us each, Vera and me, with a single role to fill, as if we were automatons moving through a prearranged scene. Can you blame me for being enticed by Vera's suggestion that we might both choose to be more? And by the idea that I might show Vera I was more than she bargained for?

# Poem by Anonymous

From the Donne School Charter and Handbook

Honesty's a girl who waits at the door
She speaks her piece without a roar.
Clarity shines a light in the dark
Her hand a torch, her mouth a spark.
To reveal is to do more
(The whisper that we're looking for;
the listing step on drunken night—

> Drunk on time and dearth and plight).

A girl who snaps to chime the hour
Knowing not her push or power.
To reveal is to bring clean
Though sometimes says more than we mean.
Perhaps it is our keenest sway
To sometimes mean more than we say.

*Editor's note: Ms. Andropov doodled lines from this poem in the margins of her later diary entries. Although it no longer exists as part of the Donne School recruitment or matriculation materials, we were able to confirm that a version of it appeared in the Charter from 1913 to 1945.*

# *Zoya*

## 54.

FOR THE TRAIN, I TIED MY HAIR INTO a ponytail and hid it under a kerchief. Brought along a packet of sandwiches in wax paper, though the ride was only a few hours long. We were to arrive in Twisted Branch before sundown, with enough time to check in to our cottage before dark. The postmaster had the key for us. The grocer had been told to anticipate our arrival with a few necessities already stashed in the cupboards, though we'd need to do a more thorough accounting the next day. Milk, yes. Milk chocolate, maybe not.

I hadn't been to the Maple Hill railway station in years—not since I stepped down onto the platform shivering with anticipation and mild scurvy from my shipboard confinement—and for ten minutes or so I amused myself by noting the changes: new newspaper stand, different hot dog vendor, better benches under the awning. But our train was set to depart in a quarter of an hour, and still Vera hadn't met me by the open cars. I was starting to get anxious when I saw her talking to the conductor some distance away, hat in hand and bags by her feet—more bags, in fact, than she could possibly need. I hurried over.

"Dear," she said when she spotted me, "why aren't you in your seat? The good places will be going fast."

I felt a splinter in my heart. *That's right*, I thought. *We aren't a team.* "I was waiting for you."

"Well, that's ridiculous. I'm sitting in first class, so my place is reserved. Surely you knew that." Her face was impassive, but I thought I saw a twinkle in her eye. She hadn't mentioned anything of the kind.

"Oh. Of course." I'd have to be quicker on my feet. Turning to the conductor I asked, "How much would it cost to upgrade my ticket?"

Vera frowned. "I don't know that—"

"I'll pay, of course." But the conductor stopped me pulling my wallet from my purse.

"My apologies, miss," he said, "but the first-class berths are all sold out."

I looked at Vera, and she looked at me.

"Well, don't I feel silly."

"Not at all, Zoya darling. It was just a misunderstanding." She gave my hand a squeeze and said, "I'll see you on the other side."

By rushing I was able to find a seat by the window, though I wasn't facing in the direction of travel and grew nauseous every time we lurched to stop or start. I had a book with me; not one of Lev's, just some popular novel set by coincidence on a train. A lonely girl who meets a mysterious young man and gets embroiled in his dangerous predicament, story and locomotive hurtling towards their final destination with shared volition. The tension was unbearable, but looking out the window made me sick, so I kept opening the book and slamming it shut, grumbling audibly each time I changed my mind. *Ridiculous*, and *Unconscionable*, and so on.

There were several middle-aged men seated near me, and one by one each of them tried to strike up a conversation, asking questions about my husband (*Oh, no husband?* they'd say, with feigned surprise) and then my work, questioning the origins of my accent, which I'd worked so hard to overcome. One fellow—I will not call him a gentleman—said, "Where are you headed? You'll probably want someone to show you around town." And it was to his grave disappointment that he learned we were not traveling to the same place, and that I would be meeting a companion. When his stop arrived he stood up with an expression of such abject sorrow I'd have felt bad for him, if only he didn't smell so strongly of onions. The rest of the men I was able to silence by distributing my sandwiches.

I reminded myself that, whatever my trials, Lev was surely enduring worse. He had such a sad grey faith in the manuscript, a belief that touching it would shade something in, make apparent the whole shape of his life. Was he now hunkering down in a field, taking cover under a tarp? Was he fishing in a local river, trying to roast his shabby meal in a tin can? White meat flaking, hot and sweet and smoked. I couldn't think of food; it made me burp. And then even my newfound friends looked at me askance, and I had to cover my mouth with a hand. *A new Leo Orlov book*, I reminded myself. *You'll be the first to see it. Almost the very first.* The train seats were green velveteen, but not as pretty as that sounds.

When I stepped down onto solid ground, it was into a wretched and drowsy world. The sea air not so cool as I'd hoped, and the sun getting ready to set. Everything was tinged with yellow and pink, which I'm sure made me look ill. Vera waved from next to a taxicab, infuriatingly refreshed. I thought she may even have changed her outfit, but I was too exhausted to be sure.

"Come on, now, we have to hurry or we'll never make the post office. I think they're holding it open for us, because business hours ended some time ago. And I for one," she said, straightening her hair, "don't want to sleep on the porch." She could've done it, though, without losing an ounce of grace; a camp-out girl in a canvas hammock. With the kerchief on my head and sallow rings beneath my eyes, I looked like a vagabond.

"Alright," I said, and heaved my single bag into the trunk along with her full coterie of matched luggage. My only comfort was that I knew more than she did; I had a plan that would surely catch her by surprise and neuter any other minor humiliations she had in store for me. Over the course of the cab ride, I refused to answer her questions with anything other than sighs and grunts, though if she found this less than gracious, she made no indication. We argued with the security man at the post office until the postmaster emerged and brought us in, handing out keys like they were candy and giving us an overview of the town. Who was nice, who was a beast: the basic gossip. Our taxi waited outside, idling and ticking up the cost, but we were afraid that if we let him go we wouldn't get another. We were right. The streets were black, abandoned. When we finally pushed our way into the cottage I heard a scrabbling that may have been either cockroaches or mice, though Vera insisted it was the trees outside, or the ocean in the distance.

Why hold on to all this, you might ask me? I don't know where else to keep it. I don't know how to put it down.

## 55.

MORNING TEA. FOR ME, MILK, FOR HER, sugar. No pills yet. We are still getting the measure of one another. Her black hair has a brown sheen to it if you look in the right light, and this makes her vulnerable to me in a way that nothing else has yet done. I wear an old robe to the table and she doesn't comment on it. We both eat toast just a tiny bit burnt. Not from preference, it's just the way the toaster is. Perhaps tomorrow, I remark, we should use forks and roast them under the broiler.

Everything has a present-tense quality when I think of it in the cabin, the cottage. Even if it was long ago. *Your eyes don't age that fast.* Or do they? I'll have to banish this shaky feeling that the past is still happening, that I could stop it if I wanted.

## 56.

WE DECIDED EARLY ON THAT FIRST MORNING to walk along the beach as far as we could go, after discussing possible routes over breakfast. It wasn't so grim in the daytime: I could see flowers growing in the front yard, and how all the streets had black concrete and fresh lines of paint. There was a café at the end of a jetty, some distance from the rest of town and only comfortably achievable in muck boots and by judging the tide right. It appealed to us right away. I can't imagine how they made their money, but this became our goal: cocoa overlooking the water, with no one else around. Before we left, Vera said, "Wait here a moment," and came back downstairs in rolled-up work pants, god knows where she got them from. Her body always seemed to be adapting based upon some hidden agenda, and I admired it. The way she existed for her own private reasons instead of existing to be seen, to be known. Though it also made me crazy. I would have liked to press her to me, whole body to whole body, whole soul, just so I'd know what I was dealing with.

Bright green grass lined the dunes and baked into yellow, receded back towards the distant inland. We had to walk through it to get to the shoreline, and already sand was starting to slip inside my shoes. Canvas sneakers, because I didn't have boots, and anyway it was so god-awful hot. Vera had decided to go barefoot, though I warned her more than once that she'd cut her foot on a quahog shell.

"A what?" she mocked.

"A quahog. Kind of clam."

"A *what?*" When I learned the word from Margaret years earlier, I'd laughed too, imagining a wee piggy burrowing beneath the sea. Now I liked it because it was funny, which wasn't a reason I liked many things. Vera just smirked. "I'll watch my step."

"If you say so."

We were bright. The sun getting high, the water cut and riveted by waves. Her pants sat loose on her little backside, and her shirt was buttoned up too high to look winning, though it did protect her chest from getting burned. We picked our way over rocks and around tide pools, cooling our heels in the salt. We passed several houses with terrible fences, picket posts all leaning out at different angles, bidden by weather or wind, strung together with bits of razor wire. The houses themselves were charming and shingled, and eventually stopped showing up.

At noon or thereabouts, we sat to rest on a piece of parched driftwood high up the tide line. We could see the café about a half mile away, and Vera inspected the soles of her feet, seeming pleased by the cuts she found there, which she claimed didn't hurt a bit. I knew I was supposed to be getting close to her, earning her trust, but every time I tried I felt like I was moving backwards.

"Doesn't it make you feel small?" I asked, indicating the ocean with my chin. "I can hardly stand it." It was less the sunny waves that made me think so, and more the memory of a gunmetal sea that my orphan ship had glided through. How I'd once spotted a big wall of water in the distance, approaching us with overwhelming speed. It would've eaten the boat and left no trace, but instead it dropped back into the horizon without getting near enough to cause a ripple. I'd been alone on deck at the time. None of the other orphans believed me when I tried to explain.

"Not at all," Vera replied.

"Really?"

"Of course. I enjoy the feeling of my own insignificance." It seemed like she might be making a joke at my expense, but her face was serious.

"You don't really think that." I was picturing Lev, his stout belief in Vera as the guiding hand that led him through his life. Point A to Point Z.

"Of course I do. It would be awful to believe that anything I did mattered, in particular. I like the ocean," she insisted. "I've always liked the ocean. It will be here forever. Not me, thank god."

Vera that day: sun-swept but not -kissed, flushed but unburnt. I kept seeing her the way Lev had told me to see her, and the way, too, I'd been imagining her since I was a child. Remarkable. Untouchable. She occasionally had things in her teeth, which didn't fit either of our renderings, but then, it often looked like blood stuck between the gums. I held her slim figure up against my own—silly girl that I still was, trying to figure out whether I could measure up. As if that was the thing that mattered: my feet being larger than hers, my prints obscuring hers in the sand when I stepped on top of them. My arms being longer than hers, long enough to wrap all the way around her shoulders and still have some to spare.

She seemed so different from how she had just the day before, standing imperious on the train platform. I wondered then how much she knew. How much she wanted me to believe she knew. Sitting here with her feet unshod and telling me she'd be perfectly happy to die if it meant she'd also disappear and leave behind something greater that obscured her completely.

# *Lev*

10 July 1931
No postmark

VERA, WHERE ARE YOU? YOU WERE not here when I got home. I swept into the bedroom expecting to find you sleeping and to kiss you awake, to see your sullen blink at being pulled out of a dream. But the bed was tidy, empty. Your suitcase missing. Mail spilled through the slot in the door and lay in a great sad stack on the floorboards. All I can do is write these notes and leave them in every room of the house, hoping that somehow they'll transmit a message to you: *come back. I love you.* Whatever I've chosen, whatever I've done, I didn't mean it. Please come back.

You know it used to confuse me, Vera, the way you got angry when I woke you up. I was so eager for your company. "Let me sleep," you'd moan, and like a brute I'd tug your arm and ask you, "Why?"

But now I understand. You imagine better things than the world can provide, and your dreams are a refuge. A place where the streets never have the scent of trash and urine, and the wind only blows newspapers into your face if they are encoded with welcome messages. Birds aren't nuisances, they're harbingers. Cats are familiars. Yes, Vera, yes. Wherever you've gone, I assume it's for similar reasons. You're in your own world while I am here, inhabiting its pale reflection. So I will not hurry you, I'll only say: please. Don't leave me here alone. I thought I could stand it, but I cannot. My life is a perpetual insomnia without you.

Signed, your limited, lonesome Lev. Lowly, left-behind, leprously forlorn.

# *Zoya*

## 57.

THE CAFÉ WAS A BIT OF A DISAPPOINTMENT, serving cocoa made from a powder. I decided that the proprietor must've lived on the premises, as his red motorboat was tied up outside, and I spotted a pillow and blanket in the corner booth. We sat by the window watching the sea, and trying to convince one another that we'd seen a whale. Great lumbering presences off in the distance. A waiter came by with extra cocoa powder and stainless-steel pots of hot water, single serving; he leaned on the table and told us it wasn't the right time of day for whales, and we both made a point of ignoring him. Oh look. Right there. Just missed. Yes, I'm sure.

On the walk back the waves were larger, and you could see the shadows of tall seaweed arms suspended in them. The beach smelled raw. At one point Vera tripped, and when I reached out a hand to help her balance she looked at me like she'd never seen me before—which, of course, she hardly had. In a book, in a story, we'd become the best of friends and take off running down the sand together, laughing wild. Each of us would've worn one of my sneakers, to save half our feet. But it wasn't like that. I thought about Lev cupping the fattest joint of my hips and pressing himself to me, hard as stone. I thought about him scratching out notes in the dark. My canvas shoes were soaked and they made my feet cold, despite the heat of the day. By the time we got back to the cabin, pulling ourselves up the rickety wooden stairs, we were both mute with exhaustion. Seabirds called out, *mock, mock, mock.*

Vera threw herself into an Adirondack chair and squinted at me, against the light. Looking young, almost girlish.

"We don't really need to carry on with this pretence, do we?" she asked. "It's awfully tiring. Let's just admit it."

"What?" I felt a cold like needles in my blood as she twisted a piece of dark hair around her finger. Her expression could've pearled an oyster.

"Lev sent you here to get rid of me." Such a simple statement, made so plainly, that I couldn't help but gasp. She smiled, perhaps assuming my shock was a put-on, but it wasn't, really. I knew I was on unsteady ground. She continued. "He thought it was a secret—but please. He can't keep secrets from me. Anyway, I'm not sure how you were thinking to do it. But I know that you won't."

"You do?" Perhaps I should've run right then. Stood up and gotten my coat from inside and hurried to the train station without looking around. It didn't feel possible, though, to walk away. I tried to make my face innocent, tried to turn my resolve to steel. She saw right through me.

"Yes. You're too smart. Or anyway, smart enough. To know a more important offer when you hear one."

"Which is?" I asked.

"Let's talk over dinner. I'm too tired now. I need a bath."

And at that she hefted her light body up and seemed to float into the house, as if having brokered an understanding with gravity. That sometimes, enough was enough.

## 58.

YOU'LL HAVE DOUBTLESS SENSED THE space closing, reader, between where I sit now, writing with my cheap black pen, and where I was, then. A time eclipse. The two moments slowly moving together until a window emerges where like meets like. You can't jump through, but you can at least peek, pressing your face against the glass to feel the heat from fading summer sun.

When I came downstairs, Vera was heating up two cans of chowder on the stove—in honor, she told me, of the *quahogs* (emphasis hers) that had shredded up her feet. The spice of seawater cut through the cream, and a box of soup crackers sat open on the table.

"So you do know how to cook," I said. She raised an eyebrow.

"I wouldn't count this as cooking."

Still I imagined her crouched over a hot plate in Paris, keeping herself and her father fed during moments of crisis. So many ration cards; unclear how the per-card items were selected, but the food always seeming to fit the ticket, through molecular sympathy or some more systematic affinity. God knows I remember from home. Yellow cards for dyed margarine, blue for salt, beige for semi-edible meats. Did she chop the salt pork into bite-sized pieces and fry it up with rice or bread? In our cottage, she stirred the soup and watched me, daring me to ask.

I imagined her, also, in Lev's arms. So small she would disappear into him as he grinned all hot and mad. His face carrying so much aristocracy in the length of the nose, the sullen, heavy eyelids. As she reduced the flame so our chowder wouldn't boil, I watched him unbuttoning her skirt. As she turned to find two clean bowls in the cupboard, I saw him take her from the back, his chin lifting in ecstasy, both of them flushing with the fever of their union. He would bite her lip, as he had sometimes bitten mine; I once bit back, too. His blood tasted different from my own, though they comingled soon enough. (And what was Vera's flavor? Cinnamon sticks grated onto pine? Pennies dipped in tea? If I pricked her finger and swallowed a drop, would she change the essence of me?)

Using her spoon as a baton, Vera directed me to sit down, and I did. Obedient as always. I was also very afraid. Was there a right thing to say now? Was that possible? She placed a bowl of soup before me, and shook the crackers farther down their sleeve so we could pick them out with ease. She nibbled the corner of one, and tested a bite of chowder: still too hot.

"So," she said. "You must be wondering."

"What in god's name you meant? It's crossed my mind." I burned my tongue and throat with one great spoonful, and it took all I had not to gag. Vera was smooth and in her element.

"Let me ask: what did Lev tell you about his trip?"

"Hmm?" I tried to play coy while also nursing my burn. The teatime plan could still work out, if I just got up in the middle of the night to adulterate the sugar bowl. "I barely know him."

"Oh please. It wafts off you like perfume."

I regarded her. Not what Lev and I had expected, but I'd known that would be the case before I set foot on the train. It occurred to me, too late, that I shouldn't have eaten anything she set before me, but my stomach wasn't cramping, and I wasn't shaking, vomiting, passing out. Which seemed like a gesture of good faith. My face dropped some ounce of pretence. "Alright. He told me he went to find the last copy of his book. The one you stole, and burned."

"Stole? That's putting it rather—incorrectly."

"Well, he didn't give it to you to destroy. What would you call it?"

"Saving him." She frowned and blew into her soup. "From himself. God, what a fool."

"Me?"

"That remains to be seen. Tell me this: did you ever read any of the book?"

"How could I?"

"No re-creations? Little bits he'd saved in a journal, or maybe a chapter he'd rewritten?"

I shook my head. I hadn't known any such pieces existed.

"Of course not," Vera said. "Because he understands, deep down, that the book's no good. I'm sure"—and here she raised an eyebrow at me—"he never told you, either, about the times he's thanked me—on his *knees*—for getting rid of it the first time around? No, of course not. It's become too big of a symbol in his head." She put down her spoon in disgust, fidgeting it back and forth on the placemat. "Flag of freedom, bluebird of unhappiness. Never mind that getting rid of that awful book was what let him write real books. That loss, it gave him a career." She exhaled. "My god. He'd ruin us all if given an inch of leash, just to say he ran to hell on his own feet."

I must've looked struck. I opened my mouth, and shut it again as Vera composed herself, tucking a strand of hair behind her ear and then licking her lips. She rarely let much emotion show, but I could see that she was genuinely perturbed from the slight twitch of her mouth, and the way she moved to crack her back as a surreptitious correction to her posture. As if she were just stretching, and not tense, uncoiling and recoiling her muscles. There had been so many moments when I feared losing my nerve, crumbling to basic cowardice. Or perhaps worried about Vera suspecting, and shooting me down with a spell from her eyes, snapping her fingers and pinching shut my windpipe. Magic death. What I hadn't counted on was this: the possibility that Vera would say she was acting for Lev's own good, and that I would think she might be telling the truth.

*How did I get here?* I suddenly wondered. Then thought, *Maybe all of this is crazy.* A little too late. I tried to remember Lev, reassuring me in bed. What it felt like when his fingers were in my hair, one leg sprawled lazily over mine. But instead my mind conjured Vera taking a sip of tea. Skipping a breath. Her hand going up to her throat and her lips turning purple as her pretty eyes bulged. Vomit, maybe, but not enough to make a difference.

"Are you listening?" she asked, and I nodded. "Good. I told you I had an offer, and I do. Better than anything Lev could promise you, one hundred percent guaranteed, because"—this, crisply—"my promises mean something. They are permanent. And I'll make you comfortable as long as you live, just so long as you do as I say." Vera perched her fingertips together in a tent, and rested her chin on the edge of them. Her voice grew quieter, but more focused, like a hose with the nozzle twisted to direct the spray.

"He thinks now that he can escape me, move on. That he needs to. And he's roped you in to the whole endeavor, because god forbid he carry a plan through on his own." She looked at me, noticing my face fall. Didn't quite smirk, but still gave a cool smile. "And I'm sure he's fond of you, too, little bee, why not. But listen. He's going to change his mind. Do you really believe he'll thank you for hurting me? He's nothing without me, and he knows it."

There was, to this, the terrible ring of truth. Her reassurance so pale: *I'm sure he's fond.* Why had I ever believed I could make her afraid of me, take anything from her? This woman who had kept Lev at heel for a decade, this girl who had played every game by her own rules for as long as she'd been alive. Lev traced my jawbone with his fingers, with his tongue. Took me to out-of-town operas and symphony performances where the strength of the music pushed me back in my seat and stunned me into letting his hand creep up my thighs. He told me stories of his wife sweeping into meetings and turning monolithic, dark-suited executives into her playthings. Why had I not noticed, or cared quite enough, how impressed she left him, how helpless? He didn't do anything on his own, anymore, if he ever had: a childhood of riches, a career made golden by the maneuvering of his wife.

But Vera's face was still serious; she wasn't triumphant. If I thought her goal was just to humiliate me, I'd misunderstood what was at stake.

"Do you see what I'm saying?" she asked. "There's something more important here than either you or me. More important than Lev, in a certain sense. Only Leo Orlov matters, really: the writer, and his public face. That's who I've built my life around, god knows. That's who I've *built*." Her fingers curled into a fist, in spite of themselves, which she set down hard on the table to emphasize her point. "Let me tell you."

The truth, according to Vera, was that Lev's beloved first novel was an atrocious failure. It showed promise in its prose, its psychological under-pinnings. But there was nothing in it to take the reader by the hand. He attached to it a romantic importance that it absolutely did not deserve. I felt sick, and said so. She shrugged. "It's juvenilia. And worse than that, it doesn't take any chances. People love Lev's work for its bold moves, and this book—well. It doesn't tell the story about him that we need to tell."

"We, then?"

"Could be *we.*" Vera sipped her soup, which had finally cooled, and crumbled a few crackers in. "I was being sincere, you know, at the beach. I don't have any interest in being remembered. In fact, I'd prefer not to be." She stirred, creating a little gyre in the bowl, and stared into the thick, spinning liquid. "It never did any favors to anyone, being picked over and kept as a memento. History's unkind in that way. Once your life leaves your hands you become—mutable. Susceptible, I suppose you might say, to anyone with an axe to grind or a tale to tell. I'd rather stay myself."

Vera frowned then, as if she knew she was straying off course, away from the inviolable Leo Orlov she meant to invoke. But she pressed on. "Lev's shadow has always kept me hidden, and let me do my real work behind the scenes. For a long time he was perfectly happy with that arrangement, because it meant he got the spotlight to himself. But now he's changed his mind." She looked at me, not quite accusing. "What he doesn't understand is that if he interrupts one part of the narrative I've set into motion, he could ruin it all—one small change and everything comes into play. Even me. And I won't have that." It was funny. She claimed not to have any personal ambition, but her goals struck me as godlike, transcendent: to be invisible, yes, but in the way of an elemental force, wind or geology. The movement of the earth beneath your feet.

*What happened to her when she left Moscow?* I wondered. Rolling her eyes through her tutoring sessions, translating expat literature in her free time, and then—nothing? It was hard to imagine her fading into black until Lev arrived to give her direction. A sparkling girl, a talented dancer, who could turn her horse at four-foot jumps and land without a bump in the saddle. A clever girl, surrounded in her youth by so many books she never bothered to count them. Tolstoy, Gogol, Chekhov, Dumas. So many ideas moving round in her brain; did she really never pick up a pen? "Vera." I reached out to grab her hand, but thought better of it, and just tapped her. The contact resonated up my bones, like the shattering of sound from a gong. She kept so many secrets. "Lev's books. You didn't *write* them, did you?" My face was hot with the shame—treason, really—of asking this question, but I had to know. Her eyes flashed.

"No." She snatched her arm away. "*No.* Lev is a great writer. There can't be any doubt." Vera of the deepest privacy, Vera of the darkest truth. "Listen, I don't want that. I don't want his credit. I just want to make sure he can't erase what I've spent *my* life doing. He doesn't get both." The house creaked around us, expanding and contracting with the stuttering cadence of a yawn. Vera looked at me from the corner of her eye. A confiding look, I guess you'd call it. "Of course, if I had, they'd say he wrote them anyway. So what would be the point of that?" I leaned in, hoping for more, but already she was settling into herself, cooling off. "Women," she said, with a little laugh. "The quieter we are, the less we're seen? The more we get done."

Small details in the room felt rich with meaning I couldn't read: the brass of the teakettle, the single cupboard left ajar. Of course, I was the one making them symbolic, but there was a strange power in that. "I want to make sure Lev's memory is established now," Vera said into the quiet, "so no one can change it too much when he's gone." Nor her memory, I suppose she thought. But in this she was wrong. You can change empty space. You can write on a blank page. It's the easiest thing in the world.

## 59.

WE SAT AT THE TABLE, SCRAPING OUR bowls long after our soup was gone.

"The fact is," she said, "he needs to go. For his own good. Before he can hurt himself much more. The story of him going after the manuscript is actually perfect, so long as he doesn't succeed in digging it out. Great golden goose lost in the bloody historical bowels. Buried treasure without a map. Lost art." She looked thoughtful. "If he's got it, you'll have to burn it."

"But the book," I said. "I don't know if I could. What makes you think I *would*?"

"You came here to save it. You can leave to save it too. You just need a new way of thinking about safety, don't you? And besides." She picked something up off the chair beside her. A stack of papers. Some of them letters, but also a manuscript tied with twine. "I didn't actually burn my copy. I just hid it from him. He probably could've found it if he looked, but for an artist he doesn't have a very inquisitive mind. If it comes out twenty, thirty years from now, no one will try to pretend it's a new novel. They'll see it as an archive. A youthful folly. Which it is." She pushed the stack over to me. "I thought you might need convincing, so I brought you this. Go ahead and read it. Then make up your mind."

"He needs," I stammered, "to go?" Without him I had nothing. The book, the man, the whole world was slipping through my fingers. Every kiss he might have given me, erased. Every minute of our future abolished. The dreams we had shared becoming nothing more than that: dreams, drifting away upon waking. My body began crumbling in on itself as under-standing overtook me, my face puckering lemon-like and my arms hugging round my chest so tight they ached. I thought that Vera looked too calm, but maybe she wasn't. Once or twice she wiped at her eye, brushing away the tears that didn't come.

"Little bee," she said. "You know what I mean. I've got my passport with me, my father's flat in Paris, when the time comes. I'm going to take you, of course, give you something brand new. But first you have to see this all through to the end." All business now, she nudged the stack again in my direction. "We'll meet back here once everything's done, and in the mean-time I'll make sure I'm seen here in town. There's a decent enough hotel for me to check in to, and no one will think to ask about you."

"About me? But how will I do it?"

"You'll think of something. Like I said, you're smart." She smiled. "That's why I like you."

"You said that before." I could hear the whine of fear in my voice, but couldn't stop it. "What in god's name makes you think so?"

Vera pushed her chair away from the table and stood. She was so petite, and yet she seemed to be made of heavier material than me, the gravity in the room all pulling towards her.

"I don't show very much of myself," she said. "I know that. You can see more than most. Maybe you look harder."

And with that she turned and left me alone with only Lev's too-familiar handwriting for company, hovering around me like a ghost.

## 60.

HE SAID HE COULDN'T WRITE TO ME, because the risk was just too much. I accepted this. His absence, his silence. As I had accepted every part of him into me, each molecule, piece and parcel. The way his ears declared themselves, and his hands defined my body. Here the thumb curves over the shoulder, here the finger flicks the nipple. Eloquent elements. Lev told me he loved me, and I had no reason to doubt it, especially considering how much I loved him. Even the first day we met, hot sweat on his brow, chasing a young girl through the trees. Crashing out of the foliage like a monster in a story.

Of course, because I loved his mind, I treasured every word he said. The ideas he came up with: our fated communion. "Everyone I ever loved was leading up to you." When we were naked, he was most loquacious, explaining our future and our past. The cosmic us-ness. He once took a razor blade and cut his name onto my arm, high up and on the underside. Not a thing that could quite heal.

All night I sat up at the table with a fat lamp and a pot of coffee, reading. First, Lev's letters: he hadn't sent a word to me, but he'd written Vera. Constantly, it seemed. Hasty letters on whatever slips of paper could be scavenged in the hounded towns Lev crawled through on his way to the border. I'd seen his notes to her before, but these had a new urgency to them, a desire to contain within them their whole life together. Trap it under glass. Perhaps he intended to make time stand still, but of course that was impossible. You could feel him, in the letters, plummeting through, even as he tried to hold on to every straw and scrap. Only to her, he wrote. Only to her. The coffee hurt my stomach and I spent an hour in the bathroom, voiding everything I could from my body. Still ending up with much too much.

The manuscript felt like a holy thing, compared. Pages curled up at the corners, paper frail. As I untied the twine a shower of dust fell as the fibers crumbled. I knew what Vera had said: it was a failure, a flop. But my hands shook as I set the title page aside; beneath, the ink was still glossy and sharp. *Untitled,* by Leo Orlov. The lost novel. The book that had started it all. I made another pot of coffee and settled in.

*Once upon a time there was a kingdom made of cardboard and glue.*

It was—a difficult experience to describe. There were moments when I felt the ghosts of my past rise around me, plucking at my clothing, tugging my hair. Kissing me straight on the lips. Exhaust rising from the Moscow streets, long lines at every corner grocery, the tyranny of the butcher shop choosing who they'd allow to buy. Sometimes there were lines to nowhere: you'd turn a corner and see a row of people outside some stucco monstrosity, and when you asked what they were waiting for they all gave different answers. A babushka saying, *"R'iba,"* fish. A little girl, holding yarn while her mother knitted, who suggested blocks of baking chocolate instead. An old man, visibly drunk, just repeating *"Xhlieb, xhlieb,"* as if incantating the bread would bring it to his hands.

There were those beautiful moments of feeling home. And then there were the rest.

## 61.

VERA FOUND ME IN THE MORNING EXACTLY as she'd left me the night before, curled up on an uncomfortable wooden chair and looking like the child of death. My face was less grim than sallow now, drawn and green from lack of sleep and the gnawing pain behind my breastbone. Heartbreak, I guess you might call it.

"So," she said, efficient. "You'll do it."

"I will," I agreed. Why did I say it? Because she was right, I suppose, and because she had always had what I did not. At a certain point it was hard not to feel like that was because she deserved it all more. Lev's body, Lev's future, his pledge of allegiance—Vera had taken all that in hand while I was still a schoolgirl, trailing Margaret like a baby duck. She had built something beautiful enough for me to fall in love with, so how could I refuse to help her protect it? Even brutally. Even mortally. Vera didn't ask me anything then, just bustled around the kitchen setting up breakfast. Not really cooking, still: we ate sliced fruit and drank the coffee cold from the pot. She did humor me by toasting our bread in the stove, as I'd suggested, though it came out just as burned from our misjudgment. That morning she was wearing a green blouse and pedal pushers, an almost American silhouette, except for the way her hair was set and her eyes so serious. I wanted to go and close them with a tender touch, mainly to stop them from looking at me with quiet triumph. Today had been my internal deadline, the time by which I should've carried out my (Lev's) plan. Which would've meant putting on gloves and moving her body in such a way as to make it look natural and suicidal. Her face held in one palm, on the table. Her shoes off, for comfort, but set nearby with care and an eye for the ordered tableau. It was windy but warm, and occasionally hard fronds of something banged against the doors and windows. Easier to imagine the aftermath than the act itself: my hair blowing into my eyes as I tugged my suitcase outside for the walk into town, which I had planned to undertake in lieu of ordering a taxi.

"You agree," Vera said. She was seated across from me, eating her toast, and she narrowed her eyes as she put the words into my mouth. "It's important that you agree that what we're doing is for the best. You'll need your strength." She had told me the night before that if he'd brought the book home, I'd have to destroy it. Just one more thing to take apart: burn it to ashes. She had fewer suggestions as regarded Lev. "You'll need your conviction."

Hadn't I had this conversation before? The two of them were more similar than I'd had cause to know. Though maybe that was just my stubborn pride. Lev had told me often enough of the bound souls, the twinned core, the psychic line that ran between them, which I took for so much hyperbole. That people could be made for one another, each one wrought in paradox from the rib of their mate. Though I believed him easily enough when he said the same of me.

"It isn't very good," I allowed. I'd re-bound the manuscript, re-tucked the flaps of every envelope. A touch unnecessary to show me all of those letters; surely one would have sufficed to make the point. "It has its moments, though."

"I never said he wasn't a genius. It's just that he refuses to see that people care about your life, once you let them into it. He thinks he can do whatever he wants and that things will just—work themselves out. I suppose I'm to blame for teaching him that."

"And you think history will forget? This? What you're asking?"

"I couldn't possibly guess. But I know it wouldn't forget a story like Lev's grand adventure leading up to a disappointment of these proportions." True enough. I imagined the newspapers: starting with an affectionate blaze and then fizzling out in polite, confused reviews. The wilting of him—after *Felice* he got terribly vain—his sickening jaunty laugh turned into a painful cry. The worst part being the way he'd think: *She was right. She was always right.*

Whereas if he died the narrative would change to a tragic man and his great lost work. Sales of his existing books would soar. People would love him to the point of distraction.

"So you're not angry about what he sent me here to do?"

She didn't flinch. Maybe twitched, at the corner of her eye, though she could also have been blinking away a spot of sand. The house was full of it.

"I've survived worse things than this" was all that she would say on the subject.

## 62.

THE TRAIN RIDE HOME WAS DIFFERENT from the ride to Twisted Branch had been. My car was almost empty, just me and an old codger sitting at the other end, periodically hacking up some ball of phlegm and spitting it into a handkerchief. I was far enough from him that I could try, at least, to ignore the sound, and sleep pressed up against the window. When the conductor woke me to say we'd arrived, I had a red circle emblazoned on my forehead. No matter how I combed my hair it was visible, and only the adults at the station were too polite to point and stare. Children are wonderfully honest in that way. I'm learning to enjoy honesty now, when I see it in others, since it hasn't been my life's foremost principle.

The town of Maple Hill seemed changed. More warble, I suppose, and fewer straight lines. This could also have been the effect of temperature: we were experiencing a heat wave, and all around town there were toddlers eating ice pops to keep from overheating. I saw quite a few on my unsteady walk home, with lips of yellow, purple, green. I realized I'd never had a Popsicle myself, and paid five cents for one at the drug store, though they were reluctant to sell it to a grown woman with so many young lives on the putative line. I think the flavor was cherry; it made my tongue numb.

In a daze, I made it to my house and fell onto the bed and into a dead slumber. When I woke up it was dusk, the fireflies starting to wink on over the lawn. Where was I? I wondered. But I was in my own room. Had I ever really been to the ocean? Looming waves, shadows in the dunes. For a hot and horrible second I couldn't recognize my limbs, not hands nor legs nor feet nor arms nor elbows. Like waking up beside a stranger, but—inside.

It wasn't until the next day that I ventured out of the house. Lev was still gone, and would be for at least two weeks, based on what he'd told me before he left. Until then I had no choice but to wander around my life as though I still belonged in it. I made occasional trips past his darkened house, but otherwise, everything was normal. I trimmed the hydrangea bushes into perfect cheery spheres, and reorganized the watering lines with manic attention to detail. I made a goulash. John invited me to dinner, just like old times, and I tried my best to have fun as he and Siobhan plied me with wine and did impressions of the faculty wives.

"And then there's the cold one," Siobhan said. "It's only once I've even seen her, and she was like an ice statuette, the kind you make with a pick."

"Oh, the writer's wife." John guffawed, then pinched his lips real thin and tried to look hawkish. "Hello. Nice to meet you. No, I don't think I've said my name." Except he fleshed out all his *h*s and *e*s: Hhhallo. Nice to myeet.

After clearing the dishes he sat beside me on the couch and asked what was wrong. I wasn't a naturally contented person, so something serious must've shown. Siobhan gave a tight nod at my miserable face.

"She has a fellow. Finally."

"You two been talking?" John asked, but his wife shook her head.

"Can just see it. Aren't I right, Zo?"

"Had, maybe," I said. "Not anymore."

"Oh, no. Either he'll come to his senses, or he wasn't worth the trouble."

"I guess."

"No, really. He should be so lucky. To go out with you? You're to die for, honey."

A few minutes later I took my leave into the dark evening so I could go cry and feel sorry for myself. I didn't want to play their guessing game about who the fellow might have been ("I'll knock some good taste into him," John offered, looking offended. "Just give me a name.") and I certainly didn't think I deserved their pity. But moreover, there was the obvious sense that we were inhabiting two different planes of existence. Two different worlds. In one, nice girls had their feelings trampled on while looking for a marriageable man. And in the other—which is to say, mine—the missions were darker, more complex, and infinitely more real.

# An Oral History of Vera Orlov, née Volkov, cont'd

*Recorded by the Maple Hill Police Department*

### THE REVEREND FATHER ALBERT PETERFFY

"I WAS INTRODUCED TO MRS. ORLOV in early July at the Grande Chez Hotel in Twisted Branch, New Jersey—I think our first interaction was a private joke she made to me at the front desk, about the name of the hotel. 'Even when they try to appreciate the old world, they do it improperly,' she said, and I agreed. The concierge looked flustered, as well he must've been—you see, she was speaking in French, and I don't think he understood. Not sure how she knew I would. Spent time in Compiègne during the war, providing relief to our boys, and perhaps I just have that look about me now.

"But yes, we spoke again. Principally because she had me booted from my room! They put me on the top floor, and I guess she tossed up a bit of a fuss about her view, and when they asked I didn't really mind moving. She hadn't realized I was the one she was kicking out (or anyway, that's what she told me), and offered to buy me a conciliatory cocktail, which—you don't say no to a drink with such an interesting lady when you get to my age.

"In the dining room, when I sat down, she already had a glass of wine for herself and a scotch for me, and she was twisting a golden chain between her fingers. Beautiful manicure, but a distant expression. Thought I must've done something to upset her, but she said no, no. Thought she was tired, but she said no, no. I wanted to put her at ease, so I asked her to tell me about herself, and she gave me this *look*—well, my parish is quite wealthy, so I see a lot of *looks*, but this was about the chilliest expression I've ever encountered. Like a thimble of ice water right into the blood.

"Then—well. Mrs. Orlov began absolutely *interrogating* me about God. About God! Not what I expected from a casual drink, I must say. I'd have guessed she was more the type to think "priest" is a political role, like "town selectman." But she jumped right in: transmigration, transubstantiation, the Holy Trinity. Some of her opinions were quite distinctive. Can't remember specifics offhand, but she wanted me to reassure her that the soul cannot be tampered with, that loss and change and external perception are not stronger than the force of the spirit. I thought I knew what she was getting at—her accent, you know. She spoke like a refugee. So I asked once again, if there was any story she could share about her youth, her childhood. Something she was fond of telling. But she just smiled. Said she met her husband at a party, that he tweaked the host's nose and she thought—maybe. She told me he was playful, if not exactly a man of great conviction. I'm not sure I really put her mind at ease.

"When we finished our drink I invited her to accompany me on a tour of the boardwalk the next day, but she declined. Didn't see her much after that. Just nodded hello if we came across one another in the halls, or raised a glass in the dining room from separate tables. Then one day she was gone. Checked out, I suppose. Though they certainly didn't offer to move me back to the penthouse. [*he snorts*] Grande Chez Hotel. [*Notes indicate that the Reverend Father was asked to clarify the dates of his encounter with Mrs. Orlov.*] Oh, I'm fairly sure about the dates. I always keep my receipts, from travel and the like. So yes, I'd estimate she was in Twisted Branch for that entire space of time. Couldn't possibly have made a trip back to— where was it? Maple Hill? No. At least, I can't imagine how."

# Zoya

## 63.

A COUPLE OF WEEKS LATER I WOKE up from a terrible dream without remembering almost any of it. Something about sitting on a platform that raised and lowered in the air. Or—a flying carpet? I could only keep it aloft by counting up and down from ten. It was the counting that woke me. *Onetwothreefourfivesixseveneight* . . . The sun was up, but not by much, and my blankets were heavy with sweat.

I'd slept on the greenhouse floor, using a skinny mattress John had procured for me a year or so earlier so I could camp out during the cold snaps. It rolled up easily, and most of the time we stored it in the shed outside; it was musty and uncomfortable. I hadn't used the thing since winter, as there wasn't much point in the nicer months. But I couldn't seem to sleep alone in my house anymore. My thoughts banged off the walls, smashed into me in bed. Shadows crawled around. In the greenhouse at least I had the company of the plants, and the comfort of their warm and even exhalations. I tied the mattress up tight and set it in the corner, not wanting to be caught out by John, and positioned myself in front of a fan to cool off. I smelled of chicken bones boiling into stock. Sleep reek.

The fan didn't work. Too much heat, or maybe not enough air. I'd had trouble pulling deep breaths lately, too. I picked a hose with a gentle spray nozzle and turned it on myself, the water cold. A mist in my face, on my arms, on my nightshirt. The light cotton clung to my chest, and I sprayed the back of my neck, letting water stream down my spine and into my underwear. Down to my feet. I stood on a grate in the concrete floor, and watched the nightmare wash off me. It looked like nothing, but I knew.

I thought about Lev. His hands all over me, arranging me like putty. His mouth on my neck. I gave a little moan. Then something banged against the door. *Not again*, I thought. I turned off the hose and ran outside, ready to confront some naughty child. But of course there was none. It wasn't even seven in the morning, and instead I found myself face to face with George Round.

"Oh," he said. "Zoe, isn't it?"

"Hello, sir." I crossed my arms over my chest and pressed my knees together. "Good morning."

"Yes, a very pleasant one. I was just taking a stroll before heading into the office. Early meetings you know, they'll be the death of me. And, may I ask—?" He stopped, seeming to reconsider his question. "Is there some problem with the greenhouse?"

"No. Well. Yes, but, no. I mean, sometimes I sleep here during extreme weather. To make sure nothing goes wrong."

"Extreme weather."

"Yes, sir."

"Awfully nice day for it."

"Actually it was rather hot inside."

George Round looked at me, then politely averted his gaze. I didn't feel him searching in me for what men usually found, but this had the odd effect of making me feel more seen. "I don't think I need to tell you this is rather strange."

"No, sir."

"When I heard a sound inside, I thought there was a vandal. Or—you know, teenagers. That's why I came to check."

I wasn't sure he'd be able to see me flush, given the water, the light. How loud had I been? Lev's hands, on every part of me.

"Listen," he said. "Just don't let me find you here again like this. I would hate for anything to complicate your position at the school."

"Of course." I couldn't meet his eye. "Thank you."

The problem, I realized once he'd left, wasn't the shame. My time at the Donne School was winding down in any case, so what did it matter if someone thought I was a little crazy? Unwholesome? I was going to kill a man. In the cottage, though, Vera had laughed and said no one would think to question me when Lev was gone, because I was just the flower girl. Invisible on campus, illegible within his life. Any investigation would pass right over me: true enough until the moment I called attention to myself, streaking half-naked out onto the lawn. There wasn't an enormous chance that George Round would put the two events together. But there was, now, a chance.

I dressed hastily in the previous day's clothes and started home to make tea; I'd gone off coffee since my night of reading at the cottage table. On the way I decided to take a quick detour into the nicer neighborhoods around campus, telling myself it was just for the pleasure of walking under the tall leafy trees, the dappled shade. Everyone was sleeping and so life seemed suspended. Birds trapped in a mailbox: I'd had that idea, once. There was a single abandoned roller skate on the sidewalk that I nudged into a flowerbed with my toe-tip, sliding it back and forth over the rough concrete before letting it go. Orange rubber, invisible in the nasturtiums. Then I was at Lev's door.

The surprise wasn't my presence. It was his. A part of me had been certain he wouldn't ever show up, would just have melted away. But. I floated up the front steps expecting the same dark rooms and empty sense that the house had exuded since my return to Maple Hill. And instead found—blazing light. Every room in the house was at peak brightness, and through the window I saw a halfway unrecognizable man standing up in front of a desk and writing something (what?) that filled him with horror. Lev. His cheekbones hollow and nose rather beaky. The lips I'd so missed red and white with chap, to such a degree they seemed to be covered with pith from an orange. His clothes were askew, his beard growing in, and when I knocked on the window his eyes searched for the sound without seeming able to find my face. It spooked me, I'll admit. There was a long moment of terror for us both, until I realized that the lamps were casting a reflection, making it impossible for him to see through the glass.

I went to the door and knocked with both hands, more a beating than an entreaty—I had to stop myself from scratching the paint. *Now, it's now,* I thought. Hating the thinking. When Lev opened the door I threw myself into his arms and kissed him once, twice, again, until we tumbled into the middle of the house to the space behind the stairs and pressed our bodies together with the desperation of two people with irreconcilable ideas about what could heal our wounds.

## 64.

AFTERWARDS, LEV SEEMED NERVOUS. He lit a cigarette and smoked it halfway before thinking to light another for me. I hadn't had a single one since leaving Vera, so the first several inhalations went to my head, leaving me woozy. Lev pressed the back of his wrist to his brow and then shook it away when the cigarette embers came too close to his skin.

"Did you?" he asked me. "Did it go off?"

I had decided several days before what to say.

"Not exactly. She never showed up at the train."

"Oh, thank god. You know, she wrote to say the trip was on but I . . ." He trailed off. I followed him into the kitchen for water, then up to his bedroom where he unrolled a gun from a silk scarf and laid it on the bed. "I shot someone," he said. "In Leningrad. She was a woman and I . . ." He shook his hand again and sparks scattered onto the carpet. I discreetly stubbed them out with my shoe, then left my own cigarette in an ashtray.

"Lev, what happened? Did you get the book?"

"You know," he went to the window and leaned against the sill. "I was excited when she told me about your plans, but then I got to thinking, I don't know, I don't know."

"She? Who? In Leningrad?"

"Oh, *her*." He laughed shrilly. "You want to know about her? Well, yes, I did it, you see. Almost. I got all the way to the station—I mean the station where it was buried, and it was nighttime, and it was dark out, and I thought, this is the best chance I'm going to have. But damn them, they'd paved over the spot, or"—his voice was hoarse—"or else I forgot where it was."

I sat down on the bed. Thinking of how he would've approached that place with perfect confidence. Did he even want to find it? Did he really care about the book, the way he said? Or did he just want to prove to himself that he could do something Vera didn't want done? *Give him an inch of leash*, she'd told me. "We were happy, weren't we?" I asked. "We could've just carried on. It didn't need to be everything, all at once." But I don't think he heard me.

"I had this idiotic shovel, I mean a *hand spade*," Lev muttered. "I mean, even if it weren't for the paving how deep could I have gotten? After how many years? Vera knew. Vera always knows. And I thought—" He turned to me, desperate. "You didn't, did you? Tell me she's alive."

"As far as I know, Lev. She wasn't there."

"Of course, of course." He looked down at his hands, wringing them. The way a raccoon washes and washes a piece of food in its fist, or some little gem it's picked up off the road. "Of course I couldn't leave it like that, so I picked a spot—I mean, I think it was the right spot—and I started trying to chip away at the cement. But it was so loud. There were actual sparks coming up where I hit." He went silent for a moment.

"And the woman?"

"Vlad, he was my guide you know, and he kept hushing me. *Tishe, tishe.* And I kept stabbing at the ground, right above where I thought it was, right towards where the book should be. And then someone came along and"—his eyes were moons, so big they scared me—"she was, I don't know, *militsia*? Secret police? But so young."

I picked up the pistol from beside me and tested the weight of it in my hand. Lev didn't seem to notice. In that moment I had no plan. He was the love of my life, you see. Fumbling towards some truth too terrible to be spoken out loud. *I kissed Daphne behind the library. You and Vera, you're exactly the same.*

"She shouted at me to put down my weapon, and I don't know—I guess she thought the sparks were something else, but she pulled out her gun and I threw down the spade, and when the sound distracted her, I—"

The shot was more than I expected. It pushed me back onto the bed and hurt my arm, leaving my ears ringing. Lev didn't shout, and for a second I thought I'd missed. But you can't miss at that range. He was four feet away at most, and it went through right under his left shoulder, and the bleeding was profuse. Tears streamed down my face, and I waited for him to say something, but he just coughed. A few drops of blood spraying out and then trickling down from his mouth as he looked at me with bemusement. Or maybe it was dreadful pain.

I dropped the gun and thought, *You have to go, you have to go right now.* But I sat there and watched him slide down to the floor and stare his questions and confusion at me, wordless. Then I went to crouch by him, at what I judged to be the last, and brought his fingers to my lips and kissed them. I could've said "It was her idea," and given him some final measure of satisfaction, but I wanted it to be us, just us again, in that room. Still, perhaps he guessed.

I didn't say good-bye. There wasn't any point. I wandered out into the street and found no one poking their head out to see what was wrong. Such a distinctive sound, a gunshot, but I suppose the neighbors all thought what they wanted to think: that a car had backfired, and they ought to get a few more minutes of sleep.

Was this the logical conclusion of hoping Lev's books would live forever? To launch him into time immemorial, where he would with tenderness caress the lives of so many women and men, whatever their troubles? The man they needed, who would bring to them books, stories. Of a girl with wings, to soar above the clean blue of the world. A girl named Felice whose little claws would grip at twig and twine and whose body would twist and dance in the air—vainglorious in her triumph, weightless in her happiness—the way they dreamed they someday might.

At home I put a few things in my bag, which had been sitting out since I got back from the seashore. I washed my hands, scrubbing off the rime of oil from the pistol so I wouldn't have to smell it. Then I walked to the train station and sat in the sun and waited for the ten-thirty express, watching with some remorse the types of bouquets men bought at the kiosk for their wives or mistresses. Unimaginative. Hardly half-inspired. I could've given them something so much better, if only things were different for us all.

# A Morning of Mourning

From the *Maple Hill Reporter*, July 11, 1931

MAPLE HILL, NJ. THE RESIDENTS OF Elizabeth Glen, a neighborhood in the center of town, were shocked yesterday morning to discover a murder in their own backyards. Leo Orlov, a teacher at the elite Donne School for Girls and renowned author of such works as the internationally bestselling *Felice* and the novels *Impresario* and *Sun Sort*, was found in his bedroom with a gunshot wound to the chest. No suspects have been identified at this time, but the police have confirmed that the novelist's wife, Vera Orlov (née Volkov), was absent at the time of the shooting, and that her current whereabouts are unknown.

"It's a very safe neighborhood," said local Sadie Kensington, who lives in Elizabeth Glen with her husband, Daryl, and two children, Samuel (6) and Denise (3). "This really makes you wonder though, what do you not know about people?" The *Reporter* will publish updates on the situation as it unfolds.

# *Zoya*

## 65.

ARE YOU EXCITED TO KNOW WE'VE ARRIVED? Or nearly so, at the moment of collision between present and past. It's quiet while I wait for Vera to return from the grocery store, where she's probably flirting with the checkout boy in that obscure way of hers. They like it very much, though she never smiles.

Sitting here, I have the almost constant urge to stand up and take myself back to the greenhouse, if only to reassure myself that it's all still there. Go about my chores. Check the moisture underneath the summer blooms, perhaps cut a bouquet of zinnias and phlox. Set them in a vase of cool water. I haven't been gone long, but it already feels like forever. I worry about when I last rotated the banana tree, and whether John will be able to tell when it needs to be moved to a brighter exposure. I would love to kiss my mother good-bye, ask my father what he did and why it was so dangerous. Ask him whether, in the end, it's really better to be happy or to be good. What he'd choose for me now, after all that's happened. All that's still to come.

I think about John, too. Imagine him leaning on the door, picking mud out of his boot with a stick, ready to pull me into a hug and tell me—well, at least to say good-bye. I know I can't stay, but I'd like to see him, even from a distance. The sunburned top of his head where he won't admit he's balding. The round pouch of his belly and the fibrous bubble of his nose. Dear man, he thought he knew me well.

## 66.

WHEN I GOT BACK TO THE COTTAGE, IT was empty. Quite according to plan: we'd agreed that Vera would join me when she saw the notice in the paper, and until then I would wait. A few days alone, no great hardship. The kitchen was stocked with tins of soup and boxes of ready-made, easy-bake, cut-and-dried concoctions. I wouldn't starve, and I wouldn't leave. That first day I spent a lot of time opening cabinets and taking inventory. There was only one kind of beans (kidney) but there were twenty cans of them, and in the cupboard above the stove I found a selection of very nice teas. Milk in the refrigerator as well as some fruit, though the apples were yellow and shriveled, the size of a child's fist.

For a while I walked around the living room, tracing the coiled pattern of the rug with my footsteps. The center moving outward, or maybe the opposite. It was dirty, grime having worn in between the layers and settled there, no matter how much they tried to beat it out. An heirloom kind of thing that someone must've made by hand, which would take weeks of work and a sack full of rags, old baby clothes and retired dress shirts and tablecloths. People wrapped bodies in rugs sometimes, I thought, wasn't that right? Then I tried to shake the thought away. It—the rug—probably just came from a craft fair in some old Shaker town, a throughway full of antiques and collectibles. It was designed to look beloved, but that kind of thing could always be had at the right price, in this country: the life you wanted, or at least the appearance of it. Finally I kicked the rug aside and went to the fireplace to try my hand at opening the flue.

Vera had thoughtfully left me several books for entertainment, but I wasn't able to read much. Mostly I wrote down everything I knew, everything I remembered, and when I was tired I walked along the seashore. I got used to the way cold water seeped into the soles of my shoes, so they made my feet chilly even after I'd left the beach, just as I got used to having sand in my hair. My bed is small, with starched white sheets, and there's sand all throughout it. I can't decide if I brought it in on my body, or if my body was, by lying down, polluted. It doesn't matter. What's done is done.

It took three days for the local paper to print the story, or at least it took three for the notice to reach Vera at her hotel in Twisted Branch. Midway through, it occurred to me that I had no assurance that she was in Twisted Branch at all: there are a number of adjacent towns, some closer to Maple Hill, some farther away. She could've just left, and I wouldn't have been able to do anything about it. All I had was her promise that we would have a new life in Paris, and that was supposed to be enough.

I spent those three days in increasing agony, crumpling the useless newspapers up into kindling after I'd paged through them. Three days of opening a book and then closing it again, washing the same pan every evening and hoping my stomach wouldn't feel too bad after another meal of beans. Then one afternoon the knob twisted on the front door, and it opened, and there she was. I do think she stayed by the ocean at least, since she's got a fresh spattering of freckles across her nose, and a pink-ness beneath: pink, like the rim of a mouse's eye. When she arrived she embraced me, and I could've sworn she'd grown much larger, her face all high and distant with a light that shone behind. She kissed me on the edge of my lips, and I felt the burn of it for some time afterwards.

She was very solicitous. She drew a hot bath and placed me in it, rubbing peppermint soap all up and down my back and asking me questions about how I left him. Were there smudges from my mouth on a cup? (Lipstick on cigarette.) Did I wipe the gun clean of fingerprints? (Hardly.) Did I touch him at all? (Entirely.) She wanted me to know that I was perfectly safe with her, though when I started to cry, heaving and phleg-matic, she didn't like it. I grabbed her wrist and she pulled it away, splashing water across the floor.

It's been a week since then. Most days, Vera seems satisfied. She floats from room to room flexing her fingers, as if new and uncomfortable strength was flowing into them. The way a child's legs hurt in a growth spurt. She's been making lists with an increasing frenzy, phone calls to her travel agent that she doesn't let me hear. I stay out of her way in my room or walking on the beach, and sometimes when I come back in I notice that a page I've been writing on has moved, though naturally this could be my imagination. Vera hasn't yet explained her plan for getting me out of the country, since I told her it would be a risk to use my pass-port. If they have any notion about what I've done, they'll be watching for me. She says I worry too much.

Sometimes when I walk into the room where's she's planning, thinking, I can feel myself crawling like a beetle over the bones of her hand. If she realized I was there, she would shake me onto the ground and she would crush me. But how can I help letting her know? It's in the nature of my trivial feet, my clicking wings. Generally if she sees me lurking, she calls me over and asks me to make tea. Which is companionable enough. But sometimes, too, she looks at me like I am dinner.

## 67.

ALL IT WOULD TAKE IS A SINGLE PHONE call: *Yes, Officer, I did notice the girl had an unnatural attachment to my husband. Of course I would appreciate being left out of the questioning, but I can tell you where she'll be at such and such time, on such and such day. I'll be heading out of the country. A period of mourning. You understand.*

I could be inventing things. But in my experience a terrible feeling is usually followed by a terrible act. I used to think if I followed the rules, every new set, I'd get to the end of the rainbow, the end of the line. Now I think I'd do better to make my own rules. It's what everyone else does.

## 68.

MAYBE YOU'RE CONCERNED ABOUT ME, dear reader. Don't be. Vera will be back from the store soon, and in the meantime I've tried on several of her dresses, plus a blouse, and that pair of work pants she wore to the jetty café. Turns out they were rolled up because they're much too long for her, which is lucky; we aren't the same size, but it's mostly a problem of length and height. I can button her nice wool skirts around my waist with ease. (Not eating well lately has helped. I've dropped five pounds, maybe ten. Dinners of oyster crackers. No matter.) They fall to just above the knee, instead of mid-calf as I'd prefer. But I only have to manage for a little while.

It's easy to want what you do not have: I would know. My life has been a study in this. In Moscow I saw girls with fox-fur coats, and when I say girls I mean ten years old. Though what I really wanted was not the coats, but the feeling of a small creature tucked around my throat. The feeling that, if I could not control the weather, at least I could gather a group of mammalian ushers to shield me from the harshest wind. I wanted my dreams to come true, even the ones I could only describe as colors or sensations. Yes, I wanted power.

The wind is high today; chilly for midsummer. Vera always overextends herself at the store, and will be wanting a cup of tea. The cabin's rent is paid through the end of the month, though of course that will soon become irrelevant.

I asked her: Don't you need to go back to Maple Hill? Not just to talk to the police and show them you're grieving (which I assume, or assume she could put on like a jacket; tears for the camera), but to gather your possessions and make an inventory? Their house was not enormous, but it was nice. There were wedding photos on the walls, Vera radiant in her white gown. She told me she has everything she needs. That she spoke by phone with a very sympathetic detective, and can withdraw cash with just a signature. She's good at letting things go, I guess. Her father passed away a long time ago; he couldn't manage the transition, postwar, and took his own life, leaving her his empty apartment in the fourteenth arrondissement, which has gone quite fashionable in the years since Lev and Vera left. *The police?* She snorted. *The police will be no trouble at all.*

In Paris she'd be *une veuve jolie,* a beautiful mourner. Black crêpe, black polished shoes, *la pauvre femme en deuil.* There would be no reason to stop her at passport control, as she isn't the official object of any investigation, and if she meets with a Parisian police inspector, that will be her duty fulfilled. If she becomes a benefactor to the Donne School, they'll lean on the local sheriff to avoid any line of questioning that places her under suspicion. That's what she says, and I believe her. She walks so confidently.

It's a step you can pick up, with care, a little like imitating a person's voice on the phone. I've made a study of her notes on Lev's manuscripts, which she didn't think to destroy along with her letters, and can now do a passable version of her handwriting.

I couldn't save much of Lev's, in the end. Not for myself. His gifts felt empty of him (presents without presence, kind without kin), so I left them behind in Maple Hill, where perhaps they'll act as clues or links between us. Twenty dollars spent on gold; a bangle abandoned in a gardener's apartment. What I did save was a folded envelope, and the tablets sliding back and forth inside. Powder held safe from the elements, lying in wait. Vera was the most glowing one of us, the kind of woman God makes as an example to the rest. *Here*, you can imagine Him saying, *is a life worth living.* A life of modesty and steam. *There will always be a Vera,* I assured myself, *one way or another.* With a dark rinse, I think our hair will look quite similar. She sets it to the side, in a style that's easy enough to replicate with the right number of pins.

My mother told me to take cues from my betters. Learn their habits, and track them like deer in a live wood. Keep watch of their movements, and, if it helps, imagine you've tied a line of bright yarn to one ankle to make their path clear. Vera puts two spoonfuls of sugar in her tea before even sipping. She and I share a soul, or so Lev insisted. Why not share a little more? I found out yesterday when she went to town for a bottle of wine that she doesn't carry her passport with her, nor check it for safety upon her return. Easy enough to move it into a clean purse, where I will slide her wallet too. Take her wedding ring from around her finger, though I doubt it will fit on mine. Something to ask a jeweler about when I arrive in France.

A fire in the fireplace might pop and get out of hand. In a place like this, made all of wood, the destruction would be catastrophic. Police, when they come, might find a woman's body burned clean of all identifying marks, except the locket—my locket—around its neck, and scraps of my clothes melted to the remaining flesh. Why would they look closer? Already they'll have found my fingerprints on the gun that shot Lev, and it can't be long before they match them to the set that's been on file since the orphan boat carried me to America. Remorse, they'll think. A murder and then a suicide. Not the most shocking idea, when you get down to it.

And then imagine: a woman walks onto an airplane and smiles, ironic and wan. She answers questions from the stewardess with an exhausted *non* or *oui* before waving her off and falling asleep with a scarf tied around her hair. I don't speak French well, but Vera doesn't talk in excess, and I can pick anything up in time. I will avoid her old acquaintances, if any still remain, and eventually it will be my face that people associate with her name, if only through the force of habit. Not such a strange thing, for a widow to hide herself away, especially when she has her husband's legacy to maintain. Correspondence. The occasional grieved statement made by postcard. A packet of papers, a yellow old manuscript, locked in a safe underneath her bed. Maybe two packets, if I can't bring myself to burn these pages after all.

With a bit of effort, a bit of distance, I know this too can be smoothed over. We forget about the atrocities of history all the time, so long as there is a fair conclusion. The poor rising up to take the place of the rich. The dead living on in our earthly memories. Practice saying it: I am Vera Petrovna Orlova. I was born Vera Volkova, just outside Moscow, on an estate that would rival Arthur's royal seat. I can make things happen with the strength of my mind, the force of my will, and it was my prerogative to disappear. I hold my secrets close, because there's no one left alive who'll understand them. No one left at all, but me.

And I am determined to be happy.

# Acknowledgments

I'm endlessly grateful to Emma Patterson for her insight, friendship, and forbearance, all of which serve to make me a better and (usually) saner writer. Thanks also to Lea Beresford for being an incredible champion for this book, and for helping me realize its best possibilities. I think we three make a pretty good team.

Thank you to Sara Kitchen, Lauren Hill, and everyone at Bloomsbury USA and UK. I'm especially grateful to my UK editor Alison Hennessey for her enthusiasm and care in bringing this novel to a readership across the pond. To my phenomenal copy editor Janet McDonald: I appreciate you. To Katya Mezhibovskaya: Thank you for designing a cover that is truly better than anything I imagined.

Love and gratitude to Branden Boyer-White (first reader, second reader, hero of my heart), Angie Dell, Rachel Andoga, Lyndsey Reese, Sam Martone, Peter Turchi, Tara Ison, T. M. McNally, and Melissa Pritchard for years of friendship and inspiration. To Reneé Bibby, Lilian Vercauteren, and everyone who is a part of Write Wednesday, for sometimes letting me pick the restaurant. To Lauren Cerand for excellent advice and generosity with her time. To Katie Adams for offering valuable feedback on an early version of this manuscript, as well as her enthusiasm writ large. To Esmé Weijun Wang, for offering joy, sharing John Wick, and being brilliant. To Edan Lepucki and Alissa Nutting for support when it was most needed. To Mairead Case, for being. To Lynn Steger Strong, Katie Coyle, Rachel Fershleiser, Jaime Green, Erika Swyler, and other friends who make my daily life better, even if it's usually through a crackling digital void.

Heartfelt thanks to the Willapa Bay Artist Residency Program, the Jentel Arts Foundation, and the Launch Pad Astronomy Workshop for offering me space and support while I worked on this book. (To my Launch Pad friends: this may not have been quite what you had in mind, but studying science fiction writers turns out to have been as valuable for me as studying science.) Thanks also to my mother-in-law, Karen Clark, for taking us on a vacation to Mexico where I drafted a huge swath of pages and got a nice suntan, too.

Thank you to my family, always.

Thank you to Dave, especially. I love you.

# A Note on the Author

ADRIENNE CELT's debut novel, *The Daughters*, won the PEN Southwest Book Award for Fiction and was an NPR Best Book of the Year and an NYPL Favorite Book of the Year. Her story "Temples" was included in *The O. Henry Prize Stories 2016* after originally appearing in *Epoch*. Celt's short fiction appears or is forthcoming in *Zyzzyva, Ecotone*, the *Kenyon Review, Prairie Schooner, Esquire, Electric Literature*, and *Carve Magazine*, among others; her nonfiction has appeared in the *Rumpus, Tin House*'s "Open Bar," *Lit Hub*, the *Toast, Catapult*, the *Millions*, and elsewhere. Adrienne has an MFA in fiction from Arizona State University, draws weekly web comics at loveamongthelampreys.com, and lives in Tucson, Arizona.